A COTSWOLD ORDEAL

A COTSWOLD ORDEAL

REBECCA TOPE

WARRINGTON BOROUGH COUNCIL	
Bertrams	16.06.05
	£18.99

First published in Great Britain in 2005 by
Allison & Busby Limited
Bon March Centre
241-251 Ferndale Road
London SW9 8BJ

http://www.allisonandbusby.com

A catalogue record for this book is available from
the British Library.

10 9 8 7 6 5 4 3 2 1

ISBN 0 7490 8349 2

Printed and bound in Wales by
Creative Print and Design, Ebbw Vale

For Morgan, Leia and Luke
and also
in fond memory of Terry Hooper

Author's Note

The villages, pubs and churches in this story are real, as are the Cotswold Canal and Siccaridge Wood. The houses and people, however, are fictitious, and any resemblance to actual persons and homesteads is pure coincidence.

Chapter One – Saturday

It was difficult to avoid the conclusion that Hepzibah did not initially like it at Juniper Court. She didn't like the geese, for one thing, and Thea could hardly blame her for that. For a small spaniel, it must have been terrifying to be faced with huge white birds in possession of necks like demented snakes, and heads that lunged and darted and hissed and squawked alarmingly.

'I'm afraid they're a bit protective,' Julia Phillips had said, shortly before she and her family had merrily climbed into the Espace and set out for Swansea. From there they planned to take a ferry to Cork, and disappear into the hills and loughs of Ireland for a fortnight. 'Or perhaps I should say *over*protective,' she added. 'My advice would be to give them a wide berth. They don't always back down if it comes to a confrontation.'

Thea and her demoralised pet were left in befuddled charge of a beautiful old stone house, an aged pony suffering from some strange condition known as laminitis, quantities of poultry, two guinea pigs , two lop-eared rabbits and a Siamese cat. Thanks to a succession of unfortunate injuries at the previous house-sit, the spaniel had lost some of her former bonhomie. Her body still carried the scars to prove that not all people and animals were benign. Thea had seriously considered abandoning the whole idea of house-sitting after everything that had happened, before giving herself a shake and assuring herself and Hepzie that lightning never struck twice.

This second venture could not be more different from the first. Here was a cluttered family home, displaying a cheerful exuberance that came as a fresh and uplifting breeze compared to the previous experience. The Phillipses clearly had respectable quantities of money at their disposal, with a five-bedroomed Cotswold house, several outbuildings, a three-acre paddock, plus two more fields (rented out to a local farmer) and sizeable woodland beyond. There was also a vintage Lamborghini housed in the garage alongside many more of the trimmings of affluence. But they clearly hadn't let it weigh them down. There had been no mention of a security system, no high-powered instructions concerning phone calls from stockbrokers. Their prevailing concern was for Pallo the pony, who had sore feet and needed close attention. He was kept indoors, because his problem was mysteriously exacerbated by access to grass. He was also to be kept on a starvation diet, Julia insisted. This, she explained, was the root of his problem – a serious excess of protein, largely thanks to his young owner's inability to refrain from overindulging him.

There were four children, introduced swiftly and superfluously as 'Naomi and Harry, aged ten and twelve – they're mine. Those two are Desmond's – Harry and Flora, aged twelve and fourteen.' Hearing their names, the foursome looked at Thea, but only Naomi smiled. The others appeared to have an ongoing disagreement simmering between them, to do with seating arrangements in the car.

'Two Harrys?' she noted.

''Fraid so. Only a few weeks difference in age, as well. Daft, isn't it. It nearly put me off marrying him, I can tell you. Sign of the times, you see. Reconstituted families, and all the chaos that results. We tried calling them Potter and Prince, for nicknames, but they both wanted to be Potter. Now they're just One and Two.'

'They all live with you and Desmond, do they?'

'Yup.' Julia was almost too cheerful to be credible. 'They all go to the Steiner school. Their terms are shorter, which is why we're beating the general rush before the other schools break up for the summer.'

Thea knew almost nothing about Steiner schools, but it sounded expensive. 'They don't board, do they?' The house felt far too lived-in for that.

'No, no. They should be so lucky. They're stuck with me more or less the whole time. Harry and Flora's mum's got ME, poor thing. Hardly ever gets out of bed.'

'Oh dear.'

'Well, it's not for me to judge or anything. It's all come on in the last year or so. She was fine when Desmond and she separated. We can't have you thinking he walked out on a sick wife, can we?'

Thea had no difficulty in displaying an entirely non-judgmental demeanour. She was much more interested in the cat and the pony. 'Does Milo object to dogs at all?' she queried. Milo was sitting on top of the kitchen dresser, his head pressed against the ceiling, tail twitching warningly.

'He objects to most things, to be honest,' Julia laughed. 'Ignore him. He thinks he's the king of the world. He and Desmond have an ongoing battle to claim Head of Family status. If it gets too much for him he'll go and have a grumble to Frannie and Robert over the way. If you can't find him, that's probably where he'll be.'

Over the way was not immediately identifiable. The Phillipses did not have close neighbours, but there was a stone cottage just visible behind a clump of trees about three hundred yards to the south, down a steeply sloping lane. Julia was too rushed to clarify the matter. Thea followed her from room to room, trying to fathom any systems or procedures she might need to know. All she had really gleaned so far was a jumble of family background.

Julia, who must have been in her late forties, had evidently started on parenthood at a fashionably tardy age. Desmond, on the other hand, had been twenty-five when Flora was born. 'He's only thirty-nine now,' Julia breezed. 'Much more sensible this way round, when you think about it.'

Thea acknowledged a stab of envious admiration. Julia's husband seemed entirely desirable: good looks, money and an easy temperament, by all appearances. The fact that he had not spoken one word to her since her arrival did not dent her approval. Few husbands could have inserted a remark into the microsecond pauses in Julia's prattle.

''Course, it meant I had time to whistle up the career ladder,' Julia burbled on. 'You wouldn't believe what I was earning before I plateaued out. It's all different now I'm working for myself, but I certainly can't complain.'

Thea didn't get a chance to enquire into the precise nature of Julia's work, but her envy expanded to uncomfortable levels. And yet the woman didn't seem to be boasting. If anything, she seemed to find the whole business rather funny.

'Look, we'll have to go,' she said, snatching up a shoulderbag. 'It's all perfectly straightforward, honestly. Just do your best to keep Pallo alive, okay? The vet's standing by if he goes off his legs, but quite frankly, that's what we're trying to stave off. Once that happens, it's the end of the road for the poor old chap. He'll miss us, I'm afraid. Try and spend time with him, talk to him, take him a carrot. He'll probably like your dog.'

'Are you leaving me a mobile number or something, so I can tell you if there's a problem?' It irked Thea to have to ask. It made her sound pessimistic and incompetent.

'Oh, I'd much rather not. The whole point is to escape from phones and all that stuff. I've told the kids we'll be out of touch with everything here.'

Thea struggled to keep her face bland. 'Well, okay then. But you appreciate that I'll have to do whatever I think best, if I can't contact you for instructions.'

Julia pulled her lips back in an exaggerated wince. 'You're absolutely right, of course.' She glanced over her shoulder before grabbing the nearest piece of paper and rapidly writing a string of digits on it. 'There! That's Des's mobile. He did finally agree to take it, in case they want his advice at work, even though it'll be switched off practically all the time, and he'll be away fishing on some remote riverbank where there won't be any signal. You can leave a message on it, if you have to. He'll probably have a quick listen every evening.'

Thea pinned the sheet of paper to a crowded corkboard beside the phone. 'I'll make a list of any phone messages,' she said, 'and pin them up here, shall I?'

Julia shrugged. 'There probably won't be many. The canal people are the biggest nuisance just now. I'd rather not know what they have to say. It'll be wonderful to escape all that for a fortnight.'

Thea badly wanted this last remark elaborated. 'Canal people?' she repeated.

'Oh, you know. They're restoring the Cotswold Canal, at the rate of about an inch a month. It runs slap bang through our woods and they're forever wanting permission for one thing or another. To be honest, it's a total nightmare.'

'Why?' In Thea's world, restoring canals was one of the most godly of all activities.

'Oh, I haven't time to explain. There's just so many implications, the mind boggles. Don't worry about it. I'm sure they're all on holiday at the moment, same as us.' Something about this final reassurance felt forced to Thea. She resolved to go and inspect the canal at the earliest opportunity.

And then, after a final skirmish which saw Flora in the front seat next to her father and Julia laughing in the back with the others, they were gone in a whirl. Thea was left to yearn briefly for the copious detailed notes she'd been given by her previous clients. Julia Phillips hadn't written a thing apart from the grudging phone number on the back of a bank statement. 'Just use your common sense,' she had said, twice.

'Well, then, Heps,' said Thea. 'Let's go out and explore the neighbourhood.'

The house was on a small road with minimal traffic. To the west was the Golden Valley, and then Minchinhampton to the south. To the north-west was Stroud. Chalford was the nearest settlement of any size, but the tiny village of Frampton Mansell was a lot closer, with Sapperton and Daneway beyond. It was the more industrial edge of the Cotswolds, with the defunct canal running through from east to west and the remnants of old woollen mills to emphasise the origins of the long-standing prosperity of the region. Woollen cloth had been the prime product of the area for many years, with place names to prove it. There was also a railway line, with a viaduct, tunnel and bridges to deal with the rises and falls of the topography as well as a network of very minor roads criss-crossing the A419. If she got too bored, she could pop into a library in Stroud and do a bit of local research. The canal had already piqued her curiosity, not only from what Julia had said, but also from a visit to the Tunnel House Inn at Coates during her previous house-sitting assignment, and she promised herself a walk along what might remain of the towpath.

Within two hours of the Phillipses' departure, Thea and her dog were embarking on their first exploratory walk. The weather was disappointing, but summer disappointment was a fact of British life, and Thea bore it with stoicism. Cool grey skies met the gaze at every compass point, draining the colour from the tidy gardens. The Cotswolds, however, had a way with grey. From the not-quite-white of the sheep to the deep slate of some of the roofs, the monochrome hues presented a spectrum that effortlessly avoided the depression often associated with an absence of brighter colours.

Thea had found a large-scale Ordnance Survey map badly folded and crammed on top of a row of books in the living room during a fruitless search for a current *Radio Times*. With the dog on a lead, she took a downward-sloping route to the bottom of the valley. A brief inspection of the map had suggested the possibility of a number of walks, in all directions, replete with dense woodland alternating with delightful views and absorbing history. The reality was even better than the map had indicated.

The levels, as in most parts of the Cotswolds, were chaotic. To the north, across the river Frome, was a settlement she had overlooked on the map, nestling on rising ground. Everywhere the classic Cotswold stone architecture added beauty to the landscape. The old buildings, surrounded by lush summer vegetation, seemed to have been there forever. Many had stone-tiled roofs, the variegated sizes of the tiles and their wobbly edges bringing all sorts of associations with fairytales and picturebooks. There were no straight lines, no clear runs. Everything was crowded and cluttered, crammed between hedges and stone walls.

Thea walked with a bounce in her step. Life was definitely improving, month on month, now that the first anniversary of her widowhood was behind her. All the birthdays and festivals without Carl had been endured, and from now on she knew the sting would steadily lessen. Money might prove to be a worry unless she found the motivation to retrain in some sort of career that offered a reasonable salary and a useful pension, but there was time enough for that. At forty-two, the thought of pensions was still amusingly irrelevant. After all, this house-sitting lark paid well enough, and she could presumably continue doing it until she was seventy or more. People did.

Her route led eastwards, into Frampton Mansell itself, where the familiar characteristics of a Cotswold village made themselves apparent. An absence of voices, music or engines laid an eiderdown of silence over the place. She found a pub with a lawn at the front, containing the usual bench-and-table furniture, but embellished by the largest garden umbrellas she had ever seen. The lane snaked down to the railway line, with a footpath heading off towards dense woodland, where Thea calculated that the defunct canal must also run, having traversed the Juniper Court woods. That, she decided, would be the next area of exploration.

She managed to find a way back that did not involve retracing her steps, taking a risk on a footpath across an open field to the south of the wooded area, where she let the dog run free, hoping her sense of direction was functioning adequately. They emerged onto a road she didn't recognise, but a helpful fingerpost directed them back to familiar ground. In a corner of the field was a stone barn, rare in having escaped conversion into a substantial house. A movement caught her eye as she climbed over the stile onto the road. One of those unnatural flickers that only human beings could create. Other species managed a harmony with the scenery that people seldom could.

This was a tall angular male individual, with hunched shoulders and something odd about one leg. He had his back to her, so all she could see was his hair – light brown and rather long. He had evidently not been aware of her or the dog, but was intent on something alongside the barn.

Thea did not investigate. She barely even registered the image before it disappeared. Hepzie showed no sign of having noticed the figure. There was no reason for either of them to show curiosity or concern.

That's what Thea said later, when questioned. 'Why would I?'

Chapter Two – Saturday into Sunday

The day proceeded slowly. On their return to the house, Thea and her dog had been severely challenged by the geese. Three of them had come at a wing-flapping run to the gate, the sinuous necks lunging unambiguously at canine head and human knee. 'This is ridiculous,' said Thea, taking hold of a convenient stick. 'I'll show them who's boss around here.'

The birds manifested absolutely no respect for her weapon, weaving and dodging as she waved it in their direction. But neither did their snapping beaks connect with flesh or fur, and Thea permitted herself a small victory. 'They're all hiss and no peck,' she told the spaniel.

A casual glance around the kitchen and living room revealed no sign of the cat. No doubt he would show up for his supper, which Julia had vaguely scheduled for 'any time after six'.

'Better go and see poor old Pallo,' Thea suggested. She had a feeling there would have to be regular hourly visits to the decrepit pony, if she were to justify her fee. In the absence of his devoted young mistress, he might simply lose the will to continue his unrewarding existence. Only frequent conversation with Thea and stimulation from an unfamiliar dog would be likely to keep him going.

Despite the greyness of the day and the confusion inherent in the Phillips household, her spirits remained light. Back home lay the usual burdens of council tax and roof repairs, dripping taps and weedy garden. The mere fact of leaving them all behind was cause for rejoicing. Some people achieved the same effect by swanning off to Barbados or Thailand; Thea had gone one better than that. She achieved a change of scene and got paid for it. And she could take the dog. Humiliating as it might be to admit, she had long ago concluded that her wellbeing mostly depended on the presence of Hepzibah.

The attractively-marked pony seemed comparatively hearty. His eye was bright and his manner alert. He ate the carrot Thea took him, and cocked a suspicious ear at the spaniel. So far, so good, Thea decided. There had been no mention of mucking out, which now struck her as a serious omission. The floor of the stable was generously covered with straw that was clearly newly-strewn, being dry and a nice bright yellow. How long, though, would it stay like that? And where were the bales with which to replace it? A glance upwards answered the second question. The substantial building was of considerable height, although quite narrow. A loft floor had been fixed at the rear of the building, projecting roughly halfway from the back wall, and on this platform were eight or ten bales of straw. A sturdy wooden ladder was fixed close to one wall, giving easy access to the upper level, some twelve feet or so above the floor. It looked high enough for a person to stand upright under the roof, and had a large square opening at the back. The pony could position himself underneath the half-floor for warmth, or move out towards the door for greater light and airiness. It seemed to Thea that he had everything an animal could wish for in this arrangement. Even the door provided options, being in two halves, so the top could be left open without risk of him escaping.

The pony did not take to Hepzibah any more readily than the dog had adjusted to the geese. It took a few arthritic steps backwards and lowered its head. Then it lifted a front hoof and made a stamping motion. A fitter animal might have managed to connect with the spaniel's head, as Hepzie stupidly stood her ground. Thea's heart lurched, first with fear, then with anger. 'Hey!' she shouted. Both creatures looked at her, and then at each other and decided to abandon their hostilities. Thea did her best to like the pony, despite its behaviour. It would be difficult to nurse it through the next two weeks if she hated it. Its main appeal was the colouring, hinted at by the name. 'Pallo' was evidently short for 'palomino', of which he appeared to be a handsome example. The mane and tail were a creamy white and the body a hue she could only describe as apricot. Despite his obvious age, he was still a beauty. She recalled her grandfather's scorn for all equines. 'Brainless beasts,' he would say. 'Not an imaginative cell in their bodies.' He would tell stories of his early years, before the advent of tractors rescued him from the moods and malaises of his working horses. Thea had never questioned his judgment on the topic, having seldom spent more than a few minutes in the presence of a horse in her entire life.

She took Hepzie on a more extended exploration of the yard and paddock, before retiring to the house for supper. The stable was a free-standing building, and they walked around it, admiring the stonework and investigating interesting smells respectively. At the back was a flight of steps running edgeways up the wall, leading to the square opening in the upper storey. It was between the house and the road, with the larger barn opposite, and a pathway running inside the road fence leading to the back of the stable. Thea imagined the games the four children could devise, hiding and chasing around all the buildings. Or were they like others of their generation, obsessed with electronic games and television, and hardly ever venturing outdoors?

There was a warmth to the house that she was increasingly appreciating. These were nice people, she decided, unspoilt by their material fortune. A reconstituted family that had, to all appearances, made a real success of the new situation. Despite their hasty attempts at tidying up, there was evidence everywhere of an openness that was rare in an age of obsession with privacy. Letters were pinned up on a cork board revealing the state of their finances, the existence of headlice in Year 6, an invitation to some sort of social evening at the Cotswold Club, and a dusty Christmas card from somebody who might have been Kate Winslet, if the signature could be believed. A large framed photo of Desmond, looking outrageously young and handsome and holding some sort of fish in the time-honoured pose of a jubilant angler was displayed on a small table in a corner of the living room. How refreshing, Thea felt, to be amongst people with no secrets.

The cat put in a stately appearance promptly at six, and delicately consumed the half-tin of meat Thea provided. He suffered himself to be stroked for a minute or so, before making an equally stately exit, tail held high and eyes straight ahead. Not an indoor cat, Thea concluded.

She had brought her laptop with her, anticipating long hours in which internet Scrabble or lengthy emails to family and friends would make all the difference. Furthermore, access to webpages had become one of life's necessities in recent times. You could never really be bored with the internet at your fingertips.

She was feeling entirely contented and relaxed, the first day having proved less strange and restless than expected. The live-stock would all settle down quickly and accept the new woman and dog who'd unaccountably replaced their usual rowdy family.

The peacocks came as a complete surprise, sometime before six the following morning. Extraordinarily, this detail had been over-looked on the day of arrival, as well as on her preliminary visit in May. The unearthly sound of their cries penetrated a rather pleasant dream causing Thea to sit up in wild alarm, staring round the unfamiliar bedroom for the banshee that was surely right beside the bed.

Hepzie was cravenly hiding under the duvet. Thea had to haul her out and speak reassuringly before she'd stop quivering. Within minutes, they'd both gone back to sleep, but the noise came again, hauntingly conjuring other worlds. But this time Thea listened with a more relaxed ear. 'Peacocks!' she told the dog. 'That's all.'

It took her quite a while to locate the birds when she went in search of them after breakfast. Three large exotic males were roosting in a cherry tree in a corner of the garden. The incon-gruity was startling. To see such big birds in a tree at all was odd; brightly coloured ones with trailing tail feathers were simply not as nature intended. She stood for several minutes admiring them, and wondering why Julia hadn't told her about them. They seemed docile enough, and the vivid blue of their breasts was enough to send any heart soaring. She decided to like them, to permit them their exotic enhancement of her sojourn and forgive them their early-morning cacophony.

The house was superficially tidy, but the first cupboard Thea opened revealed a hasty bundling-out-of-sight exercise that would inevitably mean that nothing would be found by the own-ers for the next several months. The small bedroom she'd been allocated belonged to the older daughter, Flora. 'Too many of us now for a spare room,' Julia had said. 'You'll be all right in here, won't you?'

The room's d cor had apparently been executed by the child herself. Dragons were stencilled in shades of orange and blue over two of the walls, in random clusters, while a third wall was completely covered with cut-out pictures of a pop star Thea could not recognise. He was an ill-looking fellow, apt to open his mouth much too wide when confronted by a camera, it seemed. His clothing was minimal and unstylish. Thea rather feared that his face would haunt her for some time to come.

The duvet cover was clean and plain, the curtains likewise. The carpet was equally acceptable. In fact, the tidiness was not at all as she remembered from her visit in May. Young Flora, unlike the rest of her family, had gone to a lot of trouble to tuck everything out of sight, leaving no personal items on view. Except for the dragons. There were shelves containing about thirty model dragons, made of porcelain, plastic, metal, wood, paper and other materials. One had actually been knitted. Some were a few inches high, and the largest measured a good two feet from nose to tail.

'Well, it makes a change,' Thea muttered. 'Nothing wrong with dragons.' A closer inspection persuaded her that many of the models had been skilfully made, and were far from unattractive.

Flora was not the daughter obsessed with the welfare of the pony. A glance into Naomi's room across the landing made this apparent. A large poster of a show jumper in mid-jump met the eye first, followed by a mass of other horse-related objects. A chest of drawers had a jumble of possessions littered on top of it, and there were clothes on the chair near the window. Of course, there would be no reason why she should clear it up, since nobody was intending to use it during her absence. Thea wondered whether Flora had resented the need to make her room available.

For the first time, Thea sat down and asked herself just what the definition of a house-sitter was. This was only her second assignment, and already it proved to be entirely different from the first. In the absence of detailed instructions, she felt both constrained to invent her own job description, and free to do as much or as little as she liked.

The poultry were to be shut in at night and released in the morning – except for the peacocks, which were evidently free range. The pony required some magical therapy that would maintain life until his devoted owner's return. The cat, guinea pigs and rabbits had one meal a day, and were otherwise self-sufficient. Burglars were not a worry, it seemed.

To Thea's relief, she noticed that Hepzie was cautiously pottering outside, her feathering flowing in the cool breeze. For July the weather was proving sorely defective. Thea caught regular glimpses of the dog from the front window, noting that she kept well away from the muddy patch which was obviously the preferred territory of the geese. A shallow pond was full of thick green sludge and bordered with long untidy grass. The birds seemed very attached to it. Thea heartily shared Hepzie's antipathy to the whole area. Not only was it smelly and gloopy underfoot, it was also determinedly guarded by the incumbents.

The living room window was broad and high, letting in all available light, and probably a lot of summer heat on a good day. The view extended from the green pond to the right of the main big barn that faced the house, past the front gate and lane beyond, to one corner of the pony's shed. Everything had been set at the customary odd angle, as if carelessly deposited without any planning, and yet the result was as idyllic a rural homestead as could be imagined.

Thea set up the laptop on an antique oak table close to the window, and plugged it in to charge the battery.

She saw the shiny silver car draw up in the gateway, hesitating a moment and then proceed through the open gate into the yard. She saw the wide-hipped, grey-haired woman get out. A large woman, though light on her feet, slammed the car door and stood for a moment taking in the house and yard. Thea watched her through the window trying to gauge just how welcome this visitor might be. She was assisted by her dog, who had gone running out of the open front door at the sound of the slamming car door. Two geese were waddling purposefully towards her, too.

Thea got up and went to show due hospitality. 'Hello,' she called, raising her voice to carry from the front door. The woman was not approaching, but simply standing by the car, watching Hepzibah, who was wagging ecstatically from a short distance. When Hepzie wagged, it involved most of her spine, as well as the long undocked tail. Most people instinctively smiled or laughed to see it.

This woman did neither. 'It won't jump up, will it?' The voice was tight.

'Come here, Heps,' said Thea, hearing the soppy affection in her own voice. The dog complied easily and Thea bent down to fondle the soft head. 'Good girl. Watch out for the geese,' she warned. 'They're far worse than the dog.'

This statement turned out to be false. As if barred by an invisible fence, the geese halted, exchanging muted gurgles and then diverted their attentions to microscopic morsels of food beneath their feet.

'I don't think I need worry about them,' the visitor observed. 'I take it the Phillipses aren't here?'

'That's right. I'm their house-sitter. Why, do you know them?'

'Vaguely. I'm Cecilia Clifton. I live a mile or two away. I'm afraid I've got bad news.'

Thea did not immediately feel any concern. There was only one piece of truly terrible news that could come, now, and this woman could not conceivably be the bearer of it. She did not know Jessica; there was no possibility that harm to Thea's daughter could be reported through this mouthpiece.

'What?' she said.

'The cat. Julia's Siamese. Unless I'm very mistaken, he's lying dead on the road, two or three hundreds yards that way.' She pointed eastwards.

'Oh Jesus!' said Thea, feeling suddenly sick. 'Are you sure?'

'You'd better go and see for yourself.'

The woman did not offer to accompany Thea on her unpalatable quest. 'You can't miss it,' she said, before getting back into the car. 'It's just around the corner.'

'Can't you show me?'

At last a smile flickered on the broad face. 'I would if I could, but I'm in rather a rush. You'll be all right.'

It seemed an odd thing to say. 'Will I?' she wondered.

The woman turned the key in the ignition and then seemed to reconsider. Without turning the engine off, she leaned out of the window. 'Listen – I'll be free after lunch. I'll come back then and we can have a talk, if you like. It must feel rather odd, being alone in a strange house. And you won't have bargained for dealing with a dead cat.'

Thea was rueful. 'No. But I can hardly complain about any of the other aspects, can I? I knew what it would be like. And I've got the dog.'

'So shall I come back or not?'

Thea looked into the greenish eyes that awaited her reply, seeming to say it wouldn't much matter either way. If Thea declined the offer, she felt there'd be no hard feelings. 'Yes, do,' she said. 'I'll have coffee on.'

The cat's body was limp and muddy and still not quite cold, the pelvic area crushed. Thea slid it into the plastic carrier bag she'd equipped herself with before walking down the lane. The creature's lips were drawn back in a rictus of suffering that filled Thea with pity and rage and rank despair. 'Carnage,' she muttered to herself. The word embraced a bitter pun she had been aware of since her husband had been slaughtered in a road accident. Human or animal, to die at the wheels of a motor vehicle was to pay a sacrificial price accepted almost calmly by the population at large.

'Now what?' Thea asked Hepzibah, who was as always only a few yards away. 'Better get you off the road, before you're splattered as well. Come on.'

But before they'd got any distance there was a voice calling from a gateway further down the lane. 'Hello! Has something happened?'

The gateway opened into a modest cottage garden with low-growing plants and a scrap of lawn. Behind it stood a classic Cotswold dwelling in the usual pale stone, flanked by trees.

A young woman stepped out into the lane, and Thea stayed her ground. 'I'm the Phillipses' house-sitter,' she said, raising her voice to cover the distance. 'I'm afraid I'm off to a bad start. Poor

Milo's been run over. It must have happened only a short time ago – he's still a bit warm.'

The reaction was dramatic. Covering the ground between them at a run, her mouth widened in a sob, the woman positively shrieked. 'Oh God, no! Let me see. Oh!'

'You must be Frannie,' Thea guessed. 'Julia said he visited you a lot.'

'Yes, yes, Frannie Craven. Oh Lord, this is terrible. What's Robert going to say? He'll think it's all my fault. Poor Milo. I can't bear to look at him!'

Thea had opened the carrier bag to reveal the contents. Frannie reared back in horror. 'How did you find him?'

'A woman called Cecilia Something came to tell me.'

'Bloody cars. Nothing's safe, is it. You'd think on a quiet little road like this…'

'Right. But you know – cats do dart out at just the wrong moment.' Why am I defending the motorist, she demanded of herself.

Frannie was not swayed. 'Have *you* ever killed a cat?'

'No.'

'Neither have I. It's bad driving, I don't care what you say.'

'So why will Robert think it's your fault?'

Frannie clasped her hands together and jittered on the spot. 'He says I shouldn't encourage him to come over to us. He doesn't like cats much. And the *boys*! They'll be devastated.' Her wide blue eyes gazed into Thea's. She was blonde and slight and about thirty. Just the sort to have a bossy husband, Thea noted to herself.

'Boys? You mean yours?'

'Oh, no.' Frannie put a hand over her mouth. 'I haven't got any.'

'Julia's two Harrys, then?'

'Actually…well, yes, that's right. The boys love Milo. He's a sort of mascot to them.'

'Well, it's done now. I'd better bury him, I suppose.'

'You *can't*. Not without asking Julia where she wants him. They're away for a fortnight, aren't they?'

Thea nodded. 'Maybe I could put him in a freezer or something.'

'In with the *food*?'

She wasn't at all sure she liked this Frannie. The overwrought responses to everything she said were beginning to irritate.

'I expect I could clear a compartment. And wrap him up well.' Absently she reached into the bag and stroked the dense creamy fur. It had been a very beautiful cat. She turned to go when a man came out of the house and walked towards them, his face framing intense curiosity.

'What's going on?'

'Oh, Robert. This lady's the one Julia's hired to look after their house. I'm sorry – I don't know your name? She's just found Milo, look. He's been run over.'

'My name's Thea Osborne. I only arrived yesterday. This isn't a very good start, is it.'

Robert was a lot older than his wife. He looked to be in his early forties. He did not seem the least bit distressed at the death of the cat. In fact, Thea noted, he almost shrugged.

'We'll be late, Fran, if you don't get a move on.'

'Oh, sorry.' Frannie threw Thea a glance full of helpless excuse. *He's a man, how can I withstand his instructions?* 'We're going to see Robert's mother today, and he likes to make an early start,' she explained. 'Even though it's only a few miles away.'

'Well, nice to meet you,' Thea said.

'And I'm terribly sorry about poor Milo.'

'Oh, well, at least it's not the pony,' Thea said, without really thinking.

'Don't count your chickens,' said Robert with a slight snicker that put Thea completely off him.

The immediate dilemma, once she got back to the house, was whether to tell Julia and Desmond what had happened. Her strong inclination was to leave them in cheerful ignorance, since there was nothing they could do. On the other hand, if it had been her in their shoes, she would want to be kept informed. If (fingers crossed, God forbid) anything happened to Hepzie, she would want to be told instantly. There was something dreadful in allowing a person to continue to assume all was well when it wasn't.

But Julia had given unambiguous instructions on this topic, albeit more by implication than direct speech. Only if a grim decision was required concerning Pallo should they be troubled. Otherwise it was down to Thea to use her best judgment. And the burial of a cat could wait. There was plenty of space in the large chest freezer housed in the barn that doubled as garage, general store and all-round useful space.

'Well, at least I'm meeting the neighbours,' she said, congratulating herself on finding a bright side to the sorry start to the day. And when she went to check on the pony, he stretched his neck towards her, wrinkling the soft floppy lips that for Thea was the best feature of the equine species, and snatching the carrot she proffered. The energy he displayed seemed to Thea a good omen for his survival.

Cecilia Clifton returned on schedule, just as Thea was making coffee in a machine identical to the one she had at home. She heard the car, but was too slow to prevent Hepzie rushing out and leaping at the woman as soon as she was accessible.

'Get down!' she shouted, pushing the spaniel away.

'Gosh, sorry,' said Thea, wishing for the millionth time that everybody else loved dogs as much as she did. 'She thinks you're an old friend, you see.'

'Her nails are dreadful.'

'You don't have to tell me. I'm trying to cut them, one or two at a time. She absolutely hates it, so it's rather a battle.'

'Would you like me to hold her while you do it?'

Thea knew she ought to agree to this offer. 'That's ever so kind, but somehow I'm not in the mood. You wouldn't believe how it upsets her. And after Milo... Well, I can't face it, to be honest.'

Cecilia nodded accommodatingly, and Thea warmed to her. 'What did you do with the body?' Cecilia asked.

'Put it in the freezer. According to Frannie Whatnot, that's a very insensitive thing to do.'

'Oh, Frannie. Take no notice of her. She's bonkers.'

'Really?'

'Not certifiable, but inclined to excessive emotion.'

'I know what you mean,' said Thea with a laugh. 'But what about that Robert? Are they married?'

'Oh, yes. Biggest wedding around here for years. He's from an old Chalford family. His granddad was a manager in one of the mills. Frannie's not the partner anybody envisaged for him, but after a disastrous first marriage in his twenties, I think the family was grateful that he finally seems to have settled down again, even though she is so young.'

'No kids?'

'Not yet, but I gather they're working on it. Robert's mum is the matriarchal type and so far there's just one granddaughter, born to Robert's little sister. And she lives in York.' Thea had the impression there was more family information itching to be disclosed, but Cecilia evidently decided she'd imparted quite enough.

'Do you know the family histories of everybody here?' Thea prompted.

'Not the incomers, and that's most of them. But I get around, you see, and people talk to me. Now I'm retired, I've really thrown myself into community matters.'

'Like the WI, you mean?'

Cecilia's eyes widened in horror. 'Certainly not! Listen, the Cotswolds is virtually the only area of southern England where there's still a chance – a slim one, admittedly, but not completely gone – to stem the tide of urbanisation.'

Thea gulped at this. 'Oh,' she managed. 'Good for you.'

'It's a full time job, let me tell you. Everybody thinks their little bit of desecration will go unnoticed, won't make a difference, can dodge the regulations and guidelines. But we're winning.' Cecilia paused with a smirk of satisfaction. 'We are definitely winning.'

'Well,' Thea asserted, feeling like some sort of Girl Guide, 'you can include me on your side. I'm all for conservation. My husband —'

Cecilia gave her no chance to finish. 'Let me show you around, while you're here. We've got a lot to be proud of.'

Thea nodded, struck dumb by such enthusiasm.

The woman went on. 'Not that this is a wholly rural area, of course. It actually has quite a strong industrial history, just across the river from here. It's hideous new homes and misguided attempts to attract tourists that we mainly object to.'

Thea found her voice, explaining that she was quite well apprised of the past glories of the region.

Cecilia laughed delightedly. 'Well, you are a find, to be sure. Such genuine interest is hard to come by.' She paused, before adding, 'Would you like me to show you around? What are your interests? I can do you wild flowers, William Morris, clothmaking, canals, architecture, railways, local personalities...' She ticked each topic off on her fingers.

Thea's eyes widened. 'Are you proposing to give me a tour, or just a lecture?'

'Either. Both. Chalford's just over there, as I expect you know. It's almost a ghost town now, compared to how it was less than a century ago. I never get tired of roaming its streets, imagining how it must have been. A veritable hive of industry it was.'

'Clothmaking?'

'And the rest. Dyeing, weaving, wood-turning, bone-turning...'

'What?'

'It's true. One of the mills was converted into a bone-turning works for a while. They made bone knitting needles and crochet hooks.'

Thea gulped half her mug of cooling coffee. Her lifelong knack of slipping into a different historical period had taken over. From the kitchen window at the back of Juniper Court, the slopes of Chalford were faintly visible. It did not look like a busy mill town, but with some imaginative exertion, she could visualise the streets full of workers thronging to enter the mill gates before the appointed time. Hooters would summon them from their gossip and hurried shopping forays. It was a scene more associated with Yorkshire than south Gloucestershire.

'And what's that place up there?' she asked, pointing at the settlement across the valley.

'Oakridge. Nice little village, though I hardly ever go there. Looks its best from over here, quite honestly.'

'And what about the canal? According to my map, it goes right through the woods between here and Daneway.'

Cecilia's pause was long enough to be meaningful. 'There's a terrible lot I could tell you about the canal,' she said, eventually. 'It might be best not to get me started on the canal.'

Thea seldom thought of herself as contrary or unduly argumentative, but this remark was entirely too provoking to ignore.

'But it's the canal that interests me most,' she said. 'Believe it or not, my dissertation for my degree was on English canals and railways. The period from 1870 to 1890, when the railways were in full swing, and stealing all the business from the canals. You might say I have a special interest.'

Cecilia sighed. 'I might have known it. But there isn't a lot to see. They haven't even started on any restoration along this section, although they're talking it up and trying to raise money. It's going to be a massive job, if they ever do knuckle down to it.' Her face darkened. 'And that's rather a big if, the way things are going. Besides, there's obviously nothing I could tell you. Why don't we pop along to Daneway instead? Did you know that William Morris had a house there? Quite a few houses in the area go back to the Arts and Crafts movement. We could walk from here, through the woods.'

'How far is it?'

'Barely two miles.'

'Each way?'

Cecilia nodded. 'Why? What else do you have to do?'

Thea wriggled her shoulders. 'Not a lot, really. It's just – the weather, for a start. It's going to rain, by the look of it.' She couldn't have stated precisely why she felt a reluctance to embark on a woodland walk with this woman, other than a sense of being bulldozed into too sudden an intimacy. The walk would lead to tea and cakes, in all probability, and beyond. It was Sunday, she remembered. Why did Cecilia not have a family to spend the day with? Was she so lonely she had to descend on a temporary stranger for company?

'You're probably right,' Cecilia agreed comfortably. 'I'm doing my usual trick of rushing people into things. But you must go and see Daneway House. And the tunnel. And the pub's not bad.' She gave Thea a straight look. 'And it isn't a lot of fun going to a pub by yourself, now is it?'

'That's true,' said Thea, who had a profound resistance to entering a pub alone. 'This is all very kind of you.' And it probably was, she concluded. The woman was just being kind and she was being churlish to entertain suspicions as to her motives.

Cecilia got up to go five minutes after finishing her coffee. 'Here's my phone number,' she said. 'I'm not doing very much in the coming week. I mean it about filling you in on local history. You seem interested – it's only good sense to avail yourself of somebody like me.'

'Thanks,' Thea smiled, taking the slip of paper with the phone number. 'As soon as the weather improves, I'll take you up on it.'

Even when it began to drizzle, her mood remained buoyant. Retreating to the big kitchen, she turned on the radio.

As very often happened, the programme fitted well with her situation. Tuned to a local station, there was a woman talking about Minchinhampton Common and its mysterious history. Stories of gypsy encampments, amateur golfing and perennial kite-flying made the place sound unremarkable at first. But then the voice altered to a lower key, and the talk changed to sudden thick mists, and dangerous trenches dating back to World War Two, all of it worthy of a much larger wilderness. Although people used it as if it were a country park, there were still echoes of a wilder darker history. And then, as if to lighten the mood again, the speaker went on to talk about courting couples from Thrupp and Brimscombe and Chalford spending their Sundays on the Common, walking miles for the pleasure of open grassland and bracing air.

The programme ended, to be replaced with the bland popular music that local radio tended to favour. Thea was left with a desire to visit the Common for herself. If nothing else, it sounded a perfect place for exercising a lively young spaniel. 'We'll go as soon as the rain stops,' she told Hepzibah.

But the rain got worse and the sky even darker. The house seemed to wrap itself around her, seducing her into remaining indoors, where there was a big new television with incredible sound and countless channels to choose from, slightly raising Thea's hopes of classic movies or fascinating nature programmes – if she could work out how to operate the thing. There were also books, CDs, DVDs, magazines and games.

'There aren't any no-go areas,' Julia Phillips had said. 'Help yourself to anything you might need to pass the time. I hope it won't get too tedious for you.'

At random Thea chose a recent copy of 'Cotswold Life' and found a page of listings advertising local garden fetes, barbecues, country shows and antique sales. Every village apparently had some ambitious scheme to celebrate the summer and raise some funds. Thea entertained pleasing visions of community jollity, until she remembered similar events she had attended in previous times. When Jessica was small, and Carl just embarking on his new vocation as an environmentalist in rural Oxfordshire, he had insisted they engage in as much 'grassroots activity' as they could. It had never quite been Thea's cup of tea, waiting around for the results of the raffle to be announced, and the number of currants in the kilner jar. She'd never once won anything, and only reluctantly purchased a few leggy home-grown plants and dog-eared paperbacks from the stalls.

Time was passing slowly and she was beginning to miss human company. If she'd been at home, she could have dropped in on any one of half a dozen friends. Women her age were often still encumbered by young children and therefore not generally working full time, despite the perception to the contrary. Some had given it a try for a year or two and then returned thankfully to the freedom and fulfilment of life without a job.

'Doesn't look as if this one's going to be as exciting as the last,' she muttered, with a wistfulness she almost instantly came to regret.

Neither Thea nor Hepzie heard anybody drive into the yard or come to the front door, so the first thing they knew was a loud knocking.

She trotted across the hallway with an eagerness she felt to be almost pathetic. Was she so desperate for human contact, despite the two encounters she'd already had that day? Was she going to have to admit to herself that there were aspects to this job that seriously disagreed with her?

A middle-aged man was on the doorstep, shoulders hunched against water that ran down his neck from soaking hair. His sodden trousers stuck to his legs. He shook himself and grinned at her. 'Sorry to be a bother,' he said, with no appearance of regret. 'But I'm totally lost. Where exactly does this road go?'

Thea grinned back. 'That's a very good question,' she said. 'It doesn't actually go anywhere, really. I mean, it just links to the A419. Where are you trying to get to?'

'Some Godforsaken village called Daneway. I must have missed a turning.'

Thea was not a nervous or suspicious person. She had never had cause to fear an apparently innocent stranger. But some instinct warned her not to reveal her true situation. The man was nice-looking, well-spoken. Hepzie was wagging at him from the dry of the hallway. On the surface, at least, there was no imaginable reason for doubting him. Perhaps it was his extreme wetness that she found mildly repellent. What in the world could he have been doing to get in such a state?

Glancing over his shoulder, she saw a long, low, maroon-coloured car with a soft black top. A flicker of disapproval ran through her – something so sporty and speedy should not be venturing down quiet rural lanes where Siamese cats couldn't cross to the neighbour's without being slaughtered.

'Daneway's just a couple of miles that way,' she said, pointing to the left. 'You can't really miss it.' She injected a deal more confidence into her voice than she truly felt. All she was going by was her recollection of the map, and the blithe way Cecilia Clifton had suggested they walk to the village.

'Okay,' he nodded, with a half-smile that seemed much too knowing. As if he had been testing her and found her wanting. Maybe he'd hoped for a cup of tea and a chance to dry his trousers. 'Thanks.'

'I'm sure you'll find it,' she said, retreating slightly and gripping the edge of the door. The gesture was firmly unambiguous. He understood that he was being rejected, and a flicker of something like sadness crossed his eyes. Thea felt ashamed and then impatient. This was how it was between men and women, she reminded herself. It was not wise to trust or believe the words of a stranger. If, as half her instincts were urging her, she had asked him in, she would deserve whatever happened next. Her female friends would be aghast if she were to make such a terrible mistake. Her male ones would sigh and shake their heads and talk dispassionately about vulnerability and sensible precautions. And she would never know what the right thing would have been.

'Oh, I expect I shall,' he agreed. 'Thanks very much.'

She soon forgot about him, especially as the late-afternoon routines for the livestock were due to commence. The geese had to be braved, in order to get to the henhouse, where eggs must be collected. The nesting boxes were attached to a wire run, where the birds were confined at night. The pond lay only a few feet beyond, and at the sight of her, the geese abandoned their paddling and mudlarking to waddle hurriedly towards her. Hepzie saw them coming and veered away, changing course in favour of an urgent foray into the pony's quarters. Thea tried to make herself tall and assertive, holding the egg basket before her like a shield, thankful that she was wearing her raincoat for protection against pecks as well as precipitation. Three large white birds lined up in front of her, their black eyes unblinking. Without looking at them directly, Thea marched to the henhouse, and lifted the flap to reveal five perfect brown eggs divided between two nesting boxes. The geese did not follow, and she exhaled in relief.

Collecting eggs had to be one of life's most simple satisfactions, akin to finding mushrooms or digging new potatoes. The natural bounty appearing like a small miracle couldn't fail to inflate the spirits. She would make herself an omelette for supper and think herself blessed.

The rain did not abate throughout the evening. Having fed and watered the pony, shut the birds in and mourned briefly for the poor Siamese cat, she logged onto the internet to retrieve any emails she might have.

There was one from James, her brother-in-law, who persisted in monitoring her movements and nagging her about keeping safe. In the light of events during her earlier house-sitting adventure, she could hardly criticise him for his solicitude.

I hope all's well in Minchinhampton? No strange farmers or such? You're certainly a glutton for punishment.

As it happens, Rosie and I are off to Deauville tomorrow for a week, and that means I won't be able to rush to your side if there's a crisis. So stay on the sunny side, there's a good girl. Maybe Jessica can be on standby if you need anything.

Seriously, love, do try not to get involved. Settle down with a good book, or go shopping in Cirencester. Anything that'll keep you out of trouble.

With our love, James.

Hurriedly, she keyed in a reply.

It's all perfectly fine here, thank you for asking. Apart from the weather, of course. Nice warm family house, lovely people, easy animals. There has been one disaster, though. The cat got run over this morning – or during the night, I imagine. It was a lovely Siamese, so that's quite a bummer. I've put it in the freezer for now.

I've briefly met the closest neighbour, who seems a bit of a pain on first acquaintance. A chap got lost in the rain and asked me the way. I pretended I knew, so he wouldn't guess I'm strange here myself. You'd have been proud of me.

Enjoy Deauville. (WHY Deauville, I ask myself). Love to Rosie.

Thea

The next message was from her younger sister Jocelyn, who very rarely sent emails.

> Thea, where are you? Is it that house-sitting business again? I can't get anywhere with your mobile, so this will have to be my last resort. The thing is, I've got a bit of a crisis here, and would love to get away for a couple of days. Can I use your house, do you think? If you're away, I could water the plants and answer the phone. I won't take any of the kids.
>
> Don't phone me at home. That sounds much more sinister than it really is, but I just prefer to keep it all under my hat for a while. You can email me if you get this before Sunday evening. Otherwise I'll try your mobile again on Monday.
>
> Love
>
> Joss

Thea rattled off a reply almost before she'd had time to think.

> What in the world is all this about? No, you can't just waltz into my house without me being there. And without any proper explanation. You'll have to come here first and talk to me about whatever it is that's going on. I'm at a place called Juniper Court, a mile and a half off the A419. The nearest village is Frampton Mansell. I doubt if you'd find it by yourself – we could meet in Minchinhampton or Stroud. Oh, damn, I don't know what to say until you've told me the whole story. I'll switch my mobile on, and make sure you call me as soon as you see this.
>
> Thea

Jocelyn was four years her junior, and the mother of five children. Large, cheerful and apparently contented, she was the last person Thea would have expected to be sending panicky emails. Her husband, Alex, was every bit as equable as Jocelyn, house-trained and reasonably attentive. Thea could not imagine him being the cause of her sister's crisis. The usual candidates were presumably infidelity, financial disaster, illness or trouble with the law. If forced to guess, Thea would opt for the second of these. Jocelyn was bad with money, and five children cost a lot to run. But why, in that case, would she want to get away from the family home? Impatiently, Thea awaited the call that would, she hoped, explain everything.

Chapter Three – Sunday into Monday

By the time it was dark, Thea had had more than enough of her first full day on the job. She took Hepzie outside for a swift circuit of the yard, and a glance in at the pony, who was standing passively in his stable, one back leg kinked in a picture of relaxation. Then she retreated to the house, locked all doors, closed windows and made herself a hot milky drink. At half past ten, she took herself and the dog to bed.

The dragons on the bedroom wall looked less friendly than they had the previous evening. The room felt airless, with a faint whiff of something teenage and chemical. All those potions they used on hair and skin, the odd stuff they drank, combined in a miasma that reminded Thea of Jessica in her early teens. Jessica's attempts to be a typical girl had been blessedly shortlived. 'It's all such hard work,' she complained, before having her hair cut in short layers, and leaving her face comparatively clear of make-up. 'I don't know why people bother.'

Flora was fourteen, she reminded herself, the age where life consisted of one long experiment, most of which resulted in painful disappointment or humiliation. There would be boys, inevitably, and passionate interests. If the dragons were anything to go by, this girl was capable of impressively sustained obsessions. There were magazines stacked on two shelves, which might reward a brief examination at some point.

The peacocks next morning were apparently sulking. Either that or the previous dawn had been some sort of aberration. Or perhaps the corn she'd thrown to them at poultry-feeding time had disagreed with them. But the most likely explanation for their silence was that it continued to rain. Peacocks might be expected to dislike rain, she reasoned. They came from hot sunny places, where they could rely on months of good weather. It was a small miracle that they'd adapted to the British climate at all. Idly, she played with the idea of reading up on them via the internet. It would be a good way to pass an hour or so, if nothing else. The geese were rather quiet, too, she noted. The previous morning's birdsong had definitely included some argumentative honking.

Pallo seemed to be surviving without undue difficulty. He pricked forward his ears and took a few steps towards her when she arrived with his meagre bucket of feed, which she took to be encouraging signs. She promised to bring him a carrot or two later on, and carefully secured the lower half of his door, so that he could get a view of the yard over the open top. The rain was abating, she noted with some relief, by ten o'clock.

It was Monday, with all the ingrained injunctions that went along with the first day of the working week. Despite having only a patchy employment record, Thea was not immune to these associations. On Mondays you checked that there were good stocks of groceries and household requisites. You changed the sheets and made telephone calls to set up dates and meetings for the coming week. If you were looking after someone else's house, you did a bit of vacuuming and some light dusting.

And when that was done, you chirped at your dog and set off to explore the neighbourhood, despite the threat of more rain. And in order to do that, you searched out public footpaths or bridleways in preference to the open road, however sparse the traffic might be. Remembering the dead Milo made this even more of an imperative.

She took the creased Ordnance Survey map as insurance against getting completely lost. She put on the wellington boots she'd prudently brought with her and set out with the dog. A jumbled network of footpaths seemed to offer an interesting circular walk, if roads were also used here and there. It was only two or three miles to Minchinhampton and the intriguing Common, with its history and misty trenches. There were also stately homes in the shape of Gatcombe Park and Owlpen Manor, at feasibly walkable distances. And the canal tunnel she had already discovered close to the village of Coates exerted a fascination for her. The western end of it emerged at Daneway, with another pub, mentioned by Cecilia Clifton as being an easy stroll from Juniper Court.

'Spoilt for choice,' she said to the spaniel. 'We'll be experts on the place before long, if we go on like this.'

Perhaps because of the man asking directions the previous evening, she took the path towards Daneway, through the woods – the walk she had declined to do with Cecilia Clifton the day before.

The early part, after wading through some long wet grass, involved walking across the railway line, which made her feel as if she'd stepped back in time. Keeping the dog on a tightly-clutched lead, she hurried over the track, looking repeatedly to right and left and listening hard. There was a clear view for hundreds of yards in each direction, but it was still an echo of the past, or at least of a more relaxed society, to be permitted to stride confidently in front of the train if you so chose.

Immediately, she was in the woods, which were deep and dark, but readily navigated by paths that could in no way be missed. She let the dog run free, and gave herself up to the silence and stillness. Almost deliberately she opted for smaller pathways when given a choice, but within ten minutes she was back on the trail that she only gradually understood was the one-time canal towpath. All that was discernible was a concavity in the ground to her right, until suddenly confronted by a large notice announcing dangerous locks, where children must not be permitted to play.

With utter fascination she identified the deep brick-lined pits that had once been a flight of four generous-sized locks, much wider than on other canals she had known, and puzzled as to how they came to be in such dense woodland. Surely there'd have been lockkeepers' cottages, broad basins for barges to loiter whilst waiting their turn, and the general bustle that went with the opening and closing of huge lock gates. Now there was nothing of that. The trees on all sides were mature deciduous specimens, giving an impression of permanence. But sixty or seventy years ago, when the canal ceased to be used, it was possible that all around had been much more open. Perhaps she should ask Cecilia Clifton, who would surely know all the answers. Then she found herself wondering how purist the restoration people would be. Had they any intention of clearing the trees back to where they would have been in 1786 – or even 1925? Although canals routinely passed through wooded areas, she could not recall ever seeing locks so thoroughly encroached upon.

Walking slowly along, calling once in a while for Hepzie to stay within sight, she let her thoughts drift, first to her sister and then to her daughter. Jocelyn, she remembered with a jolt, was supposed to be phoning her this morning – and she had forgotten to bring her mobile with her. The thought of it trilling its mechanical jingle in these silent woods was distasteful anyway. What was all this crisis about? They were not a family given to dramas, as a general rule. The death of Carl had not just been the biggest event they'd had to deal with – it was pretty well the *only* one. Many years ago, Damien's wife had had an early miscarriage which had been sighed over. Emily had fallen off a ladder when cleaning windows and spent a night in hospital with concussion. But over all, they were a charmed lot, taking good fortune for granted and making very little complaint.

Which was all the more reason for puzzlement now. Jocelyn simply did not behave like this. Although, Thea mentally added, if anybody in the family was going to throw a wobbly, Joss would be the one.

As for Thea's daughter, there didn't seem to be any cause for concern, touch wood. When her father had died, Jessica had wept quietly, gone off her food and lost the colour from her cheeks. But she had rallied within a month or so, and picked up more or less where she'd left off. Which had been a very focused determination to become a police officer. Only a few weeks ago, she had graduated handsomely, and was due to embark on a fast track police training, supported by her Uncle James, a Detective Superintendent, whose gratification knew no bounds. Currently, Jess was in the Rocky Mountains, touring with a group of fellow graduates in a Winnebago. She had warned her mother that there would be no communications for at least a fortnight.

Sooner than she had expected, the path emerged onto a small road, with the Daneway Inn only a short distance to her left. A quick consultation of the map showed her that she could return through the same woods, but on a lower path, the other side of the one-time canal. Mindful of the pony back at Juniper Court, and the evident imminence of rain, she turned right, and within a few yards located a second footpath roughly parallel to the first.

This was an even wider pathway, with signs of motorised vehicles and horses' hoofprints. With only a few minor mistakes, she recrossed the railway line, and cut up through a field that bordered the road leading into Frampton Mansell.

In a sudden burst of high spirits, she began to run up the sloping field through another swathe of wet grass reaching to knee height. She called to the dog and the two raced like children for a few hundred yards. Hepzie's long ears flew and flapped behind her, and her jaws parted in a doggy smile, as she bounded energetically through the grass.

Breathlessly, Thea rested against a stone wall beside the stile onto the road. 'Whew, I'm unfit,' she panted. Her chest was tight and her head quite giddy. She leaned forward, resting her hands on her knees, giving herself a chance to recover slowly. The dog nosed unconcernedly along the foot of the wall, where clumps of dock and nettles offered shelter to small rodents.

When the sound of a car engine came closer, Thea glanced at the spaniel, to ensure she wouldn't run into the road at the wrong moment. There seemed to be little risk of her so doing, but Thea moved a few steps away from the stile, to discourage any such idea.

When the car passed, she watched it over the wall. It was familiar, but it took her several seconds to connect it with the man from the day before. The maroon colour was the same, but the soft top had been folded back, so the driver was open to the rushing air. He wore old-fashioned goggles and an odd leather helmet, which concealed most of his face. It also concealed the direction of his gaze. He did not slow, or wave, or in any way suggest that he had noticed Thea standing there. But in spite of this, she knew with complete certainty that he had seen her.

She waited until the car was out of earshot before climbing back into the lane. Something was wrong. Despite the long list of perfectly innocent scenarios that would account for his presence, she was not happy. Perhaps, she reasoned, it was no more than her lasting nervousness around fast cars and potential traffic accidents. Losing her husband in a car crash was surely enough to explain this anxiety. And if it was not, then the death of the cat only a day or two ago added to the sense of vulnerability. Although not overly alarmed for herself, the real possibility of Hepzibah being run over was constantly at the back of her mind. Shakily, she attached the lead to the spaniel's collar and walked briskly back to the smallholding.

Everything seemed serenely normal as she walked in through the wide road gate. Geese were paddling in their slimy pond, peacocks perched on the roof of the barn, apparently dozing. The front door was closed, and her car was where she'd left it.

But something was different. She scanned the yard again, and the paddock beyond. It all looked entirely normal. Then she realised: the door to the pony's stable was wide open. Not simply the top half, left for Pallo to look through, but the lower section now stood at the same angle. And there was no sign at all of the animal.

A yap from Hepzie drew her to the rear of the house, and she laughed aloud with relief. The pony was placidly pulling carrots from the net hanging at a perfectly convenient height for him to reach. Ignoring the puzzle of how his door had come open, Thea approached assertively, and gripped a handful of creamy-coloured mane, in the absence of a halter. She pulled the pony around, reassured at the willing way he co-operated. 'Come on, you bad boy,' she murmured at him. 'You're not supposed to be out here. What would your young mistress say?'

Returning him to his quarters proved comfortingly easy to begin with. Only once or twice in her life had she been in such a situation, and her recollections of horses had given rise to a belief that they were not always so conciliatory. Her affection for Pallo rose in direct proportion to her relief that no harm had befallen him.

But halfway into the shed, he baulked. He pulled his head up and back, forcing Thea to release the hank of slippery hair. 'Oi!' she shouted, which only served to encourage him in his abrupt disobedience. He clattered a few steps backwards, before stopping and rolling his rheumy eyes at her. At least he didn't seem inclined to run away, and she moved calmly towards him, hoping to carry on as before.

The whole process was repeated, except that this time he dragged Thea with him as he backstepped out of his shed.

'This is getting silly,' she grumbled. 'What's the matter with you?' Tugging hard on his mane did not persuade him, and she understood that she could only lose in a trial of strength. Beneath it all, she had a sense that there was some sort of logic to the pony's behaviour. He was not acting wildly, nor exerting his superior force in any way. He simply refused to be shut in the stable again.

'Time for some lateral thinking,' Thea muttered to herself. 'Stay there,' she ordered Pallo. 'Don't you dare move.'

Then she went into the building, to check that there was no flood or goose or rat in the corner to account for the pony's reluctance.

There was no flood or goose or rat; nothing in any of the corners. But there was something guaranteed to upset a pony, however old and placid. There was a human body suspended from a beam in the roof, its feet so far off the ground that Thea would have had to jump up to touch them. A male person, sagging and leaking and slightly twisting on the end of a rope knotted appallingly tightly around his neck.

Chapter Four – Monday

A host of crazy thoughts flooded through Thea's mind, explanations entangled with the need for action. It was one of the Harrys, somehow returned home to hang himself. It was the person who'd killed Milo, struck suicidal with remorse. Even, idiotically, she imagined the body had been there for days, bizarrely forgotten or abandoned by the Phillipses, and unobserved by Thea herself. She had to keep Hepzie away for reasons she could not have explained. She had to do something with the blasted pony. And she had to call the police.

The face was inhumanly pale and lopsided, and Thea could only bear to regard it in short snatches. She didn't even consider cutting it down – and wouldn't have known how to go about it anyway. Quite how the chap had got himself there, suspended above such a long drop, was not a question she asked herself until some time later. Also much later she would analyse with some distress her total absence of sympathy or concern for the person this had been. She felt sick and angry, despairing and confused. She felt unfairly singled out, and grossly misused – but she didn't immediately feel pity.

Before calling the authorities, she led the pony to the big barn across the yard, where she found a halter hanging on a nail. This she slipped over his unprotesting head, and then tied him to an upright post. Somehow, the wellbeing of the pony now seemed more crucial than ever. Whatever happened, she was going to ensure that he would survive until his little mistress came home.

Police came, mutedly, almost secretively, with a doctor but no ambulance. First everybody went to the stable, and with some discussion and difficulty removed the body from the beam. Nobody told Thea not to watch, as they climbed up into the loft, and discovered the end of the rope securely tied to a hook above the big opening at the back of the building. Unable to see exactly what they were doing, she focused on the gentle lowering of the dead youth to the floor, where the doctor was waiting. She saw him check for vital signs, and sigh softly when none could be found. Then she saw him react as he turned his attention to the area of the neck.

When the two officers were back at ground level, the doctor must have given some invisible signal, because one of them turned to her, and ushered her firmly away. 'We'll have to ask you a few questions,' he said. 'Can we go into the house?'

Only then did he register that he had seen her before. It was a moment Thea had been anticipating with some embarrassment, ever since her realisation that one of the officers in attendance had been involved in the sudden death Thea had reported at her previous house-sit. 'Oh!' he gasped. 'Wasn't it you...?'

'I'm afraid so,' she muttered. 'Quite a grim coincidence, don't you think?'

His face wooden, the constable followed her into the house and asked rather more questions than she suspected was usual. The need to recapitulate the morning occupied all her thoughts for some time. Yes, she had gone into the stable, at about eight fifteen, to feed the pony. No, she had not seen a dead man hanging from the roof at that time. Given the behaviour of the pony subsequently, she could be almost certain that the body had not been there then. The hanging must have occurred while she was out on her walk. The door had been left open and the pony escaped. Her walk lasted for roughly two hours, from nine thirty to eleven thirty – plenty of time for the young man to do his suicidal deed.

But why choose Juniper Court? Thea strove to rationalise the fact of a second sudden death on a property under her care. 'He probably thought it made a good spot, with the people away,' she said feebly. 'And at least this one's suicide, and not murder.'

'Or so it would appear,' agreed the man. She could see bewildered suspicion leaking out of him, his eyes half closed, his teeth thoroughly sucked.

'What does that mean?'

He made no reply to that. 'We'll have to ask you not to enter that shed until further notice,' he told her. 'It'll have to be examined by Forensics. As will the yard and other buildings.'

''Seems a bit excessive for a suicide,' she commented. 'But I assume you know what's needed.' Then she added, 'The thing that docs seem just like last time is that we'll need to contact the family, I suppose.'

'Family? I thought you said you didn't know who the deceased was?'

'I don't mean *his* family. I mean the Phillipses. The people who live here.'

'Tell us about them, please.'

She enumerated the members of the Phillips family, and confirmed with effortful emphasis that this dead youth was not one of them.

'So you've never seen him before?' the police sergeant repeated.

A flash of memory occurred. 'Well…' she prevaricated. 'I don't think I have. But…'

'Yes?'

'Saturday afternoon, when I was walking, I saw somebody just for a moment, dodging behind a barn.'

'Where?'

'Somewhere over there,' she waved. 'I could show you. A fair-sized stone barn – the sort that usually gets converted into a house these days. I imagine it's the only one left for miles around. But it probably isn't the same person. There's just something…' She stopped to think, trying to pin down the elusive image. 'I saw a tall man, or boy. He had a bit of a limp. There's just something about this chap – he did seem quite tall.' She swallowed. What was she saying? 'And his hair's the same colour. You could tell, I suppose, if he had a bad leg.'

'Indeed.' The sergeant nodded at his subordinate, who made a note in his jotter. 'But you didn't speak to him at all?'

'No. I didn't even see his face. I'd forgotten all about him. He just slipped behind the barn as I walked past the field. I didn't take any notice, really. Why would I?'

Her initial sense of doom was overlaid with a growing irritation, a strong desire for this nuisance never to have happened. She wanted to relax into her assignment, to slob out, reading, walking and playing online Scrabble. She did not want to help the police with their enquiries or hear beastly stories of man's inhumanity and miserable boys choking to death in Pallo's stable.

'So why would it be him?' The policeman was nibbling his pencil, thinking hard.

It was a good question that was difficult to answer sensibly. 'I just think it probably was,' she said inadequately.

Had it been some bizarre premonition that accounted for the frisson of foreboding that she had so quickly suppressed on glimpsing the youth beside the barn? Or had there been something about the narrow hunched shoulders and painful-looking limp that screamed *victim* in those few seconds?

'He looked like some sort of outcast,' she went on. 'Ducking away out of sight, up to no good. Homeless, drug-addicted – that sort of thing.'

'All based on one quick sighting of him?'

'Right.'

She sat with her hands hanging limply between her thighs, staring unhappily at the floor. The constable's next words did a lot to revive her.

'I expect it was him, then,' he said.

She looked up. 'Really?'

'There aren't too many of that sort around here. Nobody's reported a man missing. This chap needed a shave and a wash and a haircut.'

It was only then that she thought to say something about the man in the sporty car.

The policeman gave the story full attention for about a minute, noting the detail of the man's wet trousers, and showing signs of real interest when she recounted her second sighting, earlier that morning. Then he earned Thea's admiration by asking, 'And why do you think he might be relevant?'

Most people would have skipped that particular question, if she was any judge. 'I didn't like the way he looked at me,' she said. 'As if he had some secret plans for me – or perhaps more that I was in the way of something he wanted to do. And now this has happened, I'm wondering if there's some connection. Except,' she added helplessly, 'if this was suicide, then there's no reason why anybody else would be involved, is there?'

The man didn't reply to that. He stared at the photo of Desmond Phillips with his fish for a long unfocused moment, before closing his notebook. 'If you think of anything else, please contact us,' he said, handing over a card with the phone number of the Cirencester police. 'There'll be quite a bit of coming and going outside. We'd be glad if you'd stay indoors for the next hour or so, with your dog. Oh – ' he checked himself on an afterthought, ' – and don't speak to anybody about this for the time being. Okay?'

Trying not to resent these instructions, she drifted around the house for a few minutes before settling irritably in the living room with Hepzie, flipping through more of the magazines the Phillipses had accumulated. But she wasn't seeing them. She was thinking about death.

The image of the dead boy flickered in and out of her mind, like a scene from a particularly graphic film. In fact it was less horrible than most cinematic scenes – the man with the top of his skull removed in *Hannibal* gave her a much deeper shudder when she conjured it. Equally strong were the might-have-beens, the things that had never actually happened, or even appeared on film, but *could* have done. And dreadful accidents involving animals, full of unbearable screams and futile human struggles to rescue the unrescuable. By the age of forty-two, anybody's head contained a goodly stack of such visions, to be glanced at from time to time out of some basic human need to acknowledge that life was never going to be peaceful and painless for long.

All of which highlighted the glaring omission of any actual *feelings*. Having no name or background information on the young man made it impossible to *care* directly about him. He was like a tramp found dead in a ditch. Now and then a local philanthropist would pay for a proper funeral, out of some murky motivation involving perceived obligations, perhaps – but nobody could really care, in a personal sense. 'Each man's death diminishes me' or whatever it was that John Donne said, was a fine sentiment, but Thea had never experienced it as viscerally true. Much closer to her own honest reaction was Orson Welles at the top of that big wheel in Vienna, describing the people below as ants, whose disappearance couldn't truthfully be expected to make any difference to a total stranger who couldn't even see their faces.

Films, she realised. How much of our moral reasoning apparently derived from them. How graphically they could present us with a situation, a dilemma, an act of appalling cruelty. If the hanging boy had been displayed, features blank, body slowly twisting in the warm air of the stable, a fly delightedly exploring this bounty of potential breeding ground – would Thea have been any more or less impressed than by the three-dimensional reality?

She didn't know, and this lack of certainty was much less shameful to her than other people might have expected. Thea Osborne had earned a bagful of moral credit when her husband had been snatched from her so young. She had been down to the mouth of hell, and come back again tempered by the experience. If this boy had parents and friends and siblings, then they would grieve for his loss. And rightfully so. But to Thea, he was just a boy, gone out of the world before she had known he was in it.

His death, if she was quite brutally honest with herself, was primarily a nuisance, and an embarrassment. Why hadn't he chosen some other place to finish himself off? Apart from anything else, it must surely have frightened the precious pony.

The moment the hour was up, she went outside.

The pony claimed her attention first. Police tape stretched across the doorway of his shed, and as she crossed the yard, side-stepping the continuing police activity, a van appeared containing two more police officers. Determined not to be banished to the house again, Thea marched into the barn without even giving them a wave.

It was obviously going to be impossible to return the pony to his rightful home for the foreseeable future. There was a smaller shed as well as the stone barn, but it was dark and smelt of mildew, which couldn't possibly be healthy. It seemed unkind to keep him tied up, but risky to let him loose in the barn, even if she moved the bags of food and bales of hay. Barns had hazards lurking under the scattering of straw, or behind the planks standing up in one corner.

Doggedly, Thea began to partition off one end of the space, using some of the planks, and an old metal gate that had been replaced by a newer wooden one, and was propped against the road fence. Carrying it was almost too much for her, and none of the police people offered to help, but she refused to give up. The remaining stretch was barricaded by a roll of wire netting attached to the gate and barn wall by lengths of plastic string she located neatly looped over a post by the barn door.

It took nearly an hour, and effectively prevented her from reflecting on the grisly discovery she'd made. Neither would she permit herself to envisage the coming solitary nights in the house, adjacent to the scene of pain and suffering.

What would the Phillipses expect her to do? Was the dead boy somebody they knew? A relative? By now the police would have called Desmond's mobile and told him the news. They'd probably come home, and dismiss her from her duties. She more than half hoped they would.

At least her police detective brother-in-law James wasn't going to come and interfere this time. Even if he hadn't been off to Deauville, he would hardly bother with a suicide, however unpleasant and mysterious. South Gloucestershire was not his official territory, and the local people would be unlikely to welcome a second intervention from a West Midlands Superintendent.

Presumably, anyway, once the body was identified, the family notified, the scene certified free from suspicion, things could carry on much as before. There would not be investigations and SOCOs and worries about lurking killers. Except, she realised, the police were already showing a disproportionate amount of interest in the scene of a suicide. If everything had been clear and straightforward, surely they'd have left by this time?

She went to the taped-off stable door and peered inside. There were two figures in white suits standing in the centre of the floor staring up into the roof. One of them caught sight of Thea and smiled over his face mask. 'Almost done,' he said, in a muffled voice.

'Have you come to any conclusions?' she asked.

The eyes became veiled. 'Too early to say,' he replied curtly. With no warning, Thea found herself to be quite seriously frightened. Her insides were clenching painfully, and she made a rapid departure, heading for the loo with a sudden urgency.

The ringing of her mobile phone reminded her of Jocelyn for the first time since her walk. Her sister's voice, when Thea answered the call, was strained and impatient.

'Where have you *been*?' she whined. 'I've been phoning since ten this morning.'

With some surprise Thea noted that it was already past two.

'I went for a walk. Then I was outside a lot. Sorry.' She wanted to explain, to splurge the details of this latest death and her own sense of victimisation, but not to her sister, and definitely not on the phone. Jocelyn had never been a very good confidante, and it sounded as if she was currently even more useless than usual.

'Can I *really* not have your house? It's very mean of you.'

'Not until I know what this is all about. I'm here for a fortnight. I don't want you making free with my stuff for all that time.'

'Thea, we're not children any more. I'm not going to spoil your jigsaw or scribble in your favourite storybook.'

It was enough to bring Thea up short, aware that this was very much the kind of reaction she'd been experiencing. Jocelyn had been a tremendous pest as a child, forcing the older children to hide their possessions from her, in case she broke them. It was chastening to discover that this image still hung around her, thirty-five years on.

'No, I know you're not. It's just that I need to understand what's going on first. I don't want to be accused of sheltering a wanted criminal, do I?'

'What?' Her sister sounded utterly bewildered.

Thea forced a laugh. 'That was a bit uncalled-for – sorry. It's because I've just been interviewed by the police, you see. It's the way my mind's working today.'

'Police? Why?'

Thea sighed. 'I can't tell you the whole thing over the phone. Look – can you come and see me, face to face?' A sudden idea struck her with the force of a punch on the ear. It seemed impossible that she hadn't thought of it sooner. 'Actually, if you're desperate for sanctuary, you'd be better off here, assuming I'll be staying for the agreed time. You can share the house-sitting with me, and we can talk everything through properly. And, to be honest, you'd be doing me a big favour as well.'

'But —'

'It's not so far away. And it's a lovely place. Loads to explore.'

'Oh.' Thea could hear the thinking going on at the other end. 'I suppose that might be all right. I really do have to get away from here. What's that place you put in your email? Muddlehampton or something. I've never heard of it.'

'Minchinhampton. It's south of Stroud.'

'I have no idea where Stroud is, either.'

'Hang on. I'll find a map.' Carefully, Thea directed her incompetent sister up the M5 from Bristol, and off at Junction 12. 'I'll meet you outside the church in the middle of the town, at four,' she said. 'You can't miss it – it's only a small place.'

The next half hour was occupied with assembling a quick belated lunch, and trying to guess what might be wrong with her sister. She felt jangled and stressed, but strangely upbeat after the wobbles of a short while earlier. The prospect of having Jocelyn in the house with her for a few days was primarily an appealing one, chasing away any worries about prowling strangers who might have suicide or murder on their minds. There would, she hoped, be no more police visits, once they were satisfied that the death had indeed been self-inflicted – unless they made a courtesy call to update her on the identity of the dead boy. She would focus on more local walks, and perhaps a spot of historical research if she could find a decent library, with her sister as deputy in pony care and cooking. And she could find out what in the world was the matter with Jocelyn.

Siblings, as she had recently realised, were the longest relationship anybody had in their lives, and the patterns were determined from the outset. Thea and the others had always competed, at the same time as sensibly colonising different areas of interest and experience to make the whole thing bearable. Thea had not initially elected to be clever. Her studies had come later than normal, and she was drastically outshone by Damien who got four A-levels and a first class degree and worked for British Airways doing something frightfully responsible. Neither had she been pretty in her early years. Her good looks were a feature of her adulthood, when some magic had transformed her into a beauty at twenty. The second child and first daughter, Emily, on the other hand, had been a curly-headed cherub from infancy, content to rely on this as her passport through life.

Which left Jocelyn and Thea to wrestle for more complicated ground. Thea had been her father's soulmate. She had asked questions and shown interest. She had walked alongside him, encouraging him to reminisce about his own early life, and had read books under his guidance. Jocelyn, the youngest, had inevitably been kept close to her mother for longer than the others. They boasted a telepathic bond which did at times seem impressive. Jocelyn wanted to do what her mother had done – produce a family of apparently healthy happy children. She was brilliant at nursery rhymes, fairytales, knitting, first aid. She had passed her exams half-heartedly, and taken an unambitious degree in Fine Arts, which as far as Thea could see, never taught her anything at all.

Where Jocelyn scored the highest points was in her maternity, and she had always made much of it. All of which meant that, in her unexpected abandonment of the role, Thea was left in floundering confusion as to just who her sister now was.

By two thirty all the police had left. Feeling jangled and restless, Thea felt impelled to seek out some ordinary human contact. There must be neighbours she could call on, besides the scatter-brained Frannie. But she hesitated, mindful of the policeman's injunction not to discuss the events of the morning. Could she simply stroll up to somebody's front door and engage in idle chatter, given what had happened? What if the person turned out to be the parent or sibling of the dead boy?

But she couldn't bear to stay in the house, or the surrounding yard. Without Jocelyn's providential arrival, she wondered what she would have done. The loneliness was suddenly acute, a feeling of cold emptiness, a chill wind blowing. She could get in the car now, and drive to Minchinhampton, and visit some shops before Jocelyn turned up. The dog could come too, and Juniper Court could take its chances for a couple of hours.

She dithered, wrestling with conflicting urges. Was it responsible of her to abandon the place, when she might be needed again by the police, and the pony might require attention? But she wanted to regain a sense of normality. The car and a small country town would give her that. 'Come on,' she said to the dog. 'We'll go for a drive.'

But they didn't get far. Having locked the house securely, and got out of the car to close the yard gate behind her, she heard a woman's voice calling from somewhere up the lane. Turning, she was confronted by a vision of some impact.

The woman wore a bright red skirt that reached to mid-calf, and a maroon crushed velvet jacket. Her hair was short, but vivid, dyed with expensive-looking golden highlights. At first glance she looked youngish – well under forty. With each successive minute, Thea revised this estimate upwards until it passed fifty.

'Just caught you, I see. Lucky me.' The voice was metallic, with London roots.

Thea was still trying to accommodate the arrival of this apparition, the car engine running and driver's door open. 'Er...' she said.

'I'm Valerie Innes. I live at the Manor. You must have noticed it.' Leaving no time for Thea to demur, she sailed on. 'We saw the palaver here and thought you might need some help.' She peered voraciously into the yard of Juniper Court, observing the police tape and car tyre marks. 'What on earth's going on?'

'Well,' Thea tried. 'Actually — '

Valerie Innes stepped up to Thea's car and reached in to quell the engine. Taking her for a new friend, Hepzie leaped at her, all smiles and wags. With a cry of disgust the woman backed away, slamming the car door almost on the animal's face.

'Careful!' Thea cried, furiously. 'What do you think you're doing?'

'Can't bear dogs,' said Valerie, as if this were the default position for any normal person. 'Now, are you going to tell me what's the matter here?'

'No I'm not,' said Thea, recognising that rudeness was the only way to deal with this person. 'I've been asked not to talk about it.'

'Nonsense. You can talk to *me*.' Thea heard the additional Don't you know who I am? that never quite got uttered.

'I'm afraid I've got to go.' She made a small movement towards the car.

'No, *no*. You silly girl. I've come to *help*, don't you see? I've got three valiant sons at home, ready and willing to come and lend a hand. You've obviously got troubles, you poor thing. It would be stupid to turn down any offers of help.'

'I don't think I need any help.' Thea spoke loudly, forced onto the defensive by the onslaught of this outrageous woman.

'Of course you do. You can't possibly carry on here by yourself. I don't know exactly what might have happened, but I can see it was serious. Such a little thing, too, aren't you. No match for any intruders or whatever they are.'

'I won't be by myself,' Thea almost shouted. 'I'll be perfectly all right. Now, I do have to go.' Ordinarily she would have expressed thanks for the concern, but already she was finding it impossible to be polite to somebody so pushy.

'All right. When will you be back? I'll bring the boys round to see you – just so you know what reinforcements are at hand if you need them.'

How had this happened, Thea wondered. Suddenly she was plunged into a game she didn't want to play. She found herself searching for evasions, diversions, anything that would ensure she never had to see this woman again. But already she understood that escape was impossible, resistance useless. Valerie Innes lived at the Manor, which Thea guessed had to be the large and very beautiful stone house set on rising ground half a mile to the west. And Thea was trapped here at Juniper Court for another twelve days.

'I'm not sure when I'll be back,' she said. 'But I'll have my sister with me. And we've got a lot to talk about.' Even now, she couldn't say directly – Do not visit me. Leave us alone. Go away, you pest. Women like this exploited a person's natural civility, marching through the gaps left by an inability to speak the naked truth.

'This evening, then,' said Valerie. 'I'll bring the boys.'

As she drove the few miles to Minchinhampton, Thea wondered about 'the boys'. How would it be to have a mother like that? Were they cowed little wimps, brokenly obeying her every word? Or did they somehow tune her out, going through the motions while effectively barricaded against her intrusions? Or did each one have his own strategy for dealing with her? Or, improbably, was she a whole different person at home – loving and accepting, inspiring devotion and concern from sons who must surely be in their late teens at least?

Chapter Five – Monday

Jocelyn was standing outside the lychgate of the church close to the centre of Minchinhampton as Thea drove her car into a free place only a few yards away at four o'clock. She and Hepzie had spent a soothing hour on the Common, in the meantime. Her sister didn't see her, which gave Thea a chance to examine her unawares. She looked fatter and older than she had only six weeks earlier. Her hair had been cut very short, and sat like a limp earth-coloured rag on her head. Her shoulders sloped and all her weight was on one leg, reminding Thea unpleasantly of the limping youth she'd seen a few days before.

'Here I am,' Thea announced, approaching quickly. 'Didn't you see me?'

Jocelyn shook her head. 'I was thinking,' she said. 'And trying to work out whether this place is a real town or just a sort of film set. Have you seen the churchyard?' She pointed through the lychgate, where manicured grass and paved paths surrounded very soldierly headstones, with a wooden seat and war memorial for good measure.

Thea looked. 'Unreal,' she agreed, remembering the church at Duntisbourne Abbots, which had infinitely more character.

She inspected her sister with a long steady gaze. 'You look ghastly,' she concluded.

'I know.'

'So, what the hell's going on?'

Jocelyn heaved a deep sigh, and looked around her. 'Can we go somewhere?'

'What – like a tea shoppe or something? I'm not sure there is one.'

'Well, just a bit of a walk, then. I need to stretch my legs after all that driving.'

They spent less than ten minutes walking down one side of the High Street and up the other. Two cars passed during that time, and perhaps six or seven pedestrians. There was no noise, no sign of any shoppers in the handful of smart emporiums. Two places snagged Thea's interest: a French restaurant and a pink-painted building labelled 'The Cotswold Club'.

Jocelyn followed her gaze. 'Maybe we should give that a try one evening,' she suggested, nodding at 'Sophie's'.

'Looks pricey,' said Thea. 'I'm not here for a holiday, you know.'

'Neither am I, I suppose. But we might as well have a bit of fun while we're at it.'

The Cotswold Club had opaque glass windows, boasting a recurring motif of a sheep in each one. Thea eyed it with growing curiosity. 'What do you suppose that is?' she said. 'All very secretive.'

Jocelyn glanced at the building and shrugged. 'Looks like a Freemasons' Hall for women,' she said. 'All that pink.'

'That's what I thought,' Thea agreed.

'This place is still a dump,' Jocelyn grumbled. 'I'm trying to like it, but it's beyond me. I thought towns were supposed to have people in them.'

'I expect they're all out on the Common playing golf or flying kites,' said Thea. 'There's a pub, though. I bet it'll be heaving in another couple of hours.'

Jocelyn glanced at The Crown Inn and shook her head. 'I doubt it,' she said.

Returning to their cars, they made elaborate arrangements for Thea to lead the way back to Juniper Court, the atmosphere between them spiky with untold stories. Driving slowly, constantly checking that Jocelyn was following in her elderly Volvo, Thea ran once more through the possible explanations for this descent into such uncharacteristic calamity. Illness now took first place, with adultery second. If Jocelyn could consider eating at what was obviously a highly priced restaurant, money was probably off the list.

The road gate to Juniper Court was open, as she'd left it in her haste to escape from Valerie Innes. And a police car was parked on the yard, somehow giving the impression that it had been there a long time.

Thea recognised the man sitting in the driving seat.

'Hello,' she greeted him, watching her dog jumping up at his legs as he got out of his car. 'Fancy seeing you here.' His lean face was all she could focus on, in the seconds she took to cross the yard to him. She registered as if for the first time how strong his features were, what a surge of emotions he generated within her. Surely she hadn't felt like this on their last encounter? Superintendent Philip Hollis had admittedly gone some way towards endearing himself to her three months earlier, when his leg had been in plaster and he'd manifested a genuine concern for Hepzibah when she'd been injured, but she hadn't given him more than a fleeting few thoughts since then.

'Hello *again*, I suppose you mean,' he said without the ghost of a smile. 'I do hope this won't get to be a habit. Perhaps I should ask you now where your next engagement as a house-sitter might be.'

'I haven't got another one lined up. After this, I might well abandon the whole exercise.'

'That might not be a bad idea.'

She was still completely fixated on his face, recalling how he had inexplicably frightened her when she first met him. She remembered being suspicious of him, and finally grateful for his understanding.

'So – why are you concerned with a suicide?' she asked.

'Because we don't think it *was* suicide,' he said, confirming suspicions she had so earnestly been trying to suppress.

She might never have remembered Jocelyn if her sister hadn't slammed out of her car after sitting in it for three minutes waiting for further instructions. Thea understood how odd it had been that Hollis had utterly ignored the fact of a second car coming into the yard. She understood that something was happening that she could not for a moment have predicted. Something was tugging, sucking at her insides, urging them towards the man who stood there, giving her the distinct impression that the same thing was happening to him.

'This is my sister, Jocelyn,' she introduced. 'Joss, this is Superintendent Hollis. He's a policeman.' She turned back to the man. 'I haven't explained to Joss about what happened here this morning. Let's go in, and try and get it all sorted out.'

She led the way into the living room, and then let Hollis take control. He glanced around the room at the hurriedly squared-off piles of toys, comics, CDs and videos. 'Nice and homely,' he muttered.

'They're lovely people. Did you get hold of them?'

'Mr Phillips has his mobile turned off. We left a message for him. You've no idea where they are, I take it?'

'A day or so's drive from Cork, is all I know. Nearly two days by now, I suppose. Are you going to bring them home?'

'We'll have to see about that. One thing at a time.'

In the ensuing pause, Thea glimpsed how this must look and sound to Jocelyn, who was sitting on an upright antique chair close to the window, abjuring the comfortable sofa and armchairs in the middle of the room. 'Gosh, Joss, this is dreadful timing. The thing is, I found a chap hanging in one of the sheds this morning.'

The words echoed ludicrously in her own ears. Had she really just made such a bald statement as if it was a comment on the weather?

Jocelyn went even paler than before, and put a hand to her mouth. 'I don't believe it! My God! Why aren't you screaming and running for home? What is it with you?' The final question was uttered with a profound exasperation which Thea recognised as familiar. As children when a knee was cut or a head bashed during some wild outdoor game Thea would be the calm one, cracking ludicrous jokes and refusing to join in the general hysteria. 'Come on, you're not dead,' was a refrain she was famous for in the family. Her nephews and nieces had learned of her reputation, and once experienced it at first hand when Jocelyn's little Roly had fallen spectacularly off a toboggan and Thea, who had charge of them for the afternoon, had merely scooped him up, dusted him down and plonked him right back on the sledge. 'Wow!' Noel, the eldest, had breathed. 'Mum would have really freaked at that.'

'Well, he's not dead, is he?' Thea had grinned, causing delight and hilarity all round.

'Thea,' Jocelyn tried again. 'We'll have to leave.' She glanced nervously out of the front window. 'You mean, just out there somewhere? Right *here*? Somebody hanging – I assume dead?' She was growing incoherent with the shock.

'For heaven's sake.' Thea rolled her eyes. 'It's horrible, I know. But let's not panic, okay.'

She turned back to the police detective. 'We don't need to panic, do we?'

He kept his eyes on her face, appraising her for several seconds. 'If I remember rightly, you're not the panicking type.'

Jocelyn guffawed at that. 'Ten out of ten for insight,' she applauded him. 'She's like a rhinoceros, not scared of anything.'

Thea briefly considered a sharp retort involving the catastrophic death of Carl and the way such a happening altered your perspective, but she wasn't sure Jocelyn would let her get away with it. The trouble with sisters, she thought crossly, was they knew too much about you.

'Well, I hope I've got the sense to make a proper assessment of the risks,' she said. 'If you tell me there's a maniac on the loose and there's reason to think I'm his next target, then I'd be scared. As it is, I've promised to look after this place for two weeks. I can't just bale out at a moment's notice. What about the pony?' She made a wry face. 'Although I don't have to worry about the cat any more.'

'Oh?'

'The poor thing was killed on the road yesterday morning. Not a very auspicious start.' She grimaced again. 'Even worse than I realised.'

'You didn't mention this to Sergeant Barnfield this morning, did you?'

'Why should I?'

He raised his eyebrows at her flash of defensiveness. 'No reason. But you've told me now, and I'm making a note of it.' He took out a small notebook, found the next available blank page and wrote something with a pencil kept attached to the book by a red cord. There was something old-fashioned and almost endearing about the neat efficiency of it all. He kept the book in his hand.

She paused. 'If he was hanging, why are we talking about murder? Why wasn't it suicide?'

Hollis smiled at this. 'It wasn't suicide because somebody else killed him,' he said with annoying literalness.

'Can you be sure? Isn't it more likely that he had a friend with him and they were mucking about, and this poor boy slipped? Something like that? An accident.'

'Why do you say "boy"?'

The question caught her up short. 'Oh! I'm not really sure.' She reran the image of him hanging in space. 'Something about the knobbly wrists, maybe. A look of having grown too fast. Narrow shoulders. I don't really know. Why – how old was he?'

'We think around twenty.'

'There you are then.' She was more and more impatient. 'You don't have a name for him then?'

The Inspector shook his head. 'Early days,' he said.

'I don't suppose you'll tell me why you think it was murder. Was it something to do with him being so pale? I thought people went purple when they were hanged. Or black.'

'A common misconception. Do you want details?'

Thea experienced conflicting emotions. One of them was a sharp awareness of her suffering sister, who very likely did not need to hear about the pathology of strangulation.

'Maybe not just at the moment.' She smiled at him, and something twisted or expanded or leaped within her when he smiled back. She swallowed with difficulty. 'My sister's just got here, and it seems she's going through some kind of domestic crisis.' She lifted her eyebrows at Jocelyn, trying to convey sensitivity and sisterhood. 'I feel as if I need to be in several places at once.'

'Are you staying here?' he asked Jocelyn.

She spread her hands helplessly. 'I thought so, ten minutes ago,' she muttered. 'Though I hadn't bargained for murderers in the outbuildings. I'll have to have a think about it.'

'I came here intending to order you to go home,' he said to Thea. 'But now —'

'Now I've got a minder you can stop worrying. And what makes you think you've got the right to order me to do anything?'

He cocked his head, his eyes on hers. 'I'm a policeman,' he said, with a cautious smile. 'And I do need to ask you some more questions. To start with, can you tell me exactly who you've met since arriving here on Saturday. Have there been any visitors?'

Thea stifled a snort, remembering the dreadful Valerie Innes of that afternoon. 'It's been like Piccadilly Circus,' she joked, before catching his expression and quickly sobering. 'Sorry. Well, let me see.' It wasn't easy to recapture all the events since Saturday. Hollis waited patiently while she gathered her thoughts, but Jocelyn fidgeted. Before responding to the man's questions, Thea turned to her sister. 'Why don't you take your bag upstairs and get settled? You've got the room with the picture of the horse on the wall.'

Jocelyn got heavily to her feet. 'I'm staying then, am I? Is that decided?'

'Yes.' Thea was emphatic.

'Right, then.' And Jocelyn left the room.

'A man came to the door yesterday afternoon,' Thea began, adding as much detail as she could recall, at Hollis's prompting. 'Before that, there was a woman called Cecilia something. A bridge – Clifton, that was it. She came to tell me about the cat in the road, and then she came back later and we chatted about local history. That's the only visitors, but I've also seen a couple from just down the lane. Frannie and Robert. I can't remember their surname. Cecilia knows them quite well. And this afternoon, when your lot had all gone, a ghastly creature from the Manor House intercepted me in the road and told me her three sons would come and guard me, or something. Valerie Innes.' Thea made much of the name, with the need for a pause between first and second. She had always made much of such names, since being at school with a Barbara Angus. 'She's a monster.'

Hollis jotted busily. 'Nobody else?'

'Not a soul. I think that's rather good going in such a short time.'

'And you've been for a walk, I gather? That's when you saw somebody who could have been our victim?'

'Yes, that's right. Oh, and I went for another one this morning, and saw the wet man again. I told your constable about it.'

'Tell me again.'

She supplied all the detail she could remember, including the goggles and the strange leather headgear. 'He can't be difficult to identify. Probably belongs to some daft motoring club.'

Hollis jotted again, and then got up to go. In the hallway, Jocelyn joined then, coming slowly down the stairs. The policeman addressed them both. 'I'm not going to tell you there's any direct danger to you,' he intoned. 'But I'm not going to tell you you're perfectly safe, either. Until we know a lot more about this business, all I can do is advise you to be extremely careful.'

'The police always say that, don't they?' said Jocelyn, still strung up, speaking too loudly. 'Like the threat of bombs and everything – they tell people to be vigilant and careful, but we all know there's no real safeguard. Except,' she added wildly, aware of the absence of logic in her thought processes, 'it's not like that here. Thea can just leave. She can go home where nobody's going to murder her.'

'I'm not leaving,' Thea stated firmly.

Hollis departed quickly, having issued stern instructions about staying clear of the pony shed because there might be more forensic examinations. He told Thea to keep the doors of the house firmly locked at night, and he admonished Hepzibah to be a good guard dog. He also gave a partially reassuring promise that there would be a police patrol car passing regularly throughout the night. Then he gave one last wave before turning out of the gate. Thea had walked after the car across the yard as if linked to it by a string. When he was out of sight, something hurt in the area of her navel. 'Good God,' she murmured. 'I don't believe this.'

The sheer intrusive rudeness of committing a murder in a building only a few yards from the house hit Thea repeatedly, as she tried to carry on more or less normally. The assumption that the evil deed had been deliberately timed for the Phillipses' absence really got under her skin. It implied that she was unimportant, a fleeting nuisance that could be worked around with a bit of extra care. The whole thing must have been staged and executed with cold-blooded forethought – the rope had looked new, for a start. She hadn't seen it in the shed, and could almost swear it had not been hanging where an impulsive killer could handily reach it. Even if the police were wrong, and the death was really suicide, as she supposed it was meant to appear, then that too had been premeditated.

'So who goes first in the explaining session?' Jocelyn demanded, from the front doorstep, where she had watched the parting between Thea and Hollis with interest.

'Neither of us, for a bit longer,' Thea said. 'I've got to go and look at the pony, and collect eggs and feed Hepzie.'

'I'll get my bag out of the car, then.'

Thea approached the pony's new domicile with her mind in overdrive. There were too many questions for comfort, a sense of a road only just embarked on, stretching ahead, passing through dark woods and choppy waters before it even started to think of arriving at a restful destination. She didn't understand about the murder-by-hanging, but it would certainly entail more questions about what she had seen and done since her arrival at Juniper Court.

And there was her sister, waiting not-so-patiently for her listening ear. The woman had walked out on a husband and five children, a few days before the school holidays were due to start. She looked terrible and sounded desperate. It was unnatural and unkind to delay the moment of revelation any longer.

After a quick look at Pallo, and a visit to the hens' nestboxes, she went back to the house. Jocelyn's handbag was sitting in the hall, and her sister was running water in the kitchen. 'I'm making tea,' she said, defiantly, when Thea joined her. 'That's all right, isn't it?'

'Of course. I'm sorry – everything happened at once.'

'Quite a day for you, by the sound of it.' There was no sympathy discernible in her tone.

'It is, rather. But nothing's going to stop me from hearing what your problem is. If the phone rings I'll ignore it.'

'What if somebody comes to the door?'

'They won't,' said Thea, remembering in that instant the man in the rain who'd been looking for Daneway. And then driven past wearing goggles, like somebody from the 1930s, only a short time after a murder had been committed. 'And if they do, the geese'll warn us.'

'Sit down then,' insisted Jocelyn. 'And don't change the subject.'

Thea obeyed, expecting a silence until the tea was made and set before them on the kitchen table.

'He's been hitting me.' The words flew around the room, conjuring images, gender politics, horror and confusion.

'Alex?' Thea frowned and shook her head to clear the conflict between how you were supposed to react and what her actual feelings were. 'What – hard?'

'Hard enough to scare me. And make me absolutely furious. And wear me to a frazzle, trying to decide what to do about it.'

'I'm amazed.' She knew she wasn't supposed to ask what her sister had done to provoke him, what the matter was with Alex, why such a tragic air over something that was, really, rather ordinary. They were taboo questions, suggestive of complicity or even provocation on the woman's part. But Thea wanted to ask them, just the same.

'Are you? Men do hit women, you know. Quite a lot, apparently. And yes, I know what you're thinking. I'd have been the same myself, probably. You're thinking it's all got entangled with political correctness and feminist stridency and every man's entitled to lose his rag once in a while. But, Thee, it's different when it actually happens. It shakes your whole world.'

'But *Alex*.' Thea was wrestling hard to get the picture straight.

'Precisely.'

'And you've left him in charge of the kids.'

'He won't hurt *them*. It's me he's got it in for.'

'But —' Thea's head was slowly clearing. Men hit their wives because they had a deep need to be in control, and were afraid this was slipping. They were insecure, inarticulate, frustrated. They saw their wives as deviating from the script they thought had been agreed between them. The question burst out before she could stop it. 'What have you *done* to him?'

She expected rage at this tactless question, or ice-cold withdrawal. At the very least an earnest womanly reproach.

'That's the terrible thing – I honestly don't know,' said Jocelyn quietly. 'I feel exactly like Desdemona must have felt. I remember thinking at school what an impossible position she was in. You just can't fight that sort of thing. Alex won't say what he thinks I've done, what my crime is, what he thinks he's discovered about me. It's an insane situation.'

Thea puffed her cheeks out, finally accepting the severity of the story. 'Wow,' she breathed. 'You poor thing.'

'Don't say that! I don't want to be *a poor thing*. I want to be me – without having to be scared of what I say to him, or how I look at him, or who I talk to on the phone. It's a stupid way to live.'

'How long has it been happening?'

'Nearly four months. It was Easter, the first time.'

'That's a long time.' Thea kept her tone neutral.

'Time to have worked out that I've got to do something about it. I've been through a whole load of stages since then. Trying to see it from his point of view, mainly. But now I've given up trying to explain it. I don't care any more what deep-seated psychological trouble he might be having. I just want to stay away from him. Permanently.'

'But the *kids*,' Thea wailed. 'What about the kids?'

'He can have them,' Jocelyn said, staring out of the kitchen window. 'He's welcome to them.'

Thea felt a giggle trying to erupt, impossibly wrong for the moment. She aborted it with a struggle. But the tension had broken, all the same. Jocelyn was going to be all right, thanks perhaps to her robustly secure upbringing, or the central core of self-preservation she'd learned from her position in the family – and the prospect of her sister's company while she was at Juniper Court was an increasingly engaging one.

'Tea,' she said. 'You've forgotten to make the tea.'

The evening was mild and dry, suggesting a welcome change in the weather, and the sisters sat outside facing each other across a garden table on a small fenced-off lawn at the back of the house.

Thea had fed and watered two guinea pigs and two rabbits, ranged in a collection of cages along one wall of the shed nearest the house.

'This place is a funny mixture, isn't it,' observed Jocelyn. 'Big old house, and all these outbuildings that look as if they've been thrown up at random over the years.'

'You didn't always need planning permission before you could do anything more than introduce a chicken coop,' said Thea. 'Everything must have been put here for a reason.'

'I don't doubt that. And I think it's all very pretty and every-thing. But it's awfully old-fashioned, isn't it. They're not farmers, are they? What do they do with that great barn, for a start?'

'I bet if you had a barn like that, you'd fill it to the rafters in about a week.'

'I'd be scared to go in it, in case there were rats.'

Thea chuckled indulgently. 'I forgot how daft you are about rats. Remember that one at Grandad's – when Damien chased you with it.'

Jocelyn shuddered. 'That's about the only thing I do remem-ber about Grandad's place. I don't think I've ever got over it.'

'You were such a wimp.'

'I was only about five. Damien was twelve.'

'You didn't like going there like the rest of us did.'

'I liked the baby things – those yellow chicks, and piglets.'

'Joss – you're not serious about abandoning your kids, are you? Roly's only five, for heaven's sake. And Abby – she's devoted to you. It'd break her heart.'

'I'm not talking about abandoning them. Just letting them stay with Alex in the house they've always lived in. He's very good with them – better than me in a lot of ways.'

'He's got to work, though. What time does he get home? What about homework and clothes and bedtime stories and monitoring their internet access and keeping up with who their friends are?'

'So you think I could do all that on my own, do you? I work as well, you know. Your idea of our lives is way offbeam, anyway. It might have been like that for you, with only one kid and no proper job. We just muddle along, thinking we've done well if everybody's had enough of the right sort of food by the end of the day.'

Thea stuck to the main point, ignoring the reference to her own situation. 'I just can't imagine Alex coping with it all. That's what I'm saying.'

Jocelyn shook her head impatiently. 'People cope when they have to. Never mind all that now. I've said all I want to for the time being. It sounds to me as if you've got just as urgent stuff going on here. That police person wanted you to pack up and leave, didn't he? He thinks it's dangerous for you.'

'I might just have done it, too, if you hadn't shown up. There were already a few nasty moments before I found that boy in Pallo's shed.'

'Thea, it isn't natural, the way you go on. A dead man in a shed – murdered, if I've got it right – and you're as calm as a cucumber.'

'Cool. Cucumbers are cool.'

'Same thing. Anyway – what nasty moments?'

'The cat was run over. A lovely Siamese called Milo. It's terribly sad. It made me scared for Hepzie. I can't be sure she won't go on the road – and she's not very sensible about cars. I can't seem to teach her that they're dangerous.'

'Where is it? The cat, I mean?'

'In the spare freezer. In the garage.'

'With the people food?'

'I put him in a bag, in the fast-freeze section, which was empty. I couldn't think what else to do. They'll probably want some sort of ceremony. You know what people are like about their animals.'

Jocelyn let this go. 'And what else? Besides the minor detail of the body in the pony shed, I mean.'

'Well, there was a man. He came to the door, asking the way somewhere. And I saw him again this morning. He spooked me for some reason. He's probably perfectly innocuous.'

'Have you met any of the neighbours?'

'A daft woman called Frannie, down the road, and her husband Robert. And a local history buff who found Milo and came to tell me, and then we got friendly and she told me lots about the place.

And just this afternoon a dreadful person called Valerie Innes stopped me in the road and asked what was going on.'

Jocelyn's thoughts were evidently wandering. 'Why do you do this stuff? Coming to a strange house where you've no idea what the background is? At best, it's bound to be lonely and boring. At worst, you get involved in all sorts of trouble. It's not worth it, surely?'

'It seemed like a good idea at the time,' Thea said weakly. 'And even if nothing at all happened, it wouldn't be boring. I like this area. It's genuinely fascinating. There was loads of industry here, you know. Wool, mainly, and cloth. That means mills, and workers' cottages and transportation. There's a wonderful old canal just about to be restored. Fascinating stuff.'

'I don't know how you can think about any of that sort of thing when somebody's just *died* right outside your door. Not just died, but been *murdered*. Aren't you at all frightened?'

Thea did her best to explain. 'I am a bit wobbly,' she admitted. 'And if I'd had to spend the night here by myself I might have had trouble getting to sleep. But having Hepzie does help. She'd know if there was a man hiding under the bed, for example. And she would probably wake me up if she heard anybody coming up the stairs at three in the morning.'

'That policeman wouldn't have let you stay.'

'What would he have done about the animals? The Phillipses wouldn't have been very happy about that.'

'I think the police are usually rather callous about animals,' Jocelyn said. 'Like when they evacuate an area because of a bomb scare or something. Don't they just leave all the dogs and cats and guinea pigs behind?'

'Do they? I never thought to wonder. That's terrible.'

'A lot of things are terrible,' said Jocelyn.

'So – are you going to stay and protect me? Hollis seemed to think the two of us would be okay.'

'Do I have to sleep in the same bed as you?'

Thea laughed. 'Definitely not. You can stay in the horse room. I'm sticking with the dragons.'

Jocelyn's answering smile was weak, and Thea guessed that

more than anything her sister needed sleep. 'You don't have to keep me company, if you want an early night,' she said.

'Night! It's not nine o'clock yet. Even Roly will hardly be asleep yet, these light evenings.'

That had been a mistake, they both knew as soon as the words were uttered. 'He does like me to read him his story,' she mumbled. Then, more briskly. 'Well, too late to worry about that now.'

'Joss —' Thea ventured, only to be cut off by a sharp flip of Jocelyn's hand.

'Leave it,' she warned. 'Nothing either of us can say is going to change anything.'

'I think that was a bat,' said Thea, pointedly staring at the shadows formed by the mass of the barn. 'Yes! Definitely a bat. Isn't that exciting.'

'Extraordinary,' said Jocelyn gloomily.

Next morning the peacocks gave voice at five to five, waking Thea, Jocelyn and Hepzibah with wholesale thoroughness. The haunting noise, seemingly crashing out of the sky, echoed in Thea's ears as she woke, only to be repeated for real a minute or two later.

'What the hell is that?' came a muffled voice from the room across the landing.

'Peacocks,' Thea called back. 'I forgot to warn you.'

The sisters had agreed to leave their bedroom doors open, so that if either heard a noise or had reason for alarm, a call would at least in theory awaken the other one. Hepzibah slept on Thea's bed, a warm comforting little body tucked against her mistress's legs.

'I've never heard anything so ghastly. How can anybody live with that racket?'

'I gather they don't do it all year round. Just in the mating season.'

'Are there any girl peacocks out there?'

'I think not.'

'So what's the point?'

'I imagine they're hoping to attract a female from the other side of the valley – or perhaps across the Bristol Channel in Somerset. The crazy thing is, Julia never told me about them. Imagine the shock when I woke up on Sunday morning to that.'

'Just about the same as the shock I've just had, I would guess.'

By this time they were irrevocably awake, and Jocelyn appeared in Thea's doorway, wearing a long T-shirt and nothing else. 'Shall I make some tea?' she asked. 'I bet there'll be police people turning up straight after breakfast, anyway.'

'Might as well,' Thea said. 'But we'll be horribly tired by this afternoon if we get up now.'

'We'll have a siesta, then. Looks as if it'll be a hot day.'

They drank the tea with minimal conversation. Everything had been said the night before, taking them till nearly midnight, Jocelyn far from keen to go to bed, despite being so tired. Thea tried not to worry about having less than five hours' sleep. As Jocelyn said, they could catch up during the day if necessary. In spite of their troubles and worries, there didn't seem to be any major tasks ahead of them.

'Just so long as I keep that pony alive,' Thea had said firmly. 'That's the main thing.'

Jocelyn's prediction turned out to be entirely accurate. Two police cars arrived at eight thirty, disgorging a pair of officers from one who proceeded to don white jumpsuits, and Superintendent Hollis from the other. 'And me still in my nightie,' Jocelyn muttered.

'It's still a murder investigation, then?' Thea said, as she opened the front door to him.

'That's right.' He stood looking down at her, eyes wide open and not quite focused, as if a whirl of distracting thoughts was happening behind them. Thea's heartrate accelerated stupidly.

'It's incredible that this should happen to me again,' she said. 'I feel like a jinx.'

'As well you might,' he agreed. 'Although as one of my Inspectors observed, it isn't quite as extraordinary as we first thought.'

'Really?'

'If the killer assumed the place was empty – if he knew the family were away – it might have seemed like a safe place to use.'

'But when he saw the pony, he'd have realised somebody must be here to keep an eye on him.'

'Not necessarily. A neighbour could be dropping in.'

Thea glanced back into the house. 'Do you want to come in?' she asked.

'Why don't we go for a little walk instead? I take it your sister's still here?'

'She is, yes. All right, then. Can I bring the dog?'

He hesitated, and she understood that this was not to be just a sociable stroll across the fields.

'Better not,' he said. 'Just in case.'

Thea didn't ask *just in case what?* She pushed Hepzie back indoors, and called to Jocelyn not to let her out.

Hollis led the way purposefully into the paddock behind the house, pausing halfway across it to look back the way they'd come. 'Attractive place,' he said.

Thea followed his gaze. 'I haven't seen it from this angle before. It's absolutely lovely.'

The house had its back to them, the row of windows under the roof smaller than those at the front. The stone barn was at an angle, and the duck pond with its fringe of reeds and grasses added to the timeless image. The scene of the hanging was hidden from view, but the small flower garden was between the paddock and the house, further enhancing the picture.

'The Cotswolds are the most beautiful place on earth,' he said, matter-of-factly. 'There's everything that's best about the world in this one small area. I never get tired of it.'

'It'll be spoilt eventually, though, don't you think? I saw a lot of new building on my way here on Saturday. The stone's a dreadful bright yellow in some cases.'

'It'll mellow,' he said. 'It was all that colour to start with.'

'Are you sure?' She was sceptical of his tolerance, remembering how Cecilia Clifton had spoken of new development and its effect on the residents. 'I wouldn't put it past the Phillipses to try and exploit some of their land here. They wouldn't be allowed to build a row of holiday chalets in this paddock, would they?'

Hollis snorted. 'Don't get me started on planning matters,' he warned.

'Right,' she laughed. 'Sorry. I don't know why I sounded so reactionary. I don't mind a few new buildings, if they're well built. Nothing lasts forever, I suppose.'

'Your husband died, didn't he? Have I got that right?'

'In a car crash, last year.'

'It must have been – well, you know what I'm trying to say.'

'It was. Whatever words you can find, that's more or less it. Quite predictable, on the whole. All the usual stereotypes came true, and a few new ones.'

'You look better than you did in May. Lighter.'

'As in – I've lost weight?'

'You know I didn't mean that. Lighter in spirit. More buoyant.'

'I expect I am. I've got the hang of living in the moment, which helps a lot. If I'm all right today, then I'm all right, full stop. I've been working on it for a while now, to the point where it's got fairly automatic. It really does help.'

'Hmm.' Thea did her best to ignore the note of disapproval, the doubt as to the wisdom of such a lifestyle. 'It's probably quite useful at times like this, but I wouldn't recommend it permanently.'

'Wouldn't you?'

'Just as long as it's working, who am I to criticise?' he placated. 'I must say your poor sister looks like something that's been left out in all weathers for a month or two.'

Thea laughed. 'How rude!' she spluttered. 'But yes, she's got problems. I've no idea what she's going to do, to be honest.'

'Which makes you feel even more okay yourself,' he said, perceptively.

'Maybe it does,' she admitted.

They were walking towards the woodlands at the bottom of the sloping paddock. 'Where are we going?' Thea asked.

'Did you know there's a footpath through these woods? It's the old towpath of the canal, actually.'

'Julia mentioned it, and I did a bit of exploring yesterday, but I didn't start here. I walked into Frampton Mansell and over the railway line. It felt terribly daring. I suppose I told you about Cecilia Clifton giving me a little lecture on Sunday about what there is to see. Although she seems to have rather a thing about the canal.'

'Pro or con?'

'I couldn't really tell. She changed the subject.'

'They're supposed to be restoring it,' he said vaguely.

'I know. Isn't that fantastic! But what a job! Something like twenty-five locks to rebuild, and all that scrub clearance. The mind boggles.'

'I went on a canal holiday once, about thirty years ago, with my big sister and her boyfriend. It was the most tedious week of my life.'

Thea's laugh was genuine and quite prolonged. 'You're as bad as Jocelyn,' she said. 'You've got no souls, either of you.'

'You like canals, do you?'

'I'm mad about them.'

'Hmmm. Well, don't say that too loudly in these villages. Not everybody would agree with you.'

'Julia, for one,' dismissed Thea.

'Oh?' A sudden sharpness entered his voice, reminding Thea that he was a professional, there to do a job.

'She said I might be approached by canal people, but it was unlikely. The restoration is coming this way, apparently, and it obviously affects her land. It must be right about here.'

'And she isn't happy about it?'

'That was the distinct impression I got.'

'Which puts her in the forefront of public opinion then,' he said thoughtfully.

'They're just lacking in imagination, that's all. It would be fantastic for the area to have it open again. Really invigorating.' Thea was still fighting to comprehend any viable grounds for opposing the efforts to recreate the canal in all its glory.

'Be that as it may, we won't go down to the canal. I was thinking of heading uphill to the west and doing a loop back towards Chalford. We might get as far as Cowcombe Wood.'

'Cowcombe! What a wonderful name!'

'It links up with another path, that I think must be the one you used on Sunday, when you saw the young man with a limp. The only barn I can find belongs to Greywood Manor, home of the Innes family.'

Thea groaned. 'If we see that Valerie, I warn you – I'll run away.'

'We won't see her,' he said confidently.

It took Thea several seconds to grasp the import of these words. 'Why? Is something going on?' She stared at the landscape in front of her. 'Have you got people out there, keeping the Inneses out of the way?'

'Not exactly. But we don't do things on a whim in this sort of situation.'

Thea felt young and foolish for never suspecting the background machinations. 'So we're investigating the barn, are we?'

'In a way,' he agreed. 'I thought we might have a look at it and you can show me exactly where you saw your vagrant. And at the same time, I can see if there's any sign that this path has been used recently. You haven't been this way, have you?'

'No, I came back down the lane. Shouldn't you be doing this with another police officer, rather than me?'

He turned to look at her. 'Seems as if we're getting into bad habits, doesn't it? Remember last time?'

She grinned at him. 'I remember,' she said. 'But Jocelyn's going to wonder where I am if we do the whole walk. Won't it take ages?'

'Not according to my map. It's probably less than half a mile from here to the barn you described. We'll be back in forty minutes at most. I don't think she'll panic, will she?'

Thea shook her head.

They found a path through the woods, which were largely composed of well-grown trees but with plenty of smaller saplings and underbrush. 'Looks well used,' Hollis remarked, his head turning constantly from side to side as he gave everything a forensic quality of attention.

Thea pushed at dense undergrowth. 'There doesn't seem to be a way through. The path disappears. Does this upset your intentions for our walk?'

'A bit. We'll have to go back the way we came, and then over to the corner of the woods. I think there's a stile there.'

He forged ahead of her, clearly in some haste. She began to wonder about the real motives for this expedition, and why her presence had been required.

'Are you going to tell me about the...victim? How you know it wasn't suicide, for one thing.'

'You really want details?'

'I really do. I've been thinking about all those prisoners who manage to kill themselves with a towel and a doorknob, or the taps on a basin. I've never been able to imagine how they do it.'

'We try not to publicise precise descriptions, for obvious reasons. But I can explain a bit about the pathology of it.'

'Go on, then,' she invited.

'When a person puts pressure on the carotid artery at just the right point, the result is very often an almost instantaneous cardiac arrest. The blood stops flowing, so the face doesn't become suffused.'

'Hang on. You mean it's very quick and more or less painless?'

'That's right. And terribly easy. Much easier than most people expect. Fortunately, it very rarely happens by accident.'

'But – surely that doesn't prove anything in this instance? There must be more to it.'

'The actual hanging could have happened as I've just described,' he said carefully. 'He died from cardiac arrest, not strangulation or a broken neck. That's true of the majority of suicides by a ligature around the neck. But the killer made a series of mistakes. The most serious one was the positioning of the rope for the hanging. It didn't coincide very well with the marks made by the ligature that killed him. It wasn't even the same piece of rope. And even more of a giveaway – he'd been dead for some hours before the second rope went around his neck. The police doctor had his suspicions right away and the post-mortem confirmed them.'

'So he didn't die in the stable.' The relief this brought was almost disabling. 'Somebody brought his body to Juniper Court while I was out, and strung it up from that beam. But *why*?'

'Good question,' he said. 'To which the answer possibly lies in that barn.'

'Owned by Valerie Innes and her family,' Thea added. 'Why do I suddenly hope you can pin it all on her? I don't normally take against a person like I did with her.'

'I don't think you're alone,' Hollis revealed. 'Judging from what we're beginning to glean from the interviews.'

'Interviews? Already?' She remembered belatedly that Valerie Innes had threatened to bring her boys over to Juniper Court the previous evening, but had never materialised. Had that been because they were occupied with helping police enquiries? If so, she could have hugged DS Hollis for that reason alone.

'No time to waste,' he said absently, his attention clearly on the path, the fields, and the road beyond.

'There's a gate, look.' She pointed to the further corner of the field, which they had been approaching steadily. 'We can get out onto the path that way.'

He looked at her, his eyes twinkling. 'I thought I was leading this walk,' he said.

'Carry on, captain.' She waved him forward. 'I'll maintain a respectful position in the rear.'

'We'd better speed up a bit – and I'd better concentrate. I need to confirm the way these paths connect up.' They walked more briskly for half a mile or so, saying little.

Thea noticed that he seemed quite comfortable with her joke about following in the rear – indeed when she dropped back, he made no demur. Then she realised they were alongside the barn, which looked somehow different from her glimpse of it on Sunday. 'That's it – I think,' she said. 'And this is why we didn't bring Hepzie, right? In case she roused somebody, or messed up some clues.'

'Something like that,' he agreed, his gaze scanning the building. 'Ah,' he added, in a Sherlock Holmes sort of way. 'Just as I hoped.'

Thea followed his gaze, and discovered a grey car parked unobtrusively in the lane beside the barn.

'Is that one of yours?' she asked.

'Let's go and see,' he invited, increasing his pace.

Thea enjoyed the brief scene that followed. Two figures in white jumpsuits emerged at Hollis's call, waving him into the doorway of the barn, to show him something. Nosily, Thea peered around him.

Part of the barn floor was covered with paper sacks, flattened and laid out like carpet, along the end wall of the building. There were sleeping bags and blankets folded and piled in a corner, and several cardboard boxes stacked in a corner. Everything was tidy. There was nothing overtly agricultural about the place – no old implements or dried manure. No mouldy straw bales or lengths of baler twine. Instead, Thea spotted a camping stove, a shelf stacked with mugs, plates and a saucepan. There were tins of beans and a well-wrapped loaf of sliced bread. 'Good God,' she gasped. 'Is that a computer?' It was a chunky laptop, perched on a makeshift table made from an old door.

'We'd better take that,' Hollis said to one of his officers. 'Finished collecting your samples, have you?'

'Somebody's been living here,' said Thea wonderingly. 'Was it the dead boy, do you think?'

'Not sure yet. We still don't have a name for him. Any signs of violence or struggle?' he asked the forensic people. They both shook their heads, although one seemed unsure.

'Keith?' Hollis prompted.

The man point at the opposite end of the barn from the sleeping quarters. 'A fresh scrape along the whitewash, sir,' he said. 'Probably not important. The floor's scuffed in several places, but that could be explained in all kinds of ways.'

'You've copied the prints? What sort of footwear?'

'Trainers, wellies, bare feet,' the man enumerated. 'And one pair of size 9 walking boots, which seem to have stopped in the doorway and not gone any further.'

'See if you can find some prints,' Hollis ordered the men. 'Match them with the dead lad's trainers, and we'll be getting somewhere.'

Thea realised the men must have already been at work for hours. 'Is this where he was killed, do you think?' she asked, her mind working slowly.

'Hard to say,' Hollis replied. 'Come on, we'd better go. If you could just show me exactly where you saw your man, first.'

It took her a while to orientate herself. 'I wasn't this close, you see,' she apologised. 'I must have been climbing over that stile —' she pointed. 'So he'd have been disappearing around this corner here.' She scratched her chin. 'I suppose.' The barn was positioned at the edge of a field, forty or fifty yards from the road. But a clear track had been carved from the gate to its wide wooden door. The grass had been obliterated by tyre marks in two parallel lines. 'Looks as if plenty of people come here without trying to hide the fact,' she noted.

'Planning officers, builders, tractors, and squatters for a start,'

Hollis agreed.

'Planning officers?'

'There's an application in for its conversion to a luxury four-bedroom executive home,' he quoted wryly.

'Oh,' said Thea. 'And they'll get it, won't they. Without any trouble.'

'That would have been true, up to yesterday. Now – well, there might be a bit of a delay to the proceedings.'

'Seems a shame,' she sighed. 'As a barn, it's rather romantic.'

'And as a house it's just another status symbol,' he supplied. They smiled in agreement, before Hollis spoke again to his men, suggesting they make some attempt to identify tyre marks around the front of the barn.

'So that's all you can tell me, is it? You glimpsed a male person with a limp walking around that corner. No other people? No sight of his face?'

Thea felt uneasy. She didn't want to be the sole bearer of important testimony. She danced a little jig on the spot. 'That's it. And on the strength of that, you've got all this work going on here? That makes me feel rather odd.'

'Why?'

'Well, I'm a newcomer, only here for a couple of weeks, and I'm instantly thrown into this horrible business. Why aren't there loads of other witnesses, not just me?'

'For a start, I'm sure there are. But on the other hand, you'll have noticed how empty and silent the whole place is. Hardly anybody strolls around the footpaths, even at the weekends. They stay indoors, even in July, or they drive off in their cars. You're an important witness because you actually came out here on your own two feet.'

She shrugged. 'That makes sense, I suppose. But please – I'll have to get back, if that's all you need from me,' she said. 'They'll be missing me.'

'They?'

'Jocelyn and Hepzie,' she said, in all seriousness.

His laugh was full of genuine delight in her silliness, a joyful peal of understanding and goodwill. 'Best get back to them, then,' he said. 'It's all road walking from here.'

They spent the rest of the walk side by side, touching lightly once when a car forced them to huddle into the hedge. Thea's spirits lifted with every step. She took deep lungfuls of the morning air, and walked with a bounce. Okay, so there had been a murder in these peaceful fields, and somebody somewhere had lost their beloved boy. But absence of personal guilt was a wonderful thing. None of it could remotely be construed as her fault, which made the whole business more of an intellectual puzzle than an emotional tragedy. Besides, the sun was shining, and a handsome man was walking by her side.

With Juniper Court once more in sight, Hollis cleared his throat. 'I need to be serious for a minute,' he said. 'This house-sitting malarky. It's bothering me. In general, I mean – not this place specifically – where you ought to be scared stiff and packing your bags. I mean as a general principle.'

'Why does it bother you?'

'It puts you at a disadvantage, staying where you don't know anybody.' He met her eyes, revealing a concerned little frown. 'Why do you do it?'

She performed a slow shrug. 'Why not? It's interesting. And it's *supposed* to be peaceful. Lots of time just to slop about in someone else's house, eating their food and using their bed. I think I might have overlooked a few angles, though.' She smiled. 'There must be something about an empty house that triggers a train of events.'

'But it's *not* empty. You're in it.'

'That's true. But I suppose I'm sort of invisible. For all I know, all kinds of people call in regularly, or take a short cut through the yard, or have a standing invitation to use the paddock. So I'm not going to be suspicious, am I?'

'You've been thinking about it, haven't you?'

'Of course I have. How could I not?'

He tilted his head understandingly. 'But you're still not scared? I find that amazing.'

'I might have been, without Joss, when it got dark. But it isn't very likely that anybody's going to hurt me, is it? If they were going to, surely they'd have done it by now.'

They took their slightly muddy footwear off at the back door, and Thea led the way to the kitchen. There was no sign of Jocelyn, but Hepzie had rushed to greet them, the merest hint of reproach in her eyes. 'Sorry, babes,' cooed Thea. 'I'll take you out later on for a good romp in the paddock.'

They had coffee, not saying very much. Thea wasn't even sure she'd been stringing words together coherently, with his autumn-tinted eyes steadfastly on hers the whole time. He seemed to be seeing right into her, drinking her up while at the same time keeping her safe. It was a very pleasing sensation, and she was sorry when it stopped.

'Your leg mended, then,' she said, before he left. He'd been in plaster the last time she'd met him.

'Yes, thanks. Good as new now. I won't be in any hurry to do that again.'

'That man —' she murmured. 'The one in the sporty car.'

'If you see him again, give me a call.' He handed her a card with a mobile number on it. 'Any time.'

'And should I stay here until further notice? What about the Phillipses? What happens next?'

'We get a name for the body. That's taking longer than it should, without any wallet or papers, but any time now we'll have him ticketed. Your guess is pretty much as good as mine when it comes to the Phillips family. It depends what they say when we finally reach them. But be careful, okay? Lock the doors and windows, and keep your phone in your pocket. I can't very well tell you to get off home, when you're in the middle of a job, and you've got your sister here to protect you. But I'd like to, I really would.'

'Don't worry about me,' she said. 'I'm tougher than I look.'

But just at that moment she felt far from tough.

Jocelyn was in the living room, the door firmly closed. When Thea found her, she was speaking on her mobile, huddled on the sofa, still in the long T-shirt. She took the phone from her ear and mouthed 'Won't be long,' before listening again.

Thea waited, stroking the spaniel's long ears in apology for her lengthy desertion. The animal was perched on the back of the sofa, and Thea was leaning against it, watching the yard from the window. Hollis had gone, as had the forensic men. Geese and hens drifted about, the only signs of life in the picture.

'You've been gone for ages,' said Jocelyn, pocketing her phone. 'I didn't know whether I should be doing something. How's the pony?'

'Alive. I threw him some hay and came to see how you were doing.'

'Where do those bloody peacocks go during the day? Can we shoot them, do you think? Isn't there a shotgun hidden away somewhere?'

'I doubt it. They sit on the roof of the barn, or in one of the trees at the side of the garden.'

'Actually...'

Thea leaned back against the windowsill, braced for whatever might be coming. 'What?'

'I might go home tomorrow. That was Alex.'

'Why tomorrow? Why not today, if all's forgiven?' The prospect of being left alone again was unexpectedly disagreeable. Already she'd started to think in terms of 'we' for the rest of her stay at Juniper Court. Abrupt changes of plan had always unsettled her.

'No need to be like that,' Jocelyn pouted. 'You should be pleased.'

Thea remembered all the reasons why she found her younger sister so irritating, reasons that stretched back to when Joss had been about two. The whining, the self-pity, the total absence of sensitivity – all came rushing back. Although a substantial woman well past her first youth sat before her, all Thea could see was the red-faced toddler, caught in the act of scribbling in Thea's beloved copy of *Alice Through the Looking-Glass* and utterly unrepentant.

'I'm not pleased,' she said. 'You're mucking me about. I'll have the police on my back if I'm here on my own.'

'That shouldn't be such a terrible thing. I'll be leaving you a free run with that dishy Superintendent, for a start.'

Thea clamped her lips tightly together. 'So what changed?' she asked. 'What magic words did Alex utter to lure you back home again?'

'It's not fair on the kids, that's all. They've got all the end of term stuff to do – Abby's lost a library book and they're hysterical about it. Toni's got a school trip, starting tomorrow, and can't find any clothes to take. It sounds like bedlam, even after one day. *Less* than one day. And Roly wouldn't go to bed without knowing exactly where I was.'

'But you knew all that when you left. I tried to tell you last night. You said Alex would have to do it all.'

'I know I did.'

Thea's irritation deepened. The fact that Jocelyn was belatedly coming to see the situation as Thea herself saw it was part of her annoyance. The timing was the main problem. Since the previous evening, she had come to take her sister's side against her husband, to accept that it was the only reasonable course of action for an abused wife to leave the family home. Now she wanted to go back, in the vain hope that a few hours' absence would put everything right.

'Are you thinking you've taught him a lesson, and he'll behave himself from now on?'

'He says he will. He says he had no idea how much they all needed me.'

'Well, I've got no more to say on the matter. Do whatever you want. And I still don't see why you're leaving it till tomorrow, if Toni's bag has to be packed today.'

'I've told him where all her stuff is. That was just an excuse, anyway. She knows exactly what she needs and where it all is.'

Thea blinked, thinking that if a cartoon were to be made of the scene at that moment, her head would be haloed with exclamation and question marks in equal numbers. Her sister was engaged in some grim domestic game that she had no desire to understand.

And then she found herself thinking about Hepzibah's mother. The poor dog had been thin and careworn when Thea had gone to choose her puppy, which had been one of a litter of five. She had watched as the bitch hovered indecisively outside the whelping box, obviously torn between a desire to run free in the garden outside, and the powerful instinct to protect and feed the babies. 'She's not a very good mother,' the owner had said. 'She'd much rather come for a walk with me than stay here with the pups.' A glance at the sore scratched pendulous underbelly of the wretched animal had drawn Thea's sympathy in a big way. 'I don't blame her,' she'd said. 'Poor thing.'

'Will you be breeding from yours?' the woman had asked.

Thea had made the decision once and for all. 'Oh no. I'll just keep her as a companion,' she'd said. This, she felt now, somehow summarised the difference between herself and Jocelyn. For Joss, there was no greater joy, nothing more meaningful, than the production of new lives.

'I don't know what to say,' she told her sister. 'All this seems so completely out of character for both of you. You and Alex have always been the perfect parents, with everything coming so naturally to you. I still can't believe it's gone so horribly wrong.'

'You've probably just explained it, without realising it,' Jocelyn mused, staring at the floor. 'Perfect parents don't make very good partners to each other. And anyway, we're not the perfect anything. I'm even beginning to wonder whether we had all those kids just to distract ourselves from having to look at the cracks that have always been in the marriage. That isn't very subtle, I know – but I think it's probably true.'

Jocelyn heaved herself off the sofa, making Thea aware for the first time how much weight she'd gained since their last encounter. Something in the lumbering movement raised a suspicion. 'Good God – you're not pregnant again, are you?'

Her sister stared at her, and then down at her own body. 'Of course I'm not,' she snarled. 'I'd have told you.'

'Thank heavens for that. So why are you so stiff and slow?'

Jocelyn met her gaze with a long level look. 'Isn't that obvious?' she said quietly. 'Alex hits me. He *really* hits me.' Unselfconsciously, she raised the T-shirt, in spite of the absence of any pants. 'See?'

Thea noted the brown pubic hair, the puckered stretch marks from all those pregnancies, the excess flesh in a fold across the lower abdomen. And the multi-coloured contusion on the hip bone, spreading inwards and downwards over the buttock and thigh. She moved around her sister, slowly examining the bruise.

'He didn't do that with his fist, did he?' she said at last.

'Cricket bat,' said Jocelyn. 'Three or four blows.'

Thea experienced an involuntary image of a white-clad Alex, complete with shinpads and pullover, whacking his wife with a bat. 'But he doesn't play cricket, does he?' she said, stupidly.

'It belongs to Noel. Luckily for me, it isn't a full-sized one.' She uttered a harsh humourless laugh.

'Have you been to a doctor?'

'What do you think? It isn't broken or anything. It just stiffens up if I don't keep moving. It's much better than it was.'

Thea pressed a hand over her own nauseous stomach. All the feelings of five minutes ago were gone, washed away by a new rage, and a solid steel determination to protect her little sister. Because Jocelyn had not only been a maddening interfering nuisance: she had been cherished and spoilt by the older siblings. Emily, Thea and Damien had all rejoiced when she was born, finding her fascinating and delightful, a necessary completion to the family.

'You're not going home tomorrow,' she said flatly. 'No way. You're staying here, if I have to lock you in Naomi's room for a fortnight.'

'Don't be ridiculous.' Jocelyn's tone was nowhere near as firm as the words she used. 'I told him I'd go back.'

'Does he know where you are?'

'Not exactly. *I* don't know where I am.'

'Joss,' Thea pleaded. 'You've made the break now. You must

have been desperate – you certainly *sounded* desperate. Who's to
say he won't be even more angry with you, after all this? A few
days of relief that he doesn't have to manage the kids, and then
it'll be back to square one.'

'You can't possibly know that.'

'And you can't know different. Nobody really knows another
person, and what they might be capable of.'

This remark took their thoughts straight to the murder on
their temporary doorstep, and what somebody very close by had
indeed been capable of.

'You're not thinking he'll murder me, are you?' Jocelyn gave a
shaky laugh.

'It wouldn't be the first time a husband murdered his wife,
would it,' said Thea.

They still hadn't resolved anything by mid-afternoon, but the
weather had continued to improve beyond all expectations,
which did a lot to lift their spirits. Pallo had passed inspection
twice, the geese had grudgingly called a truce, and Jocelyn had
insisted on letting the rabbits and guinea pigs out of their cages,
deftly constructing a run for them out of a wire cage she found
lurking uselessly in long grass between the barn and the paddock.
'I bet this was used for this very purpose before it got abandoned,' she said.

'Well, it's down to you to catch them, if they escape,' Thea
warned. 'There's probably a good reason why it was thrown
away.'

'At least there isn't a cat stalking them,' said Jocelyn. 'Did you
say it was a Siamese that got run over?'

'Seal point, I think. Very beautiful.'

'And lethal with guinea pigs , I shouldn't wonder.'

'Probably. I think they'll be fairly safe with Hepzie. I've never
known her kill anything.' Thea paused, savouring the scene of the
picturebook yard bathed in bright sunshine.

'Are you still cross with me?' Jocelyn asked in a baby-sister
voice.

Thea sighed. 'No, Jocelyn, I am not cross with you. I'm just
drained by everything that's happening. Nothing's turning out as

it should.'

'Oh well. Why don't we just make the best of it? As you said, it's a very nice place. I do feel better just for being here.'

'I just hope they settle this murder business,' Thea worried. 'It looks as if he wasn't killed here – but brought from half a mile away, already dead, and hanged in the stable for some unfathomable reason.'

'Yuk! That's disgusting.' Jocelyn closed her eyes against the images Thea had conjured. 'You mean, they lugged him up to the loft, tied rope round his neck and sort of *rehanged* him?'

'Something like that.'

'Presumably wanting to give some sort of message to your people – or to implicate them somehow.'

'But they weren't here, were they? So it's *me* that got implicated, and that's the bit I don't like.'

Jocelyn shook her head. 'No, I don't think they had you in mind at all. You're an incidental detail. Maybe they just wanted to ruin the family's holiday. Or divert attention from the place where he was really killed.'

Thea pondered this. 'That might be it,' she concluded. 'Especially as there was nothing to connect the victim with the barn, apart from an accidental sighting on Saturday.'

'Oh?' Jocelyn's attention was drifting. 'Who by?'

'Me,' said Thea miserably.

Her sister laughed, a loud *oof* of amusement. 'You're jinxed,' she announced. 'Let's face it.'

Before Thea could react, there was a commotion from the geese in the yard and Hepzie gave a warning yap.

'Uh oh,' said Jocelyn. 'Looks as if we've got a visitor.'

A boy of about nineteen or twenty was facing the trio of geese which had detected him before the sisters had, and had rushed to meet him at the gate. The visitor had one hand raised as if conducting the birds. Slowly he waved it from side to side, and all three heads followed in unison, beady eyes fixed on his finger. He then advanced on them, forcing them to step backwards, again in perfect synchronicity. Finally, he clapped his hands, with one sharp crack, and the birds turned and fled, casting dignity to the wind.

'How did you do that?' Thea asked in admiration.

'You haven't to take any nonsense from them,' he said care-lessly. 'That's all. Same with any animals.'

'Can you do tigers as well?' asked Jocelyn.

'Probably,' he shrugged. 'I'm Jeremy Innes, by the way. I think my mum spoke to you yesterday.'

Thea had no difficulty in recalling the woman she had taken such a strong dislike to. She had to fight to avoid transferring her antipathy to the son.

'Yes, hello,' she said. 'I'm Thea and this is my sister, Jocelyn.' She inspected the newcomer narrowly. Long dark eyelashes, thick curly hair and a charming smile. Not remotely like his mother. 'What can we do for you?'

'I've just heard the news about Nick Franklyn.'

'Who?'

'The body they found here yesterday. Nick Franklyn.'

'Hang on,' Thea put up a hand. 'Last I heard, they hadn't got an identity for him.'

'Well, they have now.' The boy gave an impatient twitch. 'Somebody told my dad. He knows everybody, my dad.'

He would, Thea thought, married to the pushiest woman in town, and living in that great mansion on the hill. Probably bribes planning officers to let him convert his barns, as well.

'Did you know him? Nick, I mean.'

'Yeah. Everybody knows Nick. He's big around here.' The boy twitched again, hunching his shoulders and clasping his hands together. Nervous, Thea diagnosed. Under quite a bit of strain.

'Oh?' She spoke gently, wondering what his motive was in coming to Juniper Court so soon after learning about his friend. She could not forget his mother, either, and her speculations as to what she'd be like to live with. 'Tell me a bit more about him.'

'He was one of the Rural Warriors. You've heard of them, I suppose?'

Thea shook her head apologetically. 'Sorry, no. I'm not from these parts, you see.'

'I know that. But they're a big outfit. I thought everybody

knew about them.'

'I've been a bit out of it lately,' she explained. 'What do they do, then? Are you one of them as well?'

Jeremy flushed. 'Sort of,' he mumbled. 'They're not illegal or anything. Not like *terrorists*. I mean, I can't get too committed, 'cause I'm going for army training in September, and I gotta keep my nose clean.' He smiled weakly at his pseudo youth-speak. His accent represented the complex conflict between generations and classes that afflicted many of his contemporaries. 'It's just local stuff, basically. They're fighting to protect the country way of life.' The words had quotation marks around them, loud and clear.

'Good for them,' Thea approved, albeit with some surprise. 'I thought people your age all wanted night clubs and bowling alleys and nice big motorways.'

'They do,' interrupted Jocelyn. 'These warriors must be very strange kids.'

Jeremy threw her such a look of contempt that Thea revised her assessment of him. There was much more to this lad than had first appeared.

'Do the police know Nick was involved with them?' she asked.

He waved an impatient hand. The police evidently didn't concern him. 'He was one of *us*, a good bloke. Brave, you know?'

Thea recalled the hunched solitary figure she'd glimpsed by the barn and wondered at this epithet. 'Brave?' she repeated.

'Right. Go anywhere, stand up to anybody, would Nick. Made a fair few enemies, that way. Specially with these canal idiots.'

'He was against the restoration of the canal?'

''Course he was. That's the main campaign just now. Dreadful news for the environment, it'd be. Nearly as bad as that bastard golf course.' The accent was into its stride now, the rhythms flowing more smoothly.

Thea did not permit herself to be distracted by the golf course. 'But surely – canals are *good* for the environment? Water birds, new plants —'

'Tourists, tree clearance, mega disturbance. You're joking,' he countered.

'So – you think that was why he was killed?' Jocelyn interrupted with the clear question, cutting through any further debate about the merits of canals.

He scratched an ear and stared at the ground for a moment. 'It must be, I think. He's made plenty of enemies. Somebody must have heard the Phillipses were away and used this place, thinking it'd be safely empty. Lucky you didn't get in the way.'

'You make it sound all done and dusted,' Jocelyn put in. She'd moved a step or two towards him, as if for a better look at the eyelashes and sharp jawline. 'Do you know who killed him?'

His colour heightened. 'Of course I don't. What makes you think that?'

'You sounded as if you'd worked it out, that's all.'

'I'm not playing detectives. I just thought I'd come and see if you were okay. Not scared or anything. I mean – dead bodies aren't very nice, are they.'

Thea had to abort a guffaw at the sheer Englishness of this remark. 'I'm not scared,' she assured him. 'At least, not of the dead. I've never really understood why people think bodies would be scary. And even if I was, he isn't here any more, is he? He's in some mortuary in Cirencester, all safely locked up.'

Jeremy coloured again. 'You're doing it on purpose. Making fun of me,' he accused. 'I wasn't suggesting you were scared of Nick – but if somebody killed him, then you'd be stupid *not* to be worried. If you don't know what's going on, or why Nick died, you can't possibly know whether you're safe or not. I only came because I felt sorry for you.'

Thea was almost seduced. 'Did you?' she challenged. 'Is that really why you're here? Or is it something a bit less altruistic? Like getting a kick out of seeing the place where somebody died. Or checking up on a few things?'

'Thea!' Jocelyn protested.

Thea did not relent. 'And what about your brothers – are they going to show up in a minute, as well?'

Jeremy's head jerked back, his eyes widening. 'What's it got to do with them?' he demanded.

'I have no idea. But your mother said there were three of you, and talked as if you came in a package. I just wondered what we might have in store for us.'

'Dominic's working. And Simon's gone on a school trip. Neither of them's going to bother you.'

'You're the eldest, are you?' Jocelyn asked.

'No, actually. Dom's twenty-three. And, if you're so interested, he's my half-brother. My dad was married before, and Dom's mum died when he was two. Then he married my mum and they had me and Simon. Satisfied?'

It seemed to Thea that the boy took some satisfaction in giving this account of himself, like a much younger child might do. There was something in the story that pleased him, gave him confidence or security. It wasn't hard to guess that it offered some sort of superiority over the motherless Dominic. And, she suspected, it said something about Valerie Innes as stepmother. That woman would be liable to play a whole host of damaging psychological games as the only female in a family of men, with the result that each one would be perpetually alert to the chance of an advantage. Jeremy saw himself as scoring a point here, if she was not much mistaken.

'And you're off to be a soldier,' said Jocelyn. 'Whose idea was that, then?'

'Mine, of course.' He was huffy at her patronising tone.

'Don't tell me – you want to be in the SAS,' she went on.

'No, I don't.' He turned away. 'I'll go now, then. Sorry if I got in your way.'

Thea remembered his hypnotism of the geese. 'It was nice to meet you,' she said, before adding, 'Do you often come here?'

He spoke over his shoulder, staring at the stable and the muddy duck pond. 'I used to, but not so much lately. I like to visit Milo, mainly. He was ours, you see, but we gave him to Julia because Simon's allergic to cat hair. I can't see him around anywhere. He usually comes to greet me.'

Jocelyn turned to Thea for elucidation. 'Who's Milo?' she asked.

Thea groaned. 'Oh, God, Jeremy, I'm afraid there's really bad news about Milo. It happened the first night I was here. He got run over.'

The boy's reaction was startling. 'No!' he screeched, raising tightly-clenched fists to the sky. 'That bastard! That bloody swine! I never thought he'd really do it. Where is he? What have you done with him? Is he at the vet's?'

Thea sorted out the pronouns before replying. 'No, no. He was killed. Surely you don't think somebody did it deliberately? Why on earth would they? He was in the road – a car must have hit him early on Sunday morning.'

Jeremy shook his head vigorously. 'It's easy to make it look like road kill,' he snarled. 'They do it after badger baiting, all the time. Milo was murdered, the same as Nick. Have you buried him?'

'He's in the freezer,' Thea admitted. 'In the garage.'

'Show me.'

Seeing no reason to refuse, Thea led the way to the part of the barn that housed the vintage Lamborghini, chest freezer and numerous cardboard boxes. Hepzibah ran ahead, nosing excitedly around the back of the car, tail wagging furiously. 'Must be mice in here,' said Thea. 'I don't expect she'll catch anything.'

Jocelyn's rat-phobia kept her hovering outside. Ignoring the dog, Jeremy marched ahead and threw open the freezer lid. Thea half expected – even hoped – the body of the cat would have disappeared, but it was evidently still where she'd left it.

'In this?' the boy said, lifting out the plastic carrierbag containing the corpse. Without waiting for an answer, he peeled it open, putting a gentle hand in to explore the frozen fur.

'I want a post-mortem done on him,' he said, his voice cracking. 'They'll know then if he was killed on purpose.'

Thea grimaced. 'We'd have to ask Julia first,' she objected. 'And somebody would have to pay – even if we could find a vet to do it.'

'That's no problem. My dad's friendly with one of the top Ministry vets in Gloucester. He'll get somebody to do it, no problem.' He had the cat fully revealed by this time, and was laying it on the top of the freezer, finding it too cold to keep hold of. He bent over it, close to tears.

'Poor Milo,' he crooned. 'Poor boy.'

Thea sought her sister's eye, but Jocelyn was completely occupied by the vision of a frozen dead cat.

'These things happen, I'm afraid,' Thea tried awkwardly to console the lad. 'I don't think there's any point in a post-mortem. If you insist on taking him with you, you'll have to bury him, or take him to a vet for cremation.'

He took a jerky few steps away from her, and then back again. 'We'll have to see about that,' he said thickly. Then, before she could stop him, he'd gathered up the defunct Milo and left Juniper Court at a run.

They sat on the minimal lawn with mugs of tea, and tried not to let the conversation get serious. The sense of waiting for something more to happen was strong, although neither mentioned it. Thea suggested a walk, but Jocelyn expressed a decided lack of enthusiasm. 'Much too hot for that,' she said. 'And you'd only take me to see your infernal canal. I know you.'

'There are forty-two locks on the whole stretch, you know,' Thea said dreamily. 'I remember that from my college course. I think there's a flight just around here, of eight or ten. It climbs fairly steeply up to Daneway, you see.'

'Shut up,' said Jocelyn. 'I don't care.'

'And then there's a tunnel. A most wonderful and prodigious tunnel. It was the widest and longest in the country for a long time. Wouldn't you like to go and have a look? The western entrance is only two or three miles from here.'

Jocelyn's interest increased by half a notch. 'Can you walk through it? I rather like tunnels, I must admit. I have very exciting tunnel dreams.'

Thea shook her head. 'The roof's fallen in by now. It's been abandoned for a century or more. And I don't think there'd be a path through, anyway. There never is with canal tunnels. The boatmen used to have to leg the barges through.'

'Huh?'

'They lay down on the roof of the boat, and did a sort of sideways walking, against the wall of the tunnel to propel the barges through. The horse met them at the other end.'

'How long is it?'

'Two miles or so. They had air vents at intervals. You can probably still see the tops of them if you know where to look.'

Jocelyn sighed. 'There's far too much history around here for my liking. Don't you feel weighted down by it?'

'Not at all. I like it. It makes me feel part of a sort of continuity. And it's not obstructing anything. People can still do modern stuff as well.'

Jocelyn's eyes hardened. 'That isn't true at all. They couldn't put a nice convenient motorway through here, or build a very-much-needed housing estate of good cheap materials like concrete blocks. Living here is like being in the Dark Ages for normal people. Imagine me trying to cope, with five kids all wanting to be somewhere different. I'd spend my entire life in the car, crashing into people on the bends and killing dozens of unwary cats. Where's the nearest shop? Or doctor? Or school, for that matter.'

'There's a school at Minchinhampton. It was right beside the church. I think it's quite new, in fact. And there's a pub in Frampton Mansell. That's no distance from here.' But then Thea remembered her house-sitting commission in Duntisbourne Abbots, where there had been no school, shop or post office. Not even a pub in the village itself. There had been a riding school, and a church and a lot of silence. And if she was honest, this second venture into the area was not so very different in those respects.

'Well, give me suburbia every time,' said Jocelyn, who lived on the edge of Bristol, with a massive out-of-town retail park almost next door, and frequent buses to the city centre. 'I can't honestly see the point of all this carefully preserved countryside.'

'You're hopeless,' sighed Thea. 'It's people like you who'll be the ruin of this country.'

'Not a bit of it. If everybody was like you, we'd all be living in grass huts with nothing to do but grow cabbages and go for senseless walks.'

'And restore lovely old canals, because they're still a valid means of transport, and one of the most benign tourist activities there is.'

'Minority interest, pet. Like camping, without any way of buying milk or newspapers. And bloody hard work opening and shutting all those locks, into the bargain.'

Thea assumed her sister was enjoying the banter as much as she was herself. It kept them away from unsettling topics like domestic violence and close-at-hand murder, for a start. And it restored the central pattern of their relationship to a familiar state. Knowing little of each other's daily routines, reading habits, or significant friendships, they instinctively reverted to this sort of theoretical debate on almost every encounter. Anything that avoided the word 'you' was a bonus.

By four o'clock, Thea was already wondering when she'd see Hollis again. He couldn't know that she had learned the identity of the dead man – so why had he not phoned her to bring her up to date? Because, she supposed, it would not be a high priority to him. Whether or not she knew the victim's name would not advance the investigation an inch. Furthermore, Thea had finally started to understand that Hollis very much needed to keep her at one remove from the murder. He was not going to discuss it with her more than was absolutely necessary. They were not going to find clues together, or rush around the uptilted countryside, through tunnels, in and out of farmyards in pursuit of criminals. Not if he could help it.

All of which suited her perfectly. She would have loved to go along with it, ignoring the smells and stains and sadnesses of mortality and murder. She would relish some midsummer romance amongst the long grasses and slow murmurings of a hot July evening. She yearned for it, acknowledging to herself that she deserved it after a year of mourning. She was ready for it. And she was tempted to believe she'd found the very man who could give it to her.

Why, then, did it feel so impossible? Such a distant unobtainable dream.

Because it was only a year and a bit since Carl died. Because her sister was there, wrestling with the breakdown of a long comfortable marriage. Because the man was a police detective and had work to do. Because thunder was forecast for later in the week.

She went to her temporary bedroom, to change from shorts and skimpy singlet to a pair of cotton trousers and a more respectable shirt. She sat on the bed for a moment, looking at the dragons stencilled on the walls, wondering at the care with which they'd been painted. Each one had a slight variation. The basic shape was consistent, done in white on the orange background of the emulsioned wall. And then delicate embellishments had been applied. Red, purple, yellow and blue touches, to the wings and tails and faces of the beasts. It must have taken hours of careful work, like painting on china. The result was a herd or flock of dragons, each one an individual with its own personality. Like horses on a circus roundabout, when they all had names and distinct characteristics. While Naomi had her ailing pony, with its needs and anxiety-provoking difficulties, Flora had her dragons, who were never going to go anywhere, and never needed more than the girl's imagination to bring them to life. Thea suspected there was a message in all this somewhere, if only she could find it.

The reflective interlude didn't last for long. At five o'clock, Thea was recalled to her duties, checking the pony yet again, feeding her own dog, returning rabbits and guinea pigs to their rightful quarters.

'What do you fancy for supper?' she asked her sister.

'Do you think we could go to that place in Mishington or whatever you call it?' Jocelyn ventured. 'I'll pay. Or rather, Alex can. It'll serve him right.'

'What place?'

'That French restaurant we passed in the main street. It's exactly the right weather for something exotic like that.'

'Sophie's,' Thea remembered. 'We'll probably have to book. And get changed. And leave Hepzie here.' She worried over this last detail for a few seconds. 'But I must admit it's a nice idea.'

'I'll go and find the number. It's sure to be in the phonebook.' Jocelyn's step was suddenly much lighter, the damaged hip forgotten in the thrill of an evening out. She'd always been one for getting out of the house, Thea remembered. Odd, in a way, that she should land herself with five children, thus curtailing her social life so dramatically.

They arrived shortly after seven, before the place had a chance to fill up. There'd been no difficulty booking a table, and Thea saw why when they stepped inside. There were two dining rooms, one each side of a passageway leading to the back of the building, which unusually boasted a small shop full of French wares. They were greeted by a woman who may or may not have been Sophie herself, ushered into the room to the left, and given a table near the window. Outside, the lowering sun was highlighting the upper storeys of the buildings opposite, warming the stone and throwing strong shadows onto parts of the street.

'Gosh, it's so beautiful,' Thea sighed. 'You couldn't improve on it, could you? Look at it!'

'It's a museum,' Jocelyn dismissed. 'Still no sign of any people, I notice. Though it looks as if something's going on at that mysterious club place.' She indicated the pink-painted Cotswold Club across the street. A small group of men was getting out of a large BMW and heading for the door. 'Not a ladies' thing, after all,' Jocelyn added.

The food was, as far as Thea could tell, entirely authentic rustic French, the soup served in bowls of monumental proportions. 'If they filled these, each one would be enough for a dozen people,' Jocelyn said, a trifle sourly. 'Seems a bit daft, really. Bad psychology, as well.'

'Oh?'

'Makes you feel cheated, with just the bottom inch or two covered.'

'But it tastes all right?' Thea wasn't having the soup.

'It tastes wonderful. I wasn't talking about the taste.'

'Oh!' Thea's attention had returned to the street outside, and a woman passing in front of the restaurant. 'I know her!'

'Mmm?'

'It's Frannie, from down the lane. I saw her on Sunday, when the cat got run over. She's seen me.' Thea waved cheerily at the figure now standing just the other side of the glass. 'Oh help – I think she's coming in.'

'You shouldn't have waved,' said Jocelyn. 'Waving's often a big mistake. People feel encouraged.'

'Shut up and smile.'

Frannie approached at a trot, ignoring the questioning look from the waitress she almost had to elbow aside to get to the sisters' table. 'Hello!' she trilled. 'Fancy seeing you here. I gather something dreadful happened, but I can't get any details. Can you tell me?'

Thea hesitated. She remembered the parting injunction to say nothing, given by the policeman who had questioned her, and Hollis had not lifted the ban. 'What have you heard?' she said.

'All sorts of rumours. Something about a boy hanging himself?' The upward inflexion might or might not have been a question. Virtually all young women spoke like that these days, even when stating plain facts.

Thea strove to be transparent. 'There was an incident, yes,' she said. 'But the police have asked me not to talk about it. I'm sure the whole story will come out in the next day or two. By the way, this is my sister, Jocelyn. She's staying with me at Julia's for a bit.'

'Pleased to meet you. I'm *dying* to know what's happened.' She squirmed girlishly. 'I hate to miss the excitement. We've been staying with Robert's mum, you see, since Sunday.'

Thea automatically logged this apparent alibi until she remembered Cecilia Clifton telling her that Robert came from a local family. 'Does she live here in Minchinhampton?' she asked casually.

'No, Chalford.' Frannie seemed surprised by the question. 'Why do you ask?'

'No reason. I remember you mentioned her on Sunday, that's all. So, what brings you here?'

Jocelyn sighed, just loudly enough to be impolite, but Frannie took no notice.

'Oh, the Club,' came the ready reply and a wave towards the street outside. 'I'd better go, actually. Robert's waiting for me.'

Robert always seemed to be waiting for her, Thea noted. 'Are you back home tonight, then?' she asked. 'It'll be nice to know there's somebody close by.'

Frannie pushed out her lips, in a coy grimace. 'Well, we *might*,' she said. 'But it'll be very late. More likely, we'll be back at Ma's. She likes having us, you see.'

Thea found herself imagining wild orgies at the Cotswold Club, lasting far into the night. Somehow its appearance suggested something very much along those lines, although common sense decreed that it was really rather unlikely.

'Well, I'm sure everything will soon be back to normal,' she said, wondering who she was trying to reassure. 'And the weather's certainly taken a turn for the better.'

Assuming that the encounter was about to conclude, Thea looked around for any sign of her fish arriving. It was with some surprise that she realised Frannie was not departing after all. Instead, she pulled a spare chair from the next table, and sat down without invitation. 'You're much better off staying out of all this bother, if you can,' she said. 'That's what I'm trying to do.' She bent closer, dropping her voice. 'The thing is, Julia and Des aren't exactly flavour of the month locally. I know they come over as happy-go-lucky and everybody's friend. But there's a lot more to it than that. They've got a lot of backs up over the past year or two.'

'Including yours?' asked Jocelyn, clearly relishing the whole situation.

'Oh, not *me*. I get along with everybody.' The winsome ingenuous smile emphasised the words. Pure Pollyanna, thought Thea.

'Robert, then?'

'Well, Robert's more critical of people, that's true. But he's away a lot, and doesn't get involved if he can help it. Of course, the people at the Club do make sure we get drawn in, sometimes.'

'The Club?'

Jocelyn interrupted. 'Do you mean the *Cotswold* Club?' She pointed with her fork at the building across the street.

Frannie's expression was undisguised bewilderment for a few seconds. Then she laughed. 'Gosh, no. That's not my sort of place at all. No – we're just a sort of gang, a *group*, I mean. We're mostly the old families – people with roots in the area. Wanting to keep things the way they've always been.'

'Like the lady who came to tell me about Milo? Cecilia some-thing.' Thea suggested on a sudden hunch.

Frannie's eyes narrowed. 'Well, Cecilia's a bit of a law unto herself. But she's pretty much on our side, I suppose. She's a friend of my mother-in-law, actually. They're wicked sometimes, the two of them.'

Thea recalled some of Sunday's conversation. 'She told me a bit about your family,' she offered. 'How Robert's grandfather was an important mill owner in Chalford.'

'That's right,' Frannie smiled. 'And mine was a drayman. Well, that was my great-grandad, actually. Did she tell you that?'

'I'm afraid not,' Thea shrugged, very aware that Jocelyn was losing patience.

'Anyway — ' she said, indicating the table. 'It was nice of you to stop and chat.'

'Oh,' Frannie got the message. 'That's all right. I was a bit wor-ried about you, to tell the truth. We don't really understand why Julia thought she needed a house-sitter, you see. I could have fed the animals for her. It's as if...' But she didn't finish. Outside a man was pressing his face to the window and beckoning imperi-ously.

'Is that your husband?' asked Jocelyn, with little effort to dis-guise her relief.

'Oh gosh. Coming!' she mouthed. 'Sorry,' she gasped. 'I'll have to go. I'm sure I'll see you again.'

'You should never have waved,' said Jocelyn, when Frannie had finally gone.

In the last light of the evening, Thea opted for a scenic drive back, thrusting a map at Jocelyn and warning her that they were highly likely to get lost. 'I want to show you the famous Common,' she said, 'and from there we might as well go up to Brimscombe, and then back along the valley. It's only a few miles.'

'Okay.' Jocelyn was lukewarm about the plan. 'If we must.'

The Common was deserted in the twilight, except for silhou-etted cattle and horses, apparently wandering freely. 'It's cer-tainly big,' Jocelyn conceded. 'Looks as if the golfers have taken most of it over, though.'

'There's more this way,' Thea pointed out, driving straight over a five-way junction, marked with an old-fashioned sign, announcing 'Tom Long's Post'.

'This isn't the way to Brimscombe,' said Jocelyn, after peering at the map. 'We're heading north now.'

'Pretty, though,' Thea countered. 'Look at that down there.' A steep valley lay to their right, the lights of scattered houses beginning to shine prominently.

'It's too dark to see,' Jocelyn grumbled. 'Take the next right, for God's sake, and see if we can get back to Brimscombe.'

Twenty-five minutes later, the light had almost gone and they were in a place called Hyde. Both tempers had frayed, and Thea had belatedly noticed that the car was almost out of fuel. 'Just get us home,' Jocelyn ordered. 'A right here will take us onto the A419. Then it's only three or four miles to the Frampton Mansell turning. You'll recognise it from there, I hope.'

'Easy,' Thea assured her.

Mercifully it was, and they turned into Juniper Court just before ten o'clock. 'Thank goodness for that,' said Jocelyn. 'Remind me to veto any more scenic routes.'

Thea was aware of something missing, as soon as she opened the car door. Why wasn't Hepzibah barking? She always greeted the well-known sound of the car engine with a special voice of welcome. Thea's insides somersaulted with terror at the implacable silence.

At a run, she approached the front door, fishing for the unfamiliar keys. 'Hepzie!' she called. 'I'm home.'

'She's here,' came Jocelyn's voice, from the other side of the car. 'She was in the barn.'

Quiveringly, Thea turned to look. A security light had come on, bathing everything in an unnatural brilliance. 'Is she all right?' she croaked.

'Seems to be. Come on, Heps. What've you been doing?'

Thea saw her spaniel approaching slowly, tail slung low. 'She's not all right at all,' Thea cried. 'Look at her!'

But when she scooped the animal into her arms, running terrified fingers over the fur, feeling for blood or broken bones, everything seemed to be in order. There were no squeals of pain or matted hair. 'What's wrong with you?' Thea demanded. 'Why are you so miserable? Who let you out of the house?'

'Oh, God!' Jocelyn groaned. The same thought hit them simultaneously: there was, or had been, an intruder in the house. 'I'm calling the police.' She extracted a mobile phone from her shoulderbag and keyed the three nines. As she did so, the yard light went out, plunging them into a darkness that seemed all the blacker for the abrupt contrast.

The eventual conclusion was that Hepzibah had been severely frightened, but not physically damaged. 'Booted out of the house by a strange intruder, and left to fend for herself in a place she hardly knows – no wonder she was in a state,' Thea crooned. 'What if she'd tried to find me, running off down these dark lanes. She might have been lost forever.'

The damage to her dog occupied considerably more of her attention than the discovery that somebody had entered Juniper Court while it was empty. The lock on the front door was an ordinary Yale, which was all that Thea had activated when she'd left the house. As far as she could see, it had not been broken in any way. Either somebody had had a key, or they'd done the trick with the credit card, which Thea had always supposed to be a myth.

Inside, some furniture had been overturned, two pictures taken down from the living room wall and scratched, and a large message spray-painted on the expanse of pale peach emulsion thus exposed.

GET OUT OF HERE

'Do they mean me, or the Phillipses?' Thea wondered aloud.

'I'd be inclined to take it personally, if I were you,' said Superintendent Hollis, who had arrived from Cirencester barely ten minutes after Jocelyn's emergency call.

'But it must be about them, rather than me. What possible reason can anybody have to take exception to a total stranger?'

'You're in the way. You might see something incriminating.'

'Mmm, maybe.' She gave this some thought. 'So I'm to go, am I?'

'That would be my personal and professional recommendation,' he nodded.

'Right. So who looks after Pallo and all those birds, and the house itself?'

Hollis shrugged. 'Not your problem.'

'I think it is,' she disagreed. 'Definitely, when it comes to the pony. He's got used to me now, and a new person might upset him.'

'Nonsense.'

'And where's a new person to be found? Are they supposed to come in once or twice a day? Or what?'

He tilted his head at her, waiting for her to hear her own words. Jocelyn was in the doorway, trying to say something. Hepzibah was on the sofa shivering miserably.

'I think we'll be all right for the night,' Jocelyn said firmly. 'After all, whoever it was waited until we were out.'

'That's right,' Thea endorsed. 'The same as when the boy was hanged in the stable. I'd taken the dog for a walk. They obviously don't want any direct confrontations.' Oh, she wanted to add, and by the way, why didn't you tell me you know who he was? But it was too late and the conversation was running down a different track.

'It would be madness to assume that,' said the police officer. 'If you don't take this hint, the whole thing's liable to escalate.'

Thea frowned, and sighed crossly. 'Well, I'm not packing up and leaving at this time of night. There are two of us now – we can barricade the door, and think it all through properly in the morning.'

'What about police protection?' Jocelyn suggested. 'Post a constable in the yard for the night.'

Hollis puffed out his cheeks in scornful amusement. 'I don't think so,' he said.

'Don't tell us you haven't got the resources,' Jocelyn said. 'Not when they send a senior rank like you for a little break-in. Shouldn't you be seeing to something a bit more serious?'

He narrowed his eyes at her. 'This, in case you've forgotten, is the scene of a recent unlawful killing. I'm the Senior

Investigating Officer on the case, and when we get a call at midnight from the same property, it would seem to me irresponsible not to investigate personally. All right?'

Thea listened to him with delight. His voice had a mellow bass range, the intonation confident and reassuring. He was well practised in dealing with argumentative females, she supposed, finding the perfect balance between patronising and bullying them. He seemed to detect her enjoyment, and turned to her with his face all open and honest-seeming.

'Well?' he demanded.

'We'd really like to stay here until morning,' she said in a small voice. 'It would be a dreadful nuisance to leave now – for you as well as us.' She glanced at the clock on the mantelpiece. 'And look at the time! It'll be light in about five hours.'

He capitulated, as she'd known he would. 'Just be sure you call me if there's the slightest cause for concern,' he ordered, as he prepared to leave. 'Put something across this door when I've gone, since it looks as if somebody out there's got a key that fits it.'

'We'll be fine,' Thea laughed. 'Honestly, you'll have scared them off long since – if they were still hanging around, which I bet they weren't.'

'I'll be back at ten tomorrow morning,' he said. 'Go and get some sleep, for God's sake.'

They slept fitfully, having debated sharing a room, only to decide it would be too much trouble to organise. Thea's head whirled with half-waking dreams, where Pallo fell down a deep crevice in the field behind the house, and the entire Phillips family came tiptoeing up the stairs, standing silently in the doorway, watching her while she slept. When she finally noticed them, Julia rushed forward and started pulling her hair and shouting that she ought to be ashamed of the mess she'd let the house get into.

But when she awoke, finally, at ten past eight, her first thoughts were all on Jocelyn, who had decided to return to her violent husband, the entirely familiar and trustworthy Alex who had somehow turned into an unknowable monster. She hadn't told Superintendent Hollis that item of news, knowing he would be implacably insistent that she leave Juniper Court, rather than stay there alone.

'Are you awake?' she called, quietly enough not to disturb a sleeper. The lack of response implied a negative answer to the question.

Hepzibah was at the foot of the bed, head raised, expression questioning. Poor little dog, Thea thought fondly. From this point on, she promised herself, she wouldn't let her out of her sight.

In bare feet, she crossed the landing, and looked through Jocelyn's open door. The bed was a jumble of duvet and clothes, with no sign of an occupant.

'Must be making breakfast,' Thea concluded, trying to identify the chink of a teaspoon or whiff of toast from downstairs. Nothing struck ear or nose, and the first flicker of anxiety occurred.

'Hepzie!' she ordered, quietly. 'Stay.' She grabbed the spaniel, in a rush of paranoia. Never mind what had happened to her sister – the dog was her first love these days, and she picked up the awkward creature before going carefully down the stairs.

The front door stood open, and sunshine was streaming into the hall. The sky outside was a tropical blue and nothing stirred. 'Joss?' she called into the yard. 'Where are you?'

'Here,' came a singing voice, full of good cheer and summer relaxation, from the lane outside the gate. 'What do you want?'

Thea put the dog down and strode towards the voice. 'What the hell are you doing?'

'Admiring wild flowers,' came the infuriating reply. 'There's an *orchid* here. Can you believe it? Right here, beside the road.'

'I was worried about you.'

'Were you? Why?'

Thea inhaled in an effort to calm herself. Had she dreamed the whole of the previous evening? Had she woken into a parallel universe? Had Jocelyn received a phonecall to say the police had arrested the intruder, who also confessed to the killing of the hanged boy?

'Why do you think?' she managed tightly.

'Oh, pooh. Nothing's going to happen to us in the broad light of day. Look at that sky! Isn't it amazing!'

'Jocelyn – are you drunk? Or have the fairies stolen my real sister and left this weird person in her place?'

Jocelyn giggled. Thea was now standing facing her in the small road, watching as she crouched over the putative orchid. 'Of course I'm not. No – it's just that I've been up since six, wandering around savouring the atmosphere and having a proper think. If I am drunk, it's on this incredible place. You were right – it's glorious. I just had to find it out for myself.'

'Did I say it was glorious?' Thea looked around herself. 'I thought I'd just wittered on about the history of canals.'

'Never mind. Now I've got to go and phone Alex. I was waiting until you were up, so I wouldn't wake you if I started shouting at him.'

'Are you likely to?'

'Quite, yes. I'm going to tell him I'm staying here after all. For at least a week.'

Thea's eyebrows lifted. 'Is this in response to a small voice emanating from the orchid? Or a bolt from the clear blue sky?'

'In a way, yes. Both of the above – and several other things. I'm due a holiday, if nothing else. Alex goes off for his reunions and camera club jaunts – why shouldn't I have a turn? Besides, somebody has to look after you, if you're intent on staying here.'

'I hate to utter the word, but what about the kids?'

'They've got two parents, damn it. They're not babies. It won't kill them. Life can be too damned comfortable sometimes. It'll be something for them to tell their shrinks when they have their breakdowns later on.'

'Right.' Thea recognised that Jocelyn was now in much the same mood she'd been in when she'd arrived. Any deviation in the meantime had probably arisen from Thea's big-sisterly adjurations. The wise course would be to accept and be glad. Wise, and also self-interested. It suited her very well to have her sister in residence for a few more days. 'Hollis'll be pleased,' she added.

'Well, you'll soon be able to tell him. Less than an hour before he shows up again. That gives me time to phone home, and you can go and wash your hair.'

But before Thea could follow this suggestion, the phone rang and a rather overdue conversation with Julia Phillips took place.

'My God, it sounds as if World War Three's broken out as soon as we turned our backs,' the householder began, with scarcely any preamble. 'It looks as if we'll have to come home,' she said. 'We can't just carry on here as if nothing has happened, whatever Desmond says.'

'What does Desmond say?'

'He's absolutely set on carrying on with his fishing. He's in some sort of competition, up in the Mountains of Morne, would you believe? Actually, it's all fallen apart a bit, with him going off like this. He only stayed with us for about ten minutes and then got talked into joining some group that were going up to the mountains. Then Flora insisted she wanted to go as well, and hopped on a bus to catch up with him. So I'm here with the others, trying to keep them occupied. At least the weather's nice. And then all this business with some dropout getting himself hanged. Quite honestly, it's turning into a bit of a nightmare.'

Thea came close to apologising for all these disappointments. 'Did you know the dead man?' she asked instead.

'What? No, I don't suppose so. Hey, Harry, quit that, will you! Listen, it's chaos here. Harry Two is in a foul mood. Poor Naomi's driving us all mad worrying about Pallo. She says somebody might murder him next.'

Thea felt cold. This was her cue to break the news about the cat. But something before that nagged at her. 'Haven't they told you his name?' she asked.

'Whose name?'

'The dead man.'

''Not yet, no. Oh, heavens – speak of the devil. It looks as if this is him now.'

Thea swallowed. 'Pardon?'

'The policeman who came to see us on Monday. He's back again. I'll have to go. Listen, I'm really sorry about all this. You must think you've walked into a madhouse. This is typical of us. Nothing ever goes to plan. But Pallo – I mean, I know it's unreasonable, but you *will* stay, won't you? I'll never be able to face

Naomi again if he's not alive and well when we get home.'

Thea felt her temper fraying. 'Considering what happened in his stable, he's surviving very nicely. I fixed up a stall for him in the barn, and he seems quite happy. I think he can go back home tomorrow.'

Julia was clearly anxious to curtail the conversation. 'Well, I'm *terribly* grateful to you. I'll call again when we've got things a bit more sorted here. Yes, yes, officer, I'm *coming*. He's looking daggers at me, I'll have to go.'

'Well, I'm happy to carry on here,' Thea said loudly, before the connection was broken.

'That's very sweet of you. Bye now.'

The conversation ended with a number of frustrations for Thea. She had found no opening into which she might insert the bad news about the break-in or the slaughtered cat. Guiltily, she realised that she had not relished being blamed for these mishaps. Neither had she referred to any of the neighbours. As for the man in the sporty car who lurked in the back of her mind as a threatening shadow, Thea was making so much effort to banish him entirely, that there was no way she was going to talk about him. Her feelings towards him were irrational, and she knew it.

And perhaps worst of all, she had neglected to inform Julia that her, Thea's, sister was currently colonising her, Julia's, daughter Naomi's bedroom, without invitation.

Then came a second phonecall three minutes later. It was Cecilia Clifton. 'How are you?' she began. 'I gather there's been some kind of incident.'

'You could say that. But I'm fine. I've got my sister here, and the police are keeping an eye on us. It's all rather exciting in a way.'

'So you're still not ready for that pub outing we're meant to be having?' There was a hint of accusation in the tone that made Thea uncomfortable. She nibbled her lip, wondering what she ought to say. Jocelyn's presence not only removed any need for socialising, it actually created a reluctance to go off and leave her sister behind. 'Well...' she began. 'I suppose...'

'Bring your sister, obviously,' Cecilia added.

But this was even more peculiar. It now felt as if Cecilia was the needy one, the one with time to kill and spaces to fill. Was she so lonely she had to batten onto visiting house-sitters for her human contact? What had Frannie Craven said? *Cecilia is a law unto herself.* Which perhaps implied a solitary habit, rather than membership of the odd-sounding 'club'.

'Okay,' she said, trying to sound enthusiastic. 'But I'm not sure what we're going to be doing.' Nothing would persuade her to make an appointment for lunchtime today, when there was a prospect of still being in DS Hollis's company by the middle of the day. 'I don't think we can manage today, anyway.'

'Goodness, I didn't mean *today*,' came the slightly unconvincing reply. 'I'm busy myself until late this afternoon.'

'And I had planned to do a bit of exploring with my sister. Thanks to your inspiration. I might take her to Daneway House.'

'It's not open to the public, you know. But you can go halfway up the drive, which gives quite a good view.' There was an impatience in the voice, a barely-concealed irritation. Thea wondered what she'd said to offend.

'Thanks. And we could explore the canal path to the tunnel, as well. I haven't seen it from this end yet.'

'Nothing much to see. The Coates entrance is infinitely more ornate.' Again the voice was scratchy with impatience.

If she didn't terminate the call instantly, there would be no time for the hair wash. 'Well, I'll see if we can manage lunch tomorrow, if that suits you,' she offered. 'Shall I phone you back this evening?'

'No, no. I'll call you. Enjoy yourselves.' And Cecilia Clifton put down the phone.

'Phone's busy,' remarked Jocelyn, coming into the kitchen.

Before Thea could agree, it rang again, raising a wry laugh between them. This time it was the Cirencester police.

'Just a courtesy call, madam, to let you know that Detective Superintendent Hollis will be paying you a visit shortly. Would you please arrange to be available, in about twenty minutes' time?' The voice held an undertone of barely-suppressed amusement, reminiscent of playground teasing where everybody knows you've got a notice attached to your back, except you.'

'That's fine,' Thea breezed, hiding the irritation. 'Thanks for calling.'

'The policeman's coming,' she told Jocelyn.

'You mean *the* policeman? Didn't we already know that? Was that him on the phone?'

'Nope. Some menial busybody.'

'They'll be enjoying this,' said Jocelyn. 'Watching their boss man falling for one of the witnesses in a murder case. It's probably totally against the rules. What if you pervert the course of justice?'

'I'll just have to promise not to, won't I? He doesn't seem worried.'

'Shall I go out for a walk, then?'

'Don't be daft. Though you can go and feed the guinea pigs if you like. I can hear them squeaking.'

'And the rabbits?'

'Of course.'

Hollis's blue Mondeo arrived four minutes late. Thea was shamelessly waiting for him in the yard, hair still unwashed. 'Hello,' she said, through the open driver's window, before he could get out. 'How's your investigating going?'

He sat unmoving for a full minute, leaning back in the seat, head turned towards her, but only flickeringly meeting her eye. His gaze took in the duck pond on one side and the stone barn on the other, with everything in between. 'Peaceful,' he murmured.

Then he got out of the car, and flexed the leg that had been in plaster three months earlier. 'I thought you said it was as good as new,' said Thea.

He blinked. 'What?'

'Your leg. The one that was broken. It looks stiff.'

He looked down at himself. 'Maybe it is a bit. I hadn't noticed.'

She waited for what might come next. 'We've got a name for the victim,' he said, without preamble. 'I thought you'd like to know.'

'Yes, I know,' she said. 'I thought you were never going to tell me.'

He gave her a look of wary reproach. 'Oh?'

'One of the Innes boys came over yesterday and shared it with us. I know quite a bit about poor Nick Franklyn now.'

'Nicholas James Franklyn. Nineteen. Student. Home address in Cirencester. Only son, last seen on Friday last week. All that?'

'Most of it,' she nodded. 'Plus he was a Rural Warrior, concerned to preserve the countryside, or some such campaign. I forget the exact words.' She watched his face, knowing she was being too flippant. 'Have you seen his parents?'

'Yes. The father's identifying the body as we speak.'

Thea was effectively sobered. 'Poor people. What a terrible thing.'

'Mmm.' The inarticulate sound contained a due measure of pity and concern, but Thea could also hear impatience. Well, she thought forgivingly, he is a policeman. His job is to find answers, explanations and rightful legal process, not to wallow in the grief and misery that went with most criminal activity.

'I was wrong, wasn't I?' she said. 'I thought he was a vagrant. What happened to his leg?'

'He had some sort of bone condition as a child. The post-mortem spotted it, and we did a search of local doctors, to see if they had anyone on their books with that particular problem. It's quite rare, apparently.'

'What's it called?' Thea had a detached curiosity about medical matters, arising from a succession of friends who found themselves or their offspring afflicted with a variety of ailments.

'Perthe's Disease. Bet you've never heard of it.'

She grinned. 'You bet right,' she admitted.

'Where's your sister?'

'Patrolling the homestead somewhere, I think. She's intent on befriending the geese, for some reason. I stay clear of them as much as possible. They're beastly if they take a dislike to you.'

'Anyway,' he pursued with a brisk display of hand-rubbing, 'I've come to warn you that the story's going to be in tomorrow's local paper, and the TV news for the region this evening. It'll put you on the map, I'm afraid.'

'Why? You won't name Juniper Court, will you?'

'No, but people will work it out.'

'So does that mean I can talk about it now? I mean, it isn't all a deep dark secret any more?'

'In what way?'

'Well, your man, on Monday, told me not to say anything. It's a bit difficult when people keep asking me what's going on.'

'All I can say to that is, use your common sense. You'll appreciate that the actual killer could be one of these people.'

Thea raised her eyebrows. 'I hope not. Anyway, I've already had most of the neighbours onto me about it.'

'Oh? Anybody I should know about?'

After a quick inspection of his face for any sign of patronage, she gave him a serious reply. 'We saw Frannie Whatever-it-is, last night. She seemed to want to warn us about something. Said Julia and Desmond weren't very popular around here. She and her husband have been staying with his mother in Chalford since Sunday – does that count as an alibi? Oh, and the mother is buddies with Cecilia Clifton. You'll remember her.'

'Indeed. And which Innes boy came to spill the beans about Franklyn – and when?'

'Jeremy. Handsome lad. It was yesterday afternoon, three-ish. He's joining the army, and is involved in an outfit called Rural Warriors, which is a very difficult phrase to say clearly. Luckily, he manages his r's quite well.'

Hollis sighed with some melodrama. 'So much for hoping to keep you out of all this. You know almost as much as I do, by the sound of it.'

Thea smirked. 'People talk to me, you see. I've just got one of those faces, they can't resist confiding their secrets.'

'Seriously,' he insisted. 'Can you be absolutely sure not to say anything about the barn? I meant to warn you of that yesterday. As far as we can work out, nobody's connected it with young Franklyn's death, so the less we say about it the better.'

'Aha!' crowed Thea. 'I understand. The first person to drop a careless reference to that being the scene of the murder is our man. Except,' she frowned, 'won't they have noticed your men crawling all over the place yesterday? They were quite visible from the road.'

'We'll have to hope they didn't. It seems to me that scarcely anybody other than the Innes family use that little road anyway. Since it's their barn, we've had to inform them that we're examining it, of course.'

'So if one of them did the murder, you're sunk.'

He sighed again. 'Thea, it really isn't as simple as that. I've got twenty people or more working on this, every one of them following up different parts of the story. There's all the forensic stuff, plus the background to these Rural Warriors, the link between the barn and your stable here – and dozens of other scraps of information, all having to be investigated. And all needing hard evidence before we can do anything as dramatic as making an arrest.'

'You make it sound awfully boring,' she pouted.

'Most of it is,' he confirmed. 'But not entirely. I'm every bit as worried as before about you and Jocelyn staying here. And if you accidentally stumble on anything that might lead to an arrest, you'll be in even more danger. A killer doesn't have a lot to lose, remember. If attacking a second person assures his escape from being caught, he's very likely to do it.'

'I know,' she said, clasping herself tightly with crossed arms. 'And I admit I wouldn't be here without Joss. But I've just promised Julia I'll stay a bit longer. Poor thing, she seems in a real old state, with her holiday falling apart.'

'When was this?'

'Just now. Half an hour ago. And Cecilia Clifton phoned as well. I'm sorry – am I supposed to report every conversation to you? Should I be taking notes?'

They were still standing out in the yard, where the sun was gaining strength and the sky was a promising blue. He took her questions manfully, treating her to one of his forward leans and intent examinations before nodding. 'I think you probably should, yes.'

Thea dropped her gaze. 'I really am a cow, aren't I. I'm not taking this half as seriously as I should be. It's not like me to be so flippant, honestly. Put it down to the weather, or something.'

He smiled. 'I'll opt for *or something*, then. Thea – you must realise —'

'Yes, I expect I must,' she dodged, her heart pounding. 'But not now. Everything's too muddled already. Shall I get coffee? Do you want to sit on the lawn for a bit?'

'Fifteen minutes, that's all,' he said, accepting the gentle rebuff. 'And then I have to be somewhere.'

'See what I mean,' she said, going briskly for the coffee.

They parted lingeringly, Thea following him to the car, and talking to him even when he was in the driver's seat.

'Thanks for coming,' she said. 'I know how busy it must all be.'

'A pleasure,' he smiled. 'Thanks for the coffee. And remember – don't say anything about the barn.'

'Sir,' she saluted. 'My lips are superglued.'

'It's a bit late to ask you this, but I'm assuming you didn't have any more trouble during the night,' he went on. 'That's the main reason I came over, after all – to check that you're both safe.'

'Not a squeak. Even the peacocks seem to have gone quiet.'

'The breeding season's over now. They don't do that cry all year.'

'Maybe not, but they were pretty raucous on Sunday. Frightened the life out of me. And again yesterday. Poor Jocelyn got the full treatment.'

'What about the geese? They're meant to be splendid alarm systems.'

'Not these. They seem to have their own inscrutable notions as to who they like and dislike. Hepzie's their main hate figure, poor love. And I think they might be pining for their people. They seem a bit droopy.'

He started the engine, glancing at the clock on the dashboard. 'I'm late,' he said. 'Don't forget to watch the news. And call me if there's anything to report.'

Thea's arm twitched as she began another mocking salute. But then she caught his eye, and the motion aborted. 'Bye,' she murmured, horrified to find tears prickling behind her eyes as she watched him go.

She stayed outside, trying to regain her equilibrium, wandering towards the field behind the house. 'Aren't you supposed to feed that wretched pony?' Jocelyn called, from the back door. 'It'll die of starvation at this rate.'

Thea remembered the phonecall from Cecilia Clifton after she and Jocelyn had had some soup and slightly stale bread. A brief discussion about shopping and future menus prompted the memory. 'We were asked out to lunch,' she told Jocelyn. 'Tomorrow, probably.'

'Who by?'

'A woman called Cecilia Clifton —'

'But I know her,' said Jocelyn, wide-eyed. 'Quite solid. Square head. Wide hips. Sergeant-major delivery.'

'That's her. How do you know her?'

'She was one of my tutors. We did textiles with her, if I remember rightly. She was terribly keen on William Morris.'

Thea considered this for a long minute. Another apparent coincidence, which might not have been so surprising when looked at logically. The area was big on Arts and Crafts, and Jocelyn's university wasn't so terribly far away, at Bath. A tutor passed a great many students through her hands, after all.

'Will she remember you?' was all she could think to say.

'I doubt it.' Jocelyn sounded rueful. 'I'm three stone heavier now, and my hair's a different colour.'

'Did you like her?'

'Terrified of the woman. More than once I stayed up all night finishing off a piece of coursework for her. I never was any good at deadlines.'

'I was. I loved them. Concentrates the mind.'

'Wow! Wouldn't it be funny if she was the murderer! Old Cissie Clifton. She must be *really* old now.'

'About sixty, I'd guess. Retired, anyway, but certainly not *old*.'

'Heavens! She seemed at least sixty twenty years ago. Isn't that weird, the way it goes? The way the age gaps seem to get smaller.'

Thea merely smiled. 'Well, we'd better have that lunch, then, so you can catch up with each other.'

'I'd much rather not. She never liked me – or any other students. We used to wonder why she'd ever gone into teaching, when she so obviously despised young people.'

'Research, probably. The teaching would be an annoying side issue from what she saw as her real work.'

'That must have been it. I wonder if she's mellowed at all.'

'I thought she was rather pleasant. She seemed interested in me.'

'Of course, she would be, with all your guff about canals and woollen mills. She must have thought you were wonderful.'

'She says we should go and look at Daneway House.'

Jocelyn sighed. 'No need. I've already been there. We had to do an essay on the pesky place. I still dream about it.'

Thea tilted her head back, eyes closed, and received the heat of the sun full blast. She could feel her skin tingling with it, the cells rushing to protect themselves.

'I should go home,' Jocelyn said, as she was repeatedly saying, but sounding sufficiently detached for Thea to ignore her. 'What do I think I'm doing?'

'Having a holiday in the sun. Helping me. Strengthening our relationship. Teaching your kids to be self-reliant.'

'Escaping my responsibilities. Hiding from my husband. Avoiding the issue.'

'All of the above. But there are worse places to do it all in, when it's like this.'

The place was uncannily silent. No vehicle had passed the gate for a good fifteen minutes. No breeze rustled the treetops. No cow bawled for its stolen calf, or flock of confused sheep for their lambs after a mass migration to new pastures. No dog barked.

They were slow to notice Valerie Innes, as she stood by the fence watching them. Hepzibah gave a single muted yap, which Thea ignored. Only when the visitor skirted the fence to the small gate opening onto the further part of the yard, did they realise she was there.

'I've been knocking for five minutes,' she said crossly. 'I thought there was nobody in.'

Jocelyn and Thea looked first at Valerie then at each other. Thea could read her sister's mind easily.

'Sorry,' she said calmly. 'What can we do for you?'

'Oh, nothing much. I just thought I'd come and see how you were. I don't think I've met...' she indicated Jocelyn with a jab of her chin.

'This is my sister. She's been here for most of the week. It's been nice to have some company.'

Jocelyn did not stir from her prone position on the grass, but flapped a limp hand in greeting. 'Hello,' she said.

'You shouldn't lie on the bare grass like that. It's bound to be wet.'

'You sound just like our mother,' Jocelyn smiled forbearingly.

The woman appeared not to hear this remark. 'It's bad for you. You ought to have a rug or something.'

'I'll risk it, thanks.'

Thea tried to conciliate, getting up from her garden chair. 'Isn't it hot!' she said.

But this strategy worked no better with Mrs Innes than any others had done. 'Not for long. They say it'll rain tomorrow and Friday. Thunderstorms.'

'Oh, well. Better make the most of it, then.'

'I gather Jeremy came to see you.'

Thea rubbed a hand across her brow, trying to think. This was Jeremy's mother, she recalled. And Jeremy had been fond of the cat, which had died in the road. Furthermore, she owned the barn which Hollis had asked her not to mention.

'That's right,' she confirmed, with a stifled sigh.

'How did he seem to you? I've been worried about him, to be honest. He's waiting for his A-level results, and seems very tense about it. I had hoped he'd have a nice relaxed summer, but it doesn't seem to be happening.' There was a thwarted look in her eye which gave Thea a fleeting satisfaction.

'Is he going to university?' Too late, Thea remembered what Jeremy had said about his future.

'Oh, yes.' Thea heard the unspoken *of course* in the tone. 'He's got a scholarship from the MoD, actually. But he has to get good grades before he can take up the place.'

'My daughter's just graduated,' she offered. 'She's going into the police.'

'Fancy,' said Valerie Innes, with a softening expression. It was enough of a connection to smooth much of the ensuing conversation.

'What's all this about Rural Warriors?' Jocelyn demanded, inserting a sharper note. 'Is your Jeremy part of it?'

Valerie huffed a rueful *Don't ask me, I'm only his mother* laugh.

'I think they're all in it, to some extent. Even young Flora Phillips seems to be involved.'

'Did you know Nick Franklyn?' Thea asked, in spite of a small warning voice. Something about Valerie Innes inspired a need to compete, to score points and keep one's end up. And why was she here anyway?

'Everybody knows him,' was the reply. 'Knew him, I should say, poor lad. He's a bit of a legend around here.'

'Not your sort, surely?' Thea challenged.

'What makes you say that? I heard him recently, when he addressed a meeting. Very articulate for his age, very thoughtful. Made quite a few of us change our minds about some things.'

Thea felt herself to be corrected. 'What sort of things?' she asked.

'To start with, this business with the canal – it'll cost millions, and take decades to achieve. And everybody knows canals were never very successful. You can see there's a case for saying they never should have been built to start with. That's what Nick said – that they were a mistake from the very outset. Now the woods have grown back, it seems vandalistic to cut them all down again, just for a few tourists. I mean – it's rather an odd way to spend your time, chugging along at four miles an hour, mostly in the pouring rain.'

'My thoughts exactly,' muttered Jocelyn.

Thea was speechless. She had never even considered there could be arguments against restoring canals until these past few days, and now suddenly it seemed to be the majority opinion.

'Do you know anybody else who's directly involved in these Warriors?' she asked.

'I've already said – they all are. Our Dominic, for one. The Cravens, as well. Various people from Oakridge and Chalford. There must have been nearly a hundred at the last meeting.'

'They have meetings? *Public* meetings?' Thea asked faintly.

'I *told* you,' snapped Valerie impatiently. 'Why don't you listen? Making me repeat everything twice. And why are you still here, anyway, with all this going on? Haven't the police given you orders to leave? You must be just another burden for them, when they're already stretched to the limit.'

Thea bristled. 'We're not causing any trouble to anybody. Why should you worry?'

'You're causing complications,' said Valerie. 'Upsetting Jeremy, telling him about the cat like that.'

Thea just stared at her, lost for words. The brief silence gave Jocelyn the opening she'd been waiting for.

'Thea,' she said, sounding very meaningful. 'Aren't we supposed to be going out?'

Thea was quick to take the hint. It had, after all, been a day slightly too full of encounters and revelations. A nice normal trip to a supermarket would be very therapeutic for them both.

'Gosh – yes. What time is it?'

'Half past three,' said Jocelyn. 'We'll be late.'

'Going where?' demanded Valerie. 'Isn't this rather an odd time to be going out?'

Mind your own business, Thea wanted to scream. But she controlled herself for a few more moments.

'We need some shopping,' she said. 'If that's all right with you.'

'No need to be rude,' came the predictable, infuriating response. 'I only came to be friendly.'

Jocelyn slowly got to her feet. 'You haven't been, though, have you?' she said, her head on one side, her voice mild. 'You started by telling me where I should sit, then you told us we were wasting police resources, and finally you stick your nose into our business. If that's friendly, then I'm a waterlily.'

Without a hint of hurt feelings or damaged dignity, Valerie took her leave. Thea was bursting by the time the woman was out of earshot.

'A waterlily!' she exploded. 'Why a *waterlily*?'

Jocelyn shrugged complacently. 'Why not?' she said.

Thea drove them to Chalford, and they spent an hour exploring the little town set on the steep-sided hill to the north of the river, with Hepzie on the lead. 'I'm not leaving her there on her own again,' vowed Thea.

'It feels so strange,' Jocelyn said, as they found themselves in a narrow street, with a high wall on one side, holding back the gardens of the houses above them. 'I can't imagine who would live in a place like this.'

'All sorts, I suppose,' said Thea. 'Probably even some descendants of the weavers and clothworkers, who made the place what it is, a century or two ago.'

'Don't start giving me a history lesson,' Jocelyn pleaded. 'I want to know about *now*.'

'I'm not very good on now,' admitted Thea. 'You'll have to work that out for yourself.'

Failing to locate a supermarket, they found instead a small high street grocery store where they bought fruit and bread and other necessities, and started back to the car with a carrierbag each. 'I'm tired,' said Jocelyn. 'This country living is exhausting.'

'You got up too early.'

'I know I did.'

'Well, we'd better get back. We need to catch the news at six.'

'Do we?'

'Didn't I tell you? There's going to be an appeal for information about the murder. If you think we've had a lot of visitors up to now, you ain't seen nuttin' yet.'

'What?'

'Honestly – you'll see I'm right. All the neighbours who haven't caught on yet will swarm on us like locusts.'

'Why?'

'Because that's what people do. They'll pretend to be offering moral support, and advice and home-baked cakes, but really they'll just want to gawp at the place where a murder happened. It's human nature.'

'You don't sound very bothered.'

'No point in fighting human nature,' Thea shrugged. 'It's understandable, when you think about it.'

'How?'

'Well, because a sudden death is just about the biggest thing that can happen. It shakes up everybody's world, and they want to satisfy themselves that they've got to grips with it. Something like that, anyway.'

'So you think people who slow down on motorways to have a

good old look at crashed cars and ambulances are okay, do you?'

'I absolutely do, yes. If the alternative is to speed on, pretending nothing's happened, then certainly I do. Did I tell you about that woman who rang me after Carl was killed?'

'I don't think so.'

'She said I might want an eyewitness account of how it had all looked, a few minutes after it happened. She was really nice. It helped a lot.'

'I chose a bad example,' Jocelyn said glumly. 'I didn't mean to remind you of Carl.'

'I don't need reminding,' Thea said gently, long since accustomed to the paradox of so often having to be the one offering consolation for a loss that was so acutely her own.

They were back soon afer five, approaching the final few yards with exaggerated trepidation. 'What d'you think we'll find this time?' Jocelyn asked in a melodramatic whisper.

'Stop it,' Thea ordered. 'Nothing else is going to happen.'

The afternoon had continued hot and sunny. The geese, ducks and bantams appeared to resent the sudden heatwave with varying degrees of passion. The peacocks, by contrast, evidently loved it. Two of them sat comfortably in their tree, heads cocked sideways in complete mirror-image of each other. The third, on a higher branch, seemed lost in atavistic dreams of India. Jocelyn tried to capture them on film.

'Why did you bring a camera?' Thea asked.

'I didn't deliberately. Alex makes me keep it in the car, in case there's an accident, and I need proof for the insurance people.'

'Why does everything keep coming back to car accidents?' Thea wondered. 'I can't believe you're doing it deliberately.'

'No, I'm not, I promise.'

'Anyway, if you want a good subject, you should use Hepzie. She's wonderfully photogenic.'

'So she might be, but all cocker spaniels look the same, don't they? It gets a bit repetitive.'

'As far as I can see, all peacocks look the same as well.'

The gentle sniping was typical of their exchanges, throughout their lives. Neither could fully relax and let the other be natural.

Thea hadn't understood this until the acute crisis of Carl's death, when all the bickering dropped away completely, and Jocelyn enfolded her sister in her fleshy arms, pulling her tight against her chest and absorbing the flood of tears with a maternal calm that was entirely new to Thea.

It hadn't lasted, of course. Six weeks later, they were arguing about some small piece of trivia, and Joss was asking one of her unreasonable favours. But they both knew that the bond between them had been confirmed and acknowledged, that it was always going to be there, even if they went through long separations or serious fights.

They missed the news, because at ten to six there was a distraction. Jocelyn had noticed a row of blackcurrant bushes, laden with fruit, at the back of the fenced-off garden. 'We can't let them go to waste,' she'd insisted, taking a colander and quickly filling it with shining dark currants. 'I'll put some in the freezer and cook the others.'

Remembering the freezer in the barn, Thea suggested Jocelyn use that one. 'It looked as if it was where they keep their own produce,' she said. 'Bags of apple slices and loads of beans and stuff.'

When Jocelyn came back seconds later, Thea was flipping through TV channels, idly waiting for the news. 'Psst!' hissed Jocelyn from the doorway of the living room. 'Come here.' The urgent whisper was so reminiscent of childhood games that Thea was momentarily transported to another time and place.

'What do you want?' she asked in a normal voice.

'There's somebody out there. Hiding in that car, in the barn.'

'What?' Thea stared. 'There can't be.'

'There is. Wrapped up in a blanket on the back seat.'

'Not dead?'

'No,' Jocelyn snapped impatiently. 'I saw a movement when I went in there, and some sort of noise. At first I thought it might be a rat. But I was fantastically brave, and went for a look. It's a youngster, I think. One of these stupid Rural Warriors, I imagine. What d'you think we ought to do?'

'Go and have a proper look,' said Thea robustly. 'If they

haven't already escaped, that is.'

They had not escaped. Or rather *she* had not. Armed with a stick she found propped against the barn wall, Thea strode to the Lamborghini and peered through the rear window. All she could see was a rolled-up sleeping bag stretched along the somewhat cramped back seat. Jocelyn hovered a few steps behind her.

She opened the driver's door, savouring the leathery smell that greeted her, and the well-balanced mechanism of the hinges, which screamed quality and money and magnificent workmanship. The bundle on the back seat wriggled slightly.

'Come out,' Thea ordered. 'I can see you. Stop playing games and show us who you are.'

Nothing happened, and feeling more irritated than apprehensive, Thea located the catch to tip the driving seat forward, before climbing in with the stowaway. 'Come on,' she said. 'Whoever you are.'

She scrabbled at the sleeping bag, unsure which was the head end, until an edge came free. She pulled, and a tousled dark head emerged. A sullen female face was almost lost amidst the disordered hair.

'Oh!' said Thea. 'Aren't you...' she groped for the name. 'Yes – you're Flora. What on earth are you doing here?'

'Who?' demanded Jocelyn at her elbow. 'Who is it?'

'Flora. She lives here. I've got her room.' Thea stared at the girl in utter bewilderment. 'But – you're in Ireland,' she said stupidly.

'No, I'm here,' said the girl with some dignity. 'I've been here for days.'

'Well, come into the house and explain what you think you're doing,' Thea ordered. 'And don't try to run away.'

'Not much danger of that,' Jocelyn remarked. 'She's like a chrysalis in that sleeping bag. You'll have to help her out of it.'

Awkwardly, the girl was extracted from the car and the bag until finally she stood rumpled and scowling before them. She was pretty, Thea noted, with the same shape head and style of hair as her own. She was also barefooted, which Thea hoped reduced the chances of a bid for freedom. Already she was wondering how she could possibly hope to restrain her if Flora decided to go.

'How've you managed for food?' she asked. 'And *why*? What's going on?'

'I got stuff out of the freezer,' the girl shrugged. 'Apples and things.'

'Have you been into the house?' Jocelyn wanted to know. A thought struck her. 'Did *you* write that stuff on the wall?'

The girl stared insolently at the beams overhead, ignoring the question.

'Of course you did,' said Jocelyn. 'It's obvious.'

'You know what happened here on Monday, don't you?' Thea demanded, too cross to be kind or sensitive. 'You being here like this looks really suspicious. I'll have to call the police and tell them.'

'Thea!' Jocelyn expostulated. 'For heaven's sake.'

Flora narrowed her eyes, looking from one sister to the other. 'Do what you like,' she muttered.

'Come into the house,' Thea ordered, 'and have some food. We can decide what to do with you after that.'

'We'll have to call your mum,' said Jocelyn. 'She must be worried sick about you.'

The effect of this attempt at a sympathetic approach was completely unexpected. Flora's eyes grew three times bigger, her head came forward like one of the defensive geese in the yard, and she almost choked on the passion behind her words. 'Don't you *dare* phone my mum. And besides, if you mean Julia, then she isn't my mum anyway. My mum's in Liverpool and can hardly get out of bed. So get your facts straight. And don't phone anybody, right? What're you trying to do? Aren't things bad enough as it is?' She kicked wildly at the sleeping bag, on the floor beside her. 'You don't understand anything, do you. You dozy cows are in the way – why don't you just go and leave us to sort it all out?' She waved at the words on the wall, in a gesture that left no doubt that they were her handiwork.

'I told you,' said Jocelyn.

'But *why* do you want us to go?' Thea persisted. 'Why did you come back?'

Flora closed her eyes tight, and shook her head. 'I couldn't tell you, if I wanted to. People would get into trouble if I did. And I wanted you to go so I could sleep in my own bed. See? Simple!'

Thea tried to think things through. 'If you've been here since Monday morning, then you're probably a witness to what happened, and the police will want to speak to you. If that happens, then one of your parents – or step-parents – will have to be with you while you're being questioned. This is very serious, Flora. Surely you understand that.'

Flora evidently found silence impossible to sustain for long. Words burst out of her. 'I don't know what the hell you're talking about. What *did* happen on Monday? I didn't get here until late, and everything seemed normal enough then – except Pallo not being in his stable.'

'She doesn't know, Thea,' Jocelyn said urgently. 'You can see she's telling us the truth.'

'So tell me,' Flora demanded.

'Darling,' said Jocelyn, 'this might come as a shock. Somebody was killed.'

'All right then – tell me,' invited Flora sturdily. 'Who's dead?'

'One of your Rural Warriors – the leader, if I've got it right. A boy called Nick Franklyn.'

They both watched her closely for a reaction. Flora didn't flinch, but her face went a greenish-white. 'Something happened to Nick?' she repeated.

'He was murdered and I found him here on Monday morning,' said Thea.

Flora's jaw bulged where she ground her teeth. Her mouth puckered as she fought to remain silent. She would not meet either woman's eyes, but stared out at the sunny yard. Her thoughts were impossible to read.

'So you see,' Jocelyn continued patiently, 'we have to make sure you're safe. You'll have to stay with somebody responsible. And your parents will have to know you're here. It's not open to discussion. That's how it'll have to be.'

'It's *your* fault,' Flora snarled at Thea, before checking herself. 'Except — When did you say it was?'

'Monday morning.'

'Ah,' sighed Flora, in a disturbingly adult way. 'I was too late then.'

'You came back to try and stop it happening?' Thea felt she was getting close to hearing something vital to understanding the whole mystery.

'None of your business,' Flora retorted. 'You can do what you like, I'm not telling you anything.'

'So what do you want to do?' Jocelyn asked, with impressive patience.

'Stay here. The car's fine. I like the car.'

It occurred to Thea that the girl might have been in the habit of using the car as a hideaway, even before the holiday. She gave Jocelyn a look, full of helpless questions about what happened next.

'You did hear what Thea just said, didn't you?' Jocelyn asked. 'You can't just ignore it and hope it'll all go away. Obviously we can't let you stay here in the car, either.' A thought struck her. 'How did you get back from Ireland, anyway?'

'On the ferry, of course.'

'By yourself?'

Flora chose not to answer that one, merely shrugging wordlessly.

'They'll be terribly worried about you,' Thea persisted. 'They've probably reported you missing by now. You'll be wasting police time.' This echo of Valerie Innes's accusation only made Thea all the more bad-tempered. 'You *stupid* girl,' she added for good measure.

'Nobody's reported anything,' the girl said. 'They don't know I'm here.'

'No – but they know you're not with them.'

Flora sighed melodramatically at the idiocy of adults. 'It's not like that. They're not together. Julia thinks I'm with Dad, and *he* thinks I'm with Julia. Simple.'

'What day did you come back? And how did you get here from Swansea or wherever the ferry docked?' Thea's questions seemed to be breeding in her mind, one leading to three or four others.

'There are such things as trains.'

Jocelyn was still in full maternal mode. 'Flora, you're obviously very shocked and upset about Nick. You must see that we have to phone your mother – stepmother – right away.' She looked to Thea for support. 'Isn't that right?'

'Definitely,' confirmed Thea, privately acknowledging that she was not in fact able to do any such thing. The only phone number she had was Desmond's mobile, and if he was still fishing in the mountains, she was unlikely to get hold of him.

'If you phone anybody, I want it to be my dad,' Flora said, struggling to maintain the hard persona. 'But you won't reach him. I tried all yesterday and he's not answering.'

'Let's see if we've got this right, then,' Thea pressed on. 'You left Julia and the others, saying you were going to join your father in the mountains. But instead you went back to Cork and got the ferry. Nobody missed you. You expect us to believe they haven't communicated by now and discovered you're not with either of them? It isn't going to work, Flora. The story's rubbish, and you know it.'

'It's not rubbish,' snapped Flora. 'You don't understand. Dad never knew I told Julia I was going with him. He won't be thinking about me at all.' She wrapped her arms around herself in her agitation. 'But if you force me, I can phone somebody. Except I'll need to borrow a mobile. Mine's run out of credit.'

'Who do you want to call?' asked Thea.

'My boyfriend, if it's any business of yours.'

'I'll have to know his name and address before I let you go to him.' Thea's anger had evaporated in the face of the girl's courage and self-control. There was a tragedy here that she had scarcely glimpsed until now. She craved the strong professional shoulder of DS Hollis, wondering how it was that she'd failed to call him minutes ago. She realised she'd been misleading the girl as to what might happen next. 'I'm sorry,' she said, 'but you really will have to speak to the police, first.'

'What for? Do they think I killed Nick? How could I, if it happened on Monday? I didn't get off the ferry till evening, and it took hours to get back here.'

Flora had something clear in her mind, that much was obvious.

And she was not inclined to disclose much of it to these two offi-
cious women who had taken over her house.

'Well, come and have something to eat,' offered Jocelyn. 'And
a proper wash. We can decide what happens next when you've got
over the shock.'

'What shock?' demanded Flora with a heart-rending effort at
bravado. 'What makes you think it's a shock?'

Hollis, when told of the new development, was almost as much
as a loss as Thea and Jocelyn had been. 'What are we going to do
with her?' he muttered. 'How old did you say she is?'

'Fourteen.'

'Bloody hell. Well, first thing, we tell her mother where she is.
Then she'll have to answer some questions. Do you think she
knows anything useful?'

Thea gave this a moment's consideration. 'I think she probably
does – I get the impression she came back hoping to prevent
some sort of violence.'

'But she hasn't told you anything specific?'

'No.'

'We'll have to find somebody to watch out for her.'

'You wouldn't expect me...?'

There was a silence. Then, 'I s'pose not,' followed by more
silence.

'She has a real mother, in Liverpool,' Thea offered. 'She's ill,
apparently, but might be useful. And she says there's a boyfriend
she wants to speak to.'

'Hmm. Well, I'll send somebody round in a few minutes. It
won't be me. Try to hold onto her till then.'

Flora sulked and refused to eat, but she did not try to escape.
She picked at her fingernails, brow furrowed in thought, her face
still very pale. Thea had not told her the news that the police were
on their way, despite a strong sense of treachery at having crept
upstairs to use the phone in the master bedroom. Both Flora and
Jocelyn seemed to be paralysed. Silence felt like the only option,
when words only led to more lies and hurt feelings.

A car arrived containing two female uniformed officers. Thea
met them at the door and took them into the living room. Flora

gave one startled look before lapsing back into her torpor. 'We'll look after you, pet,' said a smiling black policewoman with a Yorkshire accent. 'Give you somewhere comfy for the night, eh?'

Flora smiled briefly at a secret joke. 'Taking me into care, are you?' she said flatly. 'I've always wanted to be taken into care.'

Thea was left with a sense of having dodged a responsibility and ducked a duty, and a realisation, an hour and a half too late, that she was meant to be watching the six o'clock television news.

Jocelyn shrugged wearily. 'We'll have to catch it at ten, instead.'

The news had them focused unwaveringly on the television screen. After the national stories of wars and politics and the latest medical miracle, came the regional headlines. The discovery of Nicholas James Franklyn hanging in a stable in a small Cotswold village not far from Stroud was the main item.

'Mr Franklin's family have elected to make a public appeal less than twenty-four hours after learning of their son's death. The police are treating his death as suspicious, and his parents have given the following news conference. This took place earlier today, in Cirencester.'

Then came a short video of a middle-aged man and woman, flanked by people who must have been police officers.

'Oh, my Lord!' said Thea.

'What?'

'That man. The father. I've seen him before. He's the one who came to the door here, on Sunday, when it was raining. The one who drove past again, the next morning.'

'He can't be,' Jocelyn protested.

Thea's gaze didn't waver from the screen. 'It is, it's definitely him.'

'You'll have to tell the police,' Jocelyn urged her.

'Shh.' The bereaved parents were talking, first one, then the other.

Nick was a wonderful son. He was doing well in his studies, and was hoping for a place at Nottingham University. He had all sorts of plans. We just can't believe he's gone. Please, everyone, help us find out what happened to him.

That was the mother, a crumpled woman with pale ash-blonde

hair and a carefully-pressed blouse.

The father patted her arm, his eyes still on the camera. *A very fine boy. Strong social conscience. Popular.* He seemed to utter the words by rote, their meaning blurred by the fixed blankness of his features.

Then the police took over, the camera shifting to a middle-aged man with clean reliable looks. *If anybody can provide us with any information as to why Nicholas was in that particular area, or any unusual vehicles or movements, anything at all, please call the Cirencester police on this number.*

'Usual sort of stuff,' Jocelyn commented cautiously, when she was sure it was finished.

'Strong social conscience,' Thea repeated. 'That's the bit about him being an environmental activist, I suppose.'

'That father doesn't like it. You could tell.'

'Could you? He looked like a ventriloquist's dummy to me, just saying stuff he'd rehearsed in advance.'

'Most of it, yes, but not that part. And why mention it at all?'

Thea stared at the screen which had moved on to the weather forecast. 'It's extremely odd, though – him being here at the same time as the boy died. His own father.'

'Does he know you saw him on Monday?' Jocelyn looked worried.

'I'm sure he did, even though he was wearing a pair of goggles.'

'Pardon?'

'Goggles. Like old-fashioned aeroplane pilots. He had the top of his car down.'

'But he saw you? He saw you seeing him? In which case, you might have something to worry about.'

'Only if he's the murderer. Do you think he might be?'

'Well, don't ask me. Get onto your new boyfriend and chew it over with him.'

Thea knew she must do precisely that. Her reluctance stemmed mainly from the impression of hysteria given by two panicky phonecalls in one evening. And the man had sounded embroiled in work, in hard thinking and urgent claims on his time, when she'd called about Flora. Could it perhaps wait until morning? Hadn't he said he wanted her kept at a distance from the whole murder enquiry? And hadn't he also said she should watch the television news?

She picked up the phone.

But when she finally heard his voice, and gave him her news, he barely responded. 'Oh yes, we know,' was all he said.

'And you never told me?' The whining reproach was inexcusable, but unavoidable.

'I wanted you to see for yourself. It's better that way. I didn't want to sow any seeds.'

'How did you know?'

'Your description of the car, mainly. We made the connection yesterday, but he hasn't mentioned being at the scene. It'll all come out in his questioning.' Hollis spoke slowly, everything about him sluggish and drained.

'You sound dreadfully tired,' she said, realising for the first time that she knew nothing of his home situation, what his bedroom looked like, whether anybody made him a hot chocolate when he finally crawled back from work. He existed in her mind as a free-standing figure, with no contextual clutter. Except, Thea remembered, with a thumping shock, three months ago she had been told by her brother-in-law James, who knew Hollis quite well, a piece of personal history so significant that Thea wondered at her own sanity when she realised she had forgotten all about it.

Hollis, according to James, had had a daughter, who died after taking Ecstasy at a rave, not so many years earlier. If she had got it right, that had been the reason for the failure of his marriage. The sudden knowledge made her feel self-absorbed and foolish. Did Hollis know that she knew? Was he waiting for her to mention it? Trawling back over the past three days, she thought with relief that there had been no conversation about daughters. Time enough, then, to confront the man's family tragedy.

'Yes, I'm tired,' he was saying. 'I'm in a tiring line of work.'

She brought her attention back with an effort. 'Is this Franklyn man suspected of the murder?'

'I can't answer that. Now, goodnight, Thea. Sleep well, and keep the doors locked.'

She woke with a sensation of withdrawal, of needing to stay under the duvet, keeping out of other people's troubles. She and her dog would be fine if other people would only leave them alone. Then she woke up properly, opened her eyes, and saw her sister standing in the doorway, with a man's arm tightly around her throat.

They had only been there a few seconds, she concluded. The dog hadn't even noticed yet. Jocelyn's eyes were bulging, and her fingers plucked feebly at the shirtsleeve clamped between her chin and chest. Her captor's head was only half visible above and behind hers, his eyes on Thea, glittering with tension. He wore a hot-looking woollen balaclava.

'Who are you? What do you think you're doing?' Thea sat up, acutely aware of her state of undress. She put a hand on the spaniel, pressing her into the bedclothes. 'Stay, Hepzie. Stay there,' she ordered.

'We've told you to go,' the man said, his voice rather high and clear. 'What do we have to do to persuade you?'

'We?'

'You're in the way here. We don't want trouble. It's nothing personal. Just pack your things and go, will you?'

'No trouble?' Thea laughed scornfully. 'What about Nick Franklyn?'

'Never mind Nick Franklyn.'

'What about the pony and rabbits and guinea pigs ? I'm being paid to look after them. I'm staying another week. Let Joss go, will you. Stop playing idiotic games.' Joss's eyes bulged even further, but Thea was into her stride. There was no discernible knife or gun, and the man's voice did not suggest an intention to harm. He was tense but not psychotic. And he was young enough to be her son.

'I'm telling you, you've got to leave this place. It's not safe for you. Do yourselves a favour, you silly cows.' His arm was loosening visibly. Thea tried to see his eyes more clearly, already aware that she would want to identify them again. They were brown, thickly-lashed and clear. And something familiar about his words snagged at her.

'You've been talking to Flora, haven't you?' she said, out of the blue. 'She called us silly cows as well. She daubed that writing on the wall. You must be her boyfriend.' The sudden transparency came as a bracing wave of relief. 'How did you get in?'

Jocelyn began to splutter. She, like Thea, seemed to be more indignant than frightened. 'He climbed through my bedroom window,' she said thickly. 'Bloody cheek.'

'Let her go!' Thea ordered, in the voice every son would recognise. 'Just do as you're told, will you.'

It worked brilliantly. It was as if she'd activated some trigger that controlled him against his own will. Or perhaps he had simply realised that he couldn't go on standing there with his captive in an armlock for much longer. Jocelyn pulled free, and turned angrily to face him.

'Why aren't we safe here?' Thea asked, staring intently at his face. 'What are you planning to do?'

He averted his gaze, a failed attacker, an embarrassed intruder. Thea pressed her advantage. 'What's this all about anyway?'

'Mind your own business,' he growled. 'You're in the way, that's all.'

'Did you kill Nick Franklyn?' Thea asked, almost casually. 'Because I think Flora thinks you did. I think she was totally paralysed by that belief, when we told her Nick was dead.'

'Me?' The shock seemed genuine. 'Of course I didn't. He was on our side. Nick was everybody's friend.' His voice thickened, and Thea heard tears lurking. 'It's all turned into a shitty mess, because of this place.'

'Hang on.' Thea was intent on grasping his meaning. 'Are you against Julia and Desmond for some reason? Flora's parents?'

'Shut up about Flora. She's got nothing to do with it.'

'Hasn't she? You know who she is, though, don't you? You know she came back here by herself, a child of fourteen, and hid out in the barn for two nights. Did she phone you last night, from wherever they took her? Is that why you're here now?'

'You're guessing all wrong,' he said with scorn. 'I'm not Flora's boyfriend.'

'Then who is? Jeremy Innes? Simon?'

'Simon's a baby. And Jemmy's not her type.' His scorn had turned to sulks. Thea recalled her brother Damien at this age, tormented by the fickleness of girls. Flora, it seemed, was a pivotal figure in this tangled story.

Jocelyn was gently massaging her throat. 'You assaulted me,' she said, her voice still croaky. 'You're in big trouble, you know. What can be worth it? What's so important that you need to frighten us into going away?'

Thea answered for him, convinced she was on the edge of an explanation. 'They want to damage this house,' she suggested. 'Burn it down, or at least wreck it. They've got something against the family here. And they're very decently warning us about it first. Isn't that right?' she asked the intruder.

'We don't want you hurt. Nor your dog. You're a complication – that's all I'm saying.'

'Well, forget it,' Thea advised him. 'You can't hope to get away with it. We know you're linked with the Rural Warriors.'

Jocelyn turned to look into his eyes. 'And I think I know exactly who you are.'

'Go on then,' he challenged. 'Who am I?'

'I think you're the oldest Innes boy. You called Jeremy by a pet name, you're impatient of Simon. Believe me, I know about the way brothers and sisters are with each other. And, for the record, you have my sympathy over your stepmother. You might even use her as a mitigating circumstance when this all comes to court.'

'Dominic,' Thea remembered. 'That's it. Your name's Dominic.'

As the man struggled to assimilate this abrupt change of direction, and Thea waited for his reaction, all three of them slowly noticed the reality of the situation. Nobody had physical hold of anybody else, and nobody seemed likely to achieve a firm control at that stage of the proceedings. 'You can't keep me here,' said the intruder, in summary.

'And you can't make us leave,' Thea flashed back at him. 'You haven't got what you came for, so just go, why don't you. And behave yourself, you idiot. Don't get involved in whatever it is.'

'You'd better leave,' he repeated. 'You've got twenty-four hours, and then things are going to turn nasty. *Really* nasty.'

'I hope not,' said Thea. 'Have some sense, for God's sake. Now we know who you are, the police'll be looking for you.

You're in trouble, Dominic, and you'd better face up to that.'

'Stop calling me Dominic like that,' he snarled. 'You don't know who I am.' His baffled frustration increased, and Thea felt a flicker of sympathy for him. In the books and films and video games, a woman with an arm around her throat became a passive yowling creature – unless she was Lara Croft and impossibly expert at martial arts. He had not reckoned on the instinctive authority that had taken hold of first Thea and then Jocelyn. Men were stronger, in the world he thought he'd entered when he laid violent hands on Jocelyn; they were a frightening element of the culture, and could do what they liked. *Next time*, she felt like advising him, *carry a really big sharp knife. That way, you might get things to work out better.* Instantly appalled at herself, she looked into the brown eyes, that were, now she thought about it, very much like Jeremy Innes's.

'Thank you for the warning,' she said. 'But I'm afraid you're too late. The police are too close now and you've been extremely stupid to come here like this. We're not going to try and keep you here, because somebody might get hurt, but that's what we ought to do. So just go, and let *me* warn *you* that if anything at all happens here, you'll be the obvious suspect. You might run away and hide out in the back streets somewhere, but that's no way to live. Go away and have a good think. And *never* never do anything like this again. It's a very stupid game, and no campaign or protest group is worth it.'

She drew a deep breath, and suddenly saw herself, hectoring a young delinquent in her nightwear, one arm around a bemused spaniel, and her sister slumped against the wall turning a nasty shade of pale green.

Fortunately, it worked. The man took one long backward stride, and then ran along the landing and down the stairs. They heard him scrabbling at the barricaded door and then slamming it behind him.

'What time is it?' asked Jocelyn feebly and inconsequentially, and then 'Oohhh,' before Thea could answer her, or leap from the bed to catch her as she fainted.

It lasted barely a minute, and when she revived she seemed

more embarrassed than traumatised. 'Fancy fainting!' she chided herself. 'What a wimp!'

The tension dissipated, and they spent half an hour on Thea's bed, talking it all through repeatedly. 'We should call the police,' said Jocelyn. 'We've had an intruder, and he laid violent hands on me. They don't take these things lightly, you know.'

Thea was mindful of Hollis's exhaustion the night before, and never even considered speaking to a different officer. 'We'll call them at eight. It's too early now.'

Jocelyn had clearly not kept up. 'They don't just work in office hours, you know.'

'I know. But they're busy with more important things.'

'No, Thea, they aren't. This is the important thing they're busy with, remember? It's obviously got a whole lot to do with the murder, and sitting here is just letting that bloody boy get away.'

'I suppose you're right,' Thea said, aware of an odd paralysis when it came to using a phone, beyond her protective feelings towards the Superintendent. Once she'd made the call, there would be cars and men and questions and *effort*. 'You can do it, if you like.'

'Me? Why me?'

'Because you're the one he assaulted.'

'I don't want to.'

'Neither do I. Useless pair, aren't we?'

'At least he isn't likely to do it again,' Jocelyn said. 'Do you think?'

'He seemed to have every intention of burning this house down,' Thea reminded her.

'It was Dominic, wasn't it? Don't you think?'

'Yes, but we can't prove it. There might be a dozen other lads like that intent on stopping progress. That barn conversion, as well as the canal. Any new building.'

'I don't get it,' groaned Jocelyn. 'What's become of them? Where are their motorbikes and flick knives? Why don't they move to the towns where they belong?'

Thea laughed weakly. 'Maybe they've bred a mutant race down

here,' she suggested.

'Although when you think about it, they're just as bad. What they're doing is a kind of terrorism.' She frowned. 'Like the animal rights people, intimidating and attacking anybody they think is involved in vivisection.'

Thea nodded. 'That's probably where they get their methods from. I expect they're stalking the canal restoration people and sending them hate mail.'

'We have to phone the police,' Jocelyn repeated. 'They'll be furious with us as it is, for dithering all this time.'

'We'll tell them you fainted, and I had to administer first aid, before doing anything else,' Thea suggested. 'They'll give you top marks for that. They like a girl to be properly overcome in a situation like this.'

'I'm furious with myself. I don't know what came over me. It was the sudden waking up, with his hand over my mouth, I suppose. It made my heart go funny.'

Thea made the call to Hollis's personal number, and recounted the events briefly. 'We're perfectly all right,' she insisted. 'I know you'll think we should have called you sooner, but there didn't seem much point. I can give a fairly good description of him and his clothes. We think he must have been Dominic Innes. He wasn't a very competent criminal, I must say.'

'I can't come now, but I can send somebody. How about DC Herring? You know her.'

'No, no. She must have better things to do. It isn't really important. Except he said something's going to happen within the next twenty-four hours. At least – they want us to leave by then. Listen, Phil. The Rural Warriors were followers of Nick Franklyn. That means it wouldn't have been them who killed him. His death has made something more urgent for them – that's the feeling I got.'

It was the first time she'd used his Christian name and they both knew it. But he was not put off his stride.

'Why do you want to defend them? After what they've just done?'

'Good question. We've been asking ourselves the same thing. I suppose it's something to do with them being some mother's sons. And – well, it's a nice change to see young people feeling strongly about something.' It sounded crass in her own ears, and Hollis's scornful laugh made it clear that it sounded crass to him, as well.

'These early mornings are getting to be a habit,' said Jocelyn. 'What are we going to do today, then?'

'We could have lunch at Daneway with Cecilia Clifton,' Thea suggested. 'It'd be fun to see if she remembers you. And I want to go there anyway, to see the tunnel entrance.'

'Better than hanging around here waiting to see if we're going to be burned in our beds,' Jocelyn agreed.

'I wonder what they've done with Flora. I still feel a bit responsible for her. I was a fool not to take a number for Julia, when she phoned. Maybe I could try Desmond's mobile. Put his mind at rest, in case the police have upset him.'

'Stop it,' Jocelyn ordered. 'None of this is your problem. Whatever mess they're in, it's up to them to sort it out. And Julia can phone you if she wants to. All you have to do is feed the pony.'

Thea phoned Cecilia, who agreed to meet them at the Daneway Inn at midday. 'We had breakfast rather early,' Thea explained. 'So an early lunch would be nice.' Then to Jocelyn she suggested they leave an hour or so beforehand and explore the tunnel first. Jocelyn shrugged accommodatingly, her mind evidently elsewhere.

'We could walk from here,' Thea said wistfully, knowing the response she'd get.

'Not today,' said Jocelyn firmly.

They parked on the patch below the Daneway pub, which had a sloping garden devoid of drinkers at ten forty-five on a Thursday morning. Thea's map marked a footpath where the original towpath had been, as well as showing the famous Daneway House, on rising ground behind the pub. Unfortunately, dense woodland rendered it invisible.

'I definitely came here when I was a student,' Jocelyn remem-

bered. 'We were shown around Daneway House, because William
Morris used to live there.' She was gazing around, as if trying to
find something familiar. 'I don't remember all this, though.
There's no sign of the house now.'

'I think it's up the hill, behind the pub.' Thea was impatient.
'Come and see the tunnel. You said you were interested.'

'Did I? That was careless of me.'

Thea walked ahead, without replying, keeping an eye on the
dog as she left the path for forays into the long grass on their
right. They climbed a stile and proceeded along a path which
appeared to lead nowhere. 'Jolly overgrown,' grumbled Jocelyn,
pulling free of a grasping bramble.

'It's been quite well used, though, like the one I walked with
Phil the other day.'

'Oh, it's "Phil" now, is it?'

'That's his name,' said Thea coldly.

'Somebody needs to come along with a scythe.'

'Don't fuss. It's really perfectly easy to walk along.'

Jocelyn snorted and followed a few paces behind her sister.
'Where's this tunnel then?' she demanded after half a minute of
walking.

'Not far. About a quarter of a mile, I would guess.'

They found it with little warning. An arched opening, with
fanciful crenellations along the stonework above it. A flimsy-
looking wooden gate made a token attempt to prevent access into
the tunnel itself, strangely situated eight or ten yards inside the
mouth. There were only two or three inches of water on the bed
of the canal.

Jocelyn was unimpressed. 'Anybody could get in there,' she
said. 'And I still don't understand why you think it's got anything
to do with anything.'

'Did I say it had? I just wanted to see it for its own sake.
Except —' she remembered something. 'That man – the father of
the Franklyn boy – he wanted to know the way to Daneway. And
he was soaking wet.'

'He was wet *before* he came here,' Jocelyn pointed out. 'If he
ever did come here at all.'

'No, no. What if he just used that as a pretext for talking to me? For finding out if there was anybody at Juniper Court. He just said the first thing that came into his head, and it was Daneway because he'd just come from here. He'd been into the canal for some reason and got himself all wet.'

'Thea, this is pure fantasy,' Jocelyn laughed. 'You've added two and two and made seventeen.'

'But there's nothing here except the tunnel,' Thea insisted, bending forward as far as she dared, trying to peer into the gloom. 'Why else would anybody want to come to Daneway?' There were atmospheric echoing dripping sounds as water seeped through the brickwork at the top of the tunnel. She wondered whether her trainers would be totally ruined if she jumped down and started walking into the darkness.

'The pub. The William Morris house. Somebody else's house,' Jocelyn suggested. 'After all, if he was up to something sinister, he'd already know the way, wouldn't he? He wouldn't expose himself by asking how to find it. He'd have said some other place – Mishyhampton or Hyde or some other stupid backwater. And not everybody's as obsessed with canals as you are.'

Thea sighed. 'That all sounds perfectly logical. I just have a feeling he was in pursuit of his son, and the whole business concerns the canal. It's gorgeous, though, isn't it,' she diverted herself with a rapturous contemplation of the miniature castle effect over the entrance to the tunnel.

'It shows how proud they must have been of their achievement,' Jocelyn conceded. 'Is it the same at the other end?'

'Not at all. Flamboyant in a completely different way. You could get into it, from that end as well, if you didn't mind getting wet.'

'Not much water in it. Has it leaked away?'

'Here and there, possibly. But the puddling they did in those days was fantastically effective. Leaks are rare – though trees have grown in the middle of the waterway in some places. That breaks up the clay skin.'

'How on earth can anybody think it's possible to reconstruct it all? It'll take decades.'

'They've done quite a few already. The entire stretch of the Kennet and Avon is open now. Where there's a will, and all that. Some people are fanatical about it.'

'They must be.' Jocelyn cast another critical eye over the reedy canal bed, and the barricaded tunnel. 'Can't see the attraction myself.'

'You're a philistine,' said Thea. 'I think it's marvellous.'

'So you said. Pity the tunnel's blocked.' In spite of herself, Jocelyn was intrigued. 'It certainly does have atmosphere, I'll give you that.'

'Well, it is blocked, further along. But this first bit seems all right. It echoes a long way. You can tell by the drips.'

'And have you seen enough now? Even Hepzie's getting bored, look.'

'Okay,' Thea agreed. 'But we'll be early.'

They walked back to the car without speaking. Hepzibah ran cheerily ahead of them, zigzagging in her usual way. Sunlight threaded between tall trees on both sides of the waterway, promising another fine day.

It was twenty to twelve when they settled at one of the tables in the pub garden, with Hepzie comfortably curled at their feet. Pub gardens were familiar ground to her, and she knew how to behave. 'If we start drinking now, we'll be blotto by the time we get any food,' said Jocelyn.

'We'll just have to take it slowly, then,' said Thea. 'I'll go and get us some local ale, shall I?'

Jocelyn pulled a face. 'Mine's a white wine,' she instructed. 'Nice and sweet.'

'Philistine,' said Thea, again.

'Here she is,' Thea said, at two minutes to twelve. 'Nice and prompt.' A silver-coloured car had drawn up in the parking area, and the sisters watched as Cecilia got out. She was wearing a smart lightweight jacket in pale blue and darker blue slacks. Her head was up and her step confident. When Thea waved, she gave a nod of acknowledgement and quickly joined them.

'You've started without me,' she noted. 'Are you ready for

more drinks?'

The sisters shook their heads emphatically and Cecilia climbed the slope to the bar at a trot.

There did not seem to be anything to say as they waited for her to return. Then, after Thea had made the introductions, Jocelyn confessed that she had been one of Cecilia's students. 'You haven't changed a bit,' she said.

Cecilia scrutinised her. 'Well, I'm afraid I can't say the same for you. I don't remember you at all.'

'I wasn't very conspicuous,' Jocelyn smiled. 'And it was nearly twenty years ago.'

'So many students, so much wasted breath,' sighed Cecilia, as if she'd said the same thing many times before. 'But it was a living, I suppose.'

'Come off it,' said Thea. 'After last Tuesday, I don't believe a word of that. You're still devoted to your subject.'

'I'm devoted to this little part of the world, and its history,' Cecilia admitted. 'It's not at all the same thing as being an avid lecturer on the stuff.'

'You seemed quite avid on Sunday,' Thea argued mildly. 'Full of local history and gossip, you were.'

'It's completely different,' the older woman insisted. 'I really can't pretend that I ever had much of a liking for the students. Most of them had no idea why they were there and cared nothing for the subject.' She threw a mildly accusing glance at Jocelyn. 'What did you do afterwards, for example?'

'I got a job on a glossy magazine for a bit. It was wonderful while it lasted. Then I got married and had five kids.' Her tone was defiant, but there was self-mockery in her expression. 'Since then I've had a series of part-time jobs, and sold one or two articles about antique ceramics and that sort of thing. But you're right – most of us had very little feeling for the subject.'

Cecilia sipped her pint of cider and said nothing. Thea began to worry that the next hour would be rather hard going. Under the table, Hepzie was licking a paw, a sign of restlessness. 'I've seen the locks, in the woods down there,' she offered, waving a hand towards the road and the bridge across the river. 'I can't imagine how they'll ever restore them. It'll be an enormous job.'

'So everybody says,' Cecilia nodded. 'I don't expect to see it done in my lifetime.'

'Oh, but aren't they saying five years?' Too late, Thea wondered whether the remark had been an oblique revelation of a terminal illness, rendering five years well beyond Cecilia's expected survival. But this did not appear to be what she'd meant.

'Don't you find it's one of the plagues of our times – setting targets of this sort?' Cecilia's tone was conversational and calm, but Jocelyn caught Thea's eye with an alarmed look. 'It's as if these people believe that all they have to do is state an intention to achieve something by a certain time, and it'll happen, by magic. It would be laughable if it wasn't so irritatingly childish. And most of the time the target is something stupid that nobody wanted in the first place.'

Thea held up her hands. 'Let's not get into that argument,' she pleaded. In desperation she sought for a change of subject. 'Do you know Valerie Innes?' she asked Cecilia, who responded with a few seconds' blankness.

'What does she have to do with anything?' she asked.

'Nothing really. She seems to be rather a prominent personality around here, that's all.'

'She's that, yes. I can't say I have a great deal to do with her.'

'Her Jeremy was fond of the cat,' Jocelyn contributed. 'I gather you were the first one to discover the body.'

'What?' Cecilia seemed startled. 'Oh, Julia's cat. Yes – poor thing.'

Thea began to sense minefields on all sides. Not knowing how much Cecilia knew about the death of Nick Franklyn presented her with a number of brick walls when it came to conversation. Safer, then, to stick to local history. And that meant canals. 'But you would like the canal to be restored, wouldn't you?' she asked. 'So far I can't seem to find anybody who's actually in favour of it, which I find extraordinary.'

But even this was apparently an unsafe topic. Cecilia sighed heavily, suggesting exasperation and even something like anger. She shifted her feet and accidentally kicked the dog, who squeaked. 'It's all rather hard to explain,' she said. 'Life has moved on. New people have come here, who don't know or care about how things were in the past. And the canal never was all good, you know.' She leaned forward, her eyes glittering. 'People died because of that canal.'

Thea took this easily. 'Well, of course. Making that tunnel must have been an awful job. But surely —'

'And afterwards. Much more recently than the construction of the tunnel. Locks can be extremely dangerous, you see.'

Thea was unmoved. 'Just about anything's dangerous, if you get into that way of thinking,' she said. 'I'm sure the benefits would outweigh any minor hazards.'

'Well, many people would think you were wrong about that,' Cecilia said tightly.

'Let's order some food,' Jocelyn suggested. 'I'm hungry.' They duly consulted a menu and made their selections, the atmosphere heavy and slow between them.

Thea observed Cecilia as she ate – not something she would normally do. The food was absorbed impatiently, roughly chopped and certainly not savoured. The woman seemed angry and preoccupied, perhaps with the proposed canal restoration, or perhaps with the fecklessness of students. Or, more probably, as it turned out, with Valerie Innes.

'The woman's a disaster,' she said, her mouth still occupied with a large chip.

'Which woman?' Jocelyn asked with a frown and another glance at Thea.

'Valerie. She's a type, of course. Never listens, thinks the world will collapse if she doesn't take control. Gets an idea into her head and tries to force everybody to conform to it. It amazes me the way those boys have stuck around as long as they have.'

'I can't say I liked her much,' Thea agreed carefully. 'And I thought the same about the boys. Dominic must be well over twenty.' Again the sisters' eyes met, Thea trying to convey that she knew she was taking a gamble.

'Coming up to twenty-three, I think. There's a case in point, if we need one. Dropped out of Bristol after less than a year and hasn't got himself together since.'

'Too busy with his Rural Warriors, I suppose,' purred Thea. 'And girls. Isn't he involved with Flora Phillips? Which must be rather a scandal in itself, with such a big age gap.'

Cecilia had taken a second chip, which now obstructed her windpipe as she thoughtlessly inhaled. Coughing desperately, she turned red and leaned over the grass in an undignified attempt to expel the object that was preventing her from breathing. Jocelyn reached over and thumped her heartily between the shoulderblades – which clearly was not helping. Hepzibah sensed an interesting diversion and began jumping at Cecilia. Jocelyn pushed her away with an irritated comment.

All Thea could do was watch, and wonder which of her remarks had been so startling. She was not afraid that Cecilia would choke to death – if she could cough, then air must be getting through. But Jocelyn was in full panic mode. 'God, Thea, do something!' she shouted.

'She'll be all right. Just leave her to sort herself out. You're making it worse.' At the same moment, the sisters both recognised that Thea was doing it again – refusing to react to the sort of alarming event that had most people in a frenzy.

'Ohh – you,' said Jocelyn, retreating from the suffering woman. 'One of these days, somebody's going to die right in front of you, and you'll be sorry you didn't try to help.'

'Let's hope not,' gasped Cecilia, eyes streaming and voice constricted. 'But I'm all right.' She drew a long shaky breath. 'That was all my own fault.' She rubbed her bronchial area. 'What an exhibition!'

'Have a drink,' Thea suggested. 'Isn't that what people do?'

Cecilia picked up her tankard, containing barely an inch of cider. 'I'm not sure why, are you? The last thing you'd want is fluid going into your lungs as well. But let's see if it works.' She drained the glass, and set it back on the table. 'Right as rain,' she reported. 'I'm so sorry to cause such a scene.'

Jocelyn surprised them both. 'It was something to do with Flora, wasn't it?' she said. 'You weren't expecting Thea to know about her and Dominic.'

'But it isn't true,' Cecilia croaked. 'Absolute rubbish. Flora Phillips was going out with Nick Franklyn.'

'How do you know?' Jocelyn flashed.

Cecilia pursed her lips at this, and gave the question little attention. 'I just know,' was all she would say.

The lunch seemed to fizzle out after that. Thea lost any further inclination to draw gossip out of Cecilia, and Jocelyn seemed to withdraw into her own gloomy thoughts. One final unfortunate exchange centred upon the defunct Milo and Jeremy Innes's retrieval of the body.

'That was Valerie's fault, of course,' said Cecilia. 'Decided the animal would be happiest at Juniper Court, when really Frannie Craven should have had him, if anybody should.'

'Jeremy seemed to think somebody killed him deliberately,' Jocelyn said. 'He was furiously upset.'

'Jeremy's very confrontational,' Cecilia mused. 'He should do well in the Army.'

Thea laughed a little at this, but not enough to salvage the atmosphere.

Back at Juniper Court, a few minutes after one thirty, Thea idly lifted the phone and got the broken signal to indicate a 1571 message. When she listened, it was Phil Hollis, asking her to call back. He'd left it only ten minutes previously.

She got through to him quickly. 'Now brace yourself,' he said. 'This might sound a bit beyond the call of duty.'

'Go on.'

'Mr and Mrs Franklyn would like to meet you. It's not unusual, actually. You found the body, you see. It gives you a special sort of place in the story for them.'

Thea gulped. 'Well, it won't be the first time, I suppose,' she said bravely.

'Hmm?'

'In Duntisbourne. I met the entire family of the victim.'

'So you did. Well, that's okay, is it?'

'Yes, it's okay.'

'I'll be there just after two, then. Have you had lunch?'

'Yes, thanks.'

'Well I haven't. You'll have to put up with me eating sandwiches in the car.'

'No problem,' she said, wanting to add, *Yes, but what about Mr and Mrs Franklyn's lunch?* People suffering from a sudden intolerable loss forgot to eat, or they ate a jar of Marmite at three in the morning, or a whole loaf of bread, picked off with their fingers, a chunk at a time.

'And before you ask,' he added, 'no, you can't bring the dog.'

He gave her a thoroughly professional briefing as they drove to Cirencester, making her feel important and excited and involved, for the first time since Monday.

'We've questioned him, of course,' Hollis said. 'And he says he was asleep in bed with his wife until eight on Monday morning. Then he had to go and see a client in Bisley at nine thirty.'

'Bisley? Where's that?'

'You may well ask. It's north of Chalford. To get to it from Cirencester, you might reasonably opt to go through Daneway – but not Frampton Mansell, which is where you saw him, as I understand it.'

'Yes. But not before nine thirty. He must have been coming back from his client. *What* client, anyway? Has he or she backed up what Mr F. says?'

'It's a foreign family in a big house, down an impossibly steep and narrow little lane. I sent two DCs to check it out, and it sounds more or less kosher. Franklyn's a financial consultant, and he was helping them choose a pension plan, or some such stuff. They think he arrived when he said he would, and stayed about an hour. They admired his car. He charged them over a hundred quid for his services, which came as something of a shock, I gather.'

Thea thought this over while Hollis ate most of a cheese and pickle roll, driving with one hand.

'Does he know it's me?' she wondered. 'I mean, surely he does. So he'll know I saw him near Juniper Court at about eleven, just about the time when somebody was stringing up his son's body in the stable. He's had loads of time to prepare his alibi.'

'He doesn't know the exact times, and I want you to be careful not to give anything away about that. It strikes me that it's the wife who wants to see you, and the chap's been forced to go along with it.'

'But that wouldn't make him the murderer, would it? Didn't you say Nick died much earlier, probably at the barn?'

'Right. Something like four or five in the morning, they think. He was just stiffening up by the time they cut him down from your stable beam. But it's a bit convoluted to think one person killed him and another took him to Juniper Court.' He threw her a quick look. 'Don't you think?'

'I have no idea. Considering that everybody knows everybody, and they all seem to be part of the Rural Warriors outfit, I wouldn't be surprised if it was like the Orient Express, and the whole community pitched in.'

He sighed. 'I know this is going to annoy you, but what's the Orient Express reference about?'

'Oh, honestly!' she tutted. 'It's an Agatha Christie story. It turns out that everybody did it.'

'And now you've spoilt it for me.'

'Serves you right.'

'We're almost there. Just down here and it's a cul de sac on the left, if I've read the map right.'

'Hello, again,' Thea said to Mr Franklyn, when Hollis made the introductions, wondering in the sudden stillness of the detective beside her whether that was entirely the wrong thing to say. It seemed to come as a shock to Mrs Franklyn, too.

'Again?' she queried, with a puzzled frown. Thea had the impression that most things puzzled this poor woman at the moment.

The man turned to her. 'You remember, dearest – I met this lady on Sunday. When I was out looking for Nick.'

'Oh, did you?' Interest lapsed into lethargy. Thea remembered the sense of fragility that she could see on the woman's face – the conviction that if you moved or spoke too violently, your arms and legs and head would all come off.

The Franklyns were hollow-eyed but controlled. The man held his wife's hand, stroking her fingers, one by one, feeling the joints, bending them slightly. Thea understood his need to believe in warm living flesh, to convince the bereaved mother, at the same time, of the same reality. Mrs Franklyn kept her free hand pressed against her sternum, as if monitoring her own breathing.

'I saw your appeal on the telly,' Thea pressed on. 'You did it very well. It must have been nerve-wracking.'

'We badly want to find who did this, you see,' said the father.

'Not that that will bring him back,' his wife put in, as if this needed to be said repeatedly, before she could properly believe it.

'Did you find Daneway?' Thea asked, feeling unkind and irrelevant. It was now blatantly obvious to her that the man had not slaughtered his son.

He stared at her blankly. 'Where?' he said.

'Daneway. You asked me the way, remember? On Sunday afternoon. I hope I directed you the right way.'

'I was looking for Nick,' he repeated. 'We were worried about him. He'd phoned us that morning and said something about the canal. He said there was trouble over the plans for the canal and he had to confront some people. It didn't make very much sense.' He turned to Hollis in appeal. 'I've already told you all this.'

'I don't think Mrs Osborne is asking you to explain yourself,' Hollis said. 'She's here because you and your wife said you'd like to meet her.'

Franklyn subsided, shaking his head gently as if it was hurting him. 'Angie thinks it might help her to hear about his...how he was.' He tilted his head towards his wife, but didn't look at her.

Obediently, Thea turned to the mother. 'I'm not sure what I can tell you,' she said. 'I assume you've had the medical details from the Coroner's Officer?'

'His face,' said the mother, leaning forward, suddenly urgent. 'What was his face like?'

'Very pale,' said Thea. 'His eyes were open, but not bulging or anything. I suppose they told you the same as they told me – that he must have died very quickly from heart failure.' She looked to Hollis for confirmation. 'Isn't that right?'

'I didn't know whether to believe them,' the woman said.

'Hanging, you see. It's always been a horror with me. I used to dream it was happening to me, gasping for breath, kicking my legs in empty air. My sister always said I must have been hanged in a former life, but that sounds daft, doesn't it. It seems so terribly cruel that it should happen to Nick. He's my only one, you know.'

'I'm so sorry,' said Thea, with a great sigh. 'I can't really say anything that could make you feel better. If my daughter died, I'd be annihilated. Even though I don't see so much of her now.'

She'd obviously pressed a button. The woman seemed to imbibe these words as if they were saving her life. 'Don't you! I hadn't seen Nick for a long time, either. We weren't even sure where he was. He'd been quite...difficult...last time we met. Argumentative, rebellious. You know how they get.'

'I'd gathered something like that, from what you said at the appeal.' Thea looked at Mr Franklyn, who stared unwaveringly at the floor.

'Yes, well, I never thought it was very important. Just one of those family tiffs. But now – well, now it makes me feel so *guilty*.' She wailed the last word. 'If only I'd made more effort to find him sooner, none of this might have happened. When he phoned, he sounded...strange. As if he had to do something unpleasant, and wanted to hear our voices first. It scared me, and I sent Nigel out to look for him. When we realised he'd been to the *very same house* where Nicky was going to die the next morning, just imagine how we felt.' Mrs Franklyn clutched her husband more tightly. 'Have I understood it right?' she asked. 'I'm in a terrible muddle.'

Thea felt Hollis go tense beside her. 'Yes, that's right,' he said tersely.

Thea heard the words *unlikely coincidence* ring in her head. She looked at Nigel Franklyn. 'What *did* you feel?' she asked.

'As if Fate was playing with me. I only came to you because your gate was open and it was wet, so anywhere I could drive close to the front door seemed a good idea.'

'You were very wet,' she observed.

'I'd been walking across fields, and all sorts, trying to find the damned canal. I just knew about the tunnel at Daneway. I still don't understand why Nick thought it was so important.'

'We've never really kept up with Nicky's activities, you see,' said the mother. 'We couldn't really understand why he was so hot-headed about such – well, *dull* things. He never had a proper job, you know, because he said it would distract him from what really mattered.' Her eyes seemed to sag, elongating in her face. 'I wish I'd tried harder to share it all with him.'

'It sounds to me as if he was very popular,' Thea attempted. 'He seems to have inspired a lot of enthusiasm in others.'

'Maybe he did,' came the dubious response. 'But that's just another way of saying he was like an outlaw, isn't it? He was such a quiet little boy, too. Right up to when he was sixteen and started messing about with that Club. I'll never forgive myself for not taking more care to check up on what that was all about. Especially when he let himself get so *scruffy*. But he only laughed when I said something about it.' The woman's voice was slow and slack with misery.

'I'm sure you couldn't have prevented it,' Thea said, hurrying to reassure, while knowing she couldn't be the least bit certain that it was true.

'I might have talked him out of this stupid business about the canal, and being some sort of campaign leader. That must be what got him killed.'

'Don't be silly,' chided her husband affectionately. 'Nobody would kill for the sake of a canal.'

Abruptly, the woman jerked her hand away from him. 'What then?' she flared. 'What made somebody hate our son enough to kill him? Answer me that!'

His response was to pull her to him, and press her head against his shoulder. Loud sobbing filled the room. Thea and Hollis stood up in unison and made an unobtrusive exit.

'Poor, poor woman,' she said as they got back into the car.

Thea and Hollis didn't say much on the return drive, except that Thea wanted to know if she'd done what he'd wanted her to. 'You did fine,' he told her.

'He wasn't telling the whole truth, though, was he?' she said. 'Apart from anything else, how could he not know where Daneway was, if he had an appointment in Bisley the next morning? Presumably he travels the whole area all the time. He must know every little lane and shortcut.'

'That's what we thought,' said Hollis. 'And I'll share one other little snippet with you, even though I shouldn't. Nigel Franklyn knows Desmond Phillips. In fact, he's his financial advisor. What do you think about that?'

'I think he must be an awful fool if he thought you wouldn't find that out,' she said slowly.

'Or maybe he just doesn't care,' said the policeman.

'When will I see you?' she asked, when he delivered her back to Juniper Court, not even attempting to hide her desire to be with him.

Before responding to her question, he gave her one of his looks, full of guarded hope and a kind of disbelief. 'You can give me some tea, if you like,' he said. 'I think I've earned a few hours off, and I haven't really had much chance to speak to your sister.'

Thea forced herself to assess the moment. When had all this begun? This easy acceptance that she and he were somehow already linked. The semi-professional way in which he was involving her in his murder enquiries and his obvious personal concern for her welfare? The answer to the question hardly mattered, she decided. The fact was, it had happened, and she liked it.

'Right,' she said.

Chapter Eleven – Thursday

They took tea and biscuits out to the garden, and tried to relax. Jocelyn was quiet and serious, not at all the teasing younger sister that Thea had anticipated. Hollis waited for her to make the first conversational move, after a brief exchange of greetings. Thea gave an account of their visit to the Franklyns.

'I bet you feel rather differently about their son now, don't you?' Jocelyn said. 'Now you know he's not just some sad vagrant nobody needs to care about.'

'I never thought that,' Thea defended herself uncomfortably.

'You did,' said Jocelyn equably. 'Anybody would. It's the way of the world. Some people are little more than detritus, drifting about on the polluted edges of society.'

Hollis made a murmuring sound, suggestive of interest and partial agreement.

Thea heaved a sigh. 'Don't get all poetic on us. It's too hot for that.'

Jocelyn subsided, with a glance at Hollis. After a moment she said, 'That poor woman. It doesn't bear thinking about, losing her one and only.' She turned to Thea, her voice becoming stronger. 'Mind you, I've always said it's dangerous only to have one. Haven't I always said?'

Thea found herself unable to respond naturally with Hollis at her side. She remembered with a wince his own dead daughter. What's more, she did not feel that he ought to be learning about her in this indirect fashion. It was bad of Jocelyn to force these matters into the open. But she had to say something. 'Many times,' she said. 'And I agree with you in theory. On the other hand, it would be wonderful if people knew when to stop. In my case, if I had produced another one, it would have been for Carl and Jess, not for myself.'

'So?'

'So I'm not that self-sacrificing a person. Anyway, there could be a dozen reasons why Nick Franklyn was an only child. It makes no sense to criticise.'

'I wasn't really. Just saying, that's all.'

'How many have you got?' Hollis jumped in at last.

'Five. Two boys and three girls. Ages range from twelve down to five.'

'I'm impressed,' he smiled. 'We only managed two.' Thea held her breath, waiting for reference to the daughter, but it never came. Instead she was constrained to digest the *we*, understanding for the first time that she had achieved an age where she was never again going to be somebody's first significant partner. There would always be 'baggage': assumptions, painful experiences, habits, and wariness. It was a gloomy thought, and she tried to drown it in a large mouthful of tea.

'Has anybody come forward after the appeal?' Jocelyn asked Hollis.

He seemed to find this question as surprising as Thea did. 'Not that I've heard,' he admitted. 'We never really expected them to.'

'So why do it?'

He put his cup down and folded his arms across his chest, settling back in the expensive garden chair. 'It sometimes rattles somebody's cage,' he said. 'Gives the message that we're taking it seriously. Quite subtle stuff, basically.'

'And hasn't it almost become routine that the person doing those appeals on TV turns out to be the murderer?' Thea put in. 'Like a sort of double bluff? I can think of at least four instances in the past three years or so where that's happened.'

Jocelyn seemed to find this irritating. 'How can you remember them? It's in one eye and out the other with me.'

'I don't know. I get interested. It's something to do with the way people can tell absolutely outright lies, with extraordinary skill sometimes. Not just in court, which must be hard enough, but sitting in front of all those cameras and microphones. It fascinates me.' She looked at Hollis, who was looking at Jocelyn. Nobody spoke for a moment.

'I think they convince themselves it's true,' he suggested. 'They split off. Somebody else did it. It wasn't really them at all. That's what they actually believe sometimes.'

Jocelyn nodded. 'A sort of Doctor Hyde thing.'

'*Mr* Hyde. Doctor Jekyll,' said Thea automatically.

'For God's sake, don't *do* that!!' Jocelyn snapped. 'You're always correcting me.'

'Well, you're always getting things wrong.'

'It interrupts the flow. You make me forget what I was saying. You know what I mean, and you still have to catch me out, and show me who's the clever one.' It was a moment that should have been acutely embarrassing, but somehow it wasn't. Thea felt herself to be showing in a bad light, but Jocelyn was definitely overreacting. And Hollis merely looked from one to the other with something like fondness in his expression. It was obvious that he didn't mind cross words or flaring tempers. He could cope with imperfection and choppy emotion.

'Sorry,' Thea addressed her sister. 'You're absolutely right. I'll try not to do it again.'

'No you won't,' grumbled Jocelyn. 'You're far too old to change.'

All three laughed and Thea's heart expanded at the thought that this man of such rare maturity and balance just might be hers for the taking. She came close to feeling grateful to Jocelyn for affording him the opportunity of revealing his qualities.

Inevitably they returned to the subject of the murder. 'But in this case,' Thea said emphatically, needing to explain herself, 'I'm sure the man didn't kill his son. You only have to look at him to know that.'

Hollis looked at her with naked affection. 'So that's all right then,' he smiled.

Thea made a valiant effort to stick to the subject. 'Everybody keeps talking about the canal,' she said. 'Surely that can't be what's behind Nick's killing? I'm really amazed at the opposition to it being restored, I must say.'

'The canal people have been getting backs up for years around here. They don't mean to, most of the time, but they seem incapable of grasping the fact that not everybody thinks it's a good idea to look back. After all, they do a fair amount of damage in the process.'

'Yes, I know. I've had it all explained to me.'

He wasn't deterred. 'And they put a lot of pressure on

landowners to let the conservationists have access to their bit of the canal. Moral blackmail, some would call it. People resent it. Plus they do a lot of fundraising, competing with other charities that are dear to people's hearts. They tread on toes. And not everybody wants a whole new lot of tourists spoiling the peace.'

'Nick Franklyn was a leader of the Rural Warriors, wasn't he?'

'He's not on record as a rioter or anything. We've checked the Rural Warriors, and they're involved in a whole range of things. Mostly, at the moment, they're busy opposing a planning application for a massive new mansion not far from here. They also resist road widening, landfill sites and new supermarkets.'

'Good for them. I think I'll sign up.'

'Very funny. They also passionately condemn all efforts to restore the canal, so you're at odds with them there.'

'And you think Nick was more involved in roads and mansions than canals?'

'I didn't quite say that. The canal is a very live issue around here.'

'So who's your chief suspect?' Jocelyn demanded. 'Thea seems to suspect the father, with that awful Valerie Innes in second place. Or is it the other way round?' she asked Thea, who clamped her lips together and waited for Hollis to speak.

He looked at them both with an expression of amused forbearance. 'It doesn't work like that,' he said. 'We have to keep an open mind.'

'Oh, pooh!'

'I assure you that's how it is. We're collecting evidence. Getting to know the boy, and what his last movements were. Talking to everyone who knew him.'

'Including Flora Phillips? And her family?' Thea frowned at a sudden thought. 'Where are Julia and Desmond, anyway? Isn't it time they came back, and stopped pretending they're having a happy holiday? Flora's sure to have knocked that on the head by this time.'

'I've handed all that over to Social Services,' he said, with unmistakable relief. 'Flora was just a distraction, silly girl. If the social workers think her people should come back, then it's up to them to say so. But I imagine they'll settle for the mother in Liverpool.'

'But why did she come back? And who exactly is her boyfriend? Was it Nick, as Cecilia said?'

'I have no idea,' Hollis admitted wearily. 'Except that nobody has suggested to us that she was involved with Nick. Of course, we've been asking it from the other end, as it were. Who he might have been involved with. And the answer seems to be nobody.'

'We thought she seemed very shocked when we told her he was dead,' Jocelyn informed him. 'Don't you think she might have some idea who did it?'

He shook his head slowly. 'I'm sure she has an idea. We all have an idea. That isn't the problem.'

'Oh?' Thea frowned at him suspiciously. 'What is, then?'

'Proving it,' he told her.

A faint jingle from the house made them all raise their heads and listen, until Jocelyn realised, 'That's my phone. I left it in the living room,' and went to answer it.

She was pale when she came back. 'What's the matter?' Thea asked.

'That was Noel. He thinks Alex is going to come and find me.'

This sounded complicated. Jocelyn's eldest, the placid twelve-year-old cricket-playing Noel, had warned his mother about his father. 'And?' she prompted, aiming for the safe non-judgmental line.

Jocelyn eyed Hollis doubtfully. 'You don't really want to hear this,' she said.

He was instantly alert. 'But Thea does. I get it. I'll take myself for a little walk, then, shall I? Just around the paddock. Maybe the dog will come with me.'

'Oh, she'll go with anybody,' said Thea, inattentively, hardly noticing when he left.

'Thea, that wasn't very polite,' Jocelyn admonished. 'The poor man.'

'What did Noel say?'

'That was it, really. Alex has run out of patience and I suddenly feel scared. My insides are all shivery.'

'Hmm. Scared he'll hit you, or just that he'll talk to you?'

'He wouldn't hit me in front of you, so it must be the talking.'

'I thought he didn't know where you were.'

'That's why Noel called. He caught Alex reading my emails. He's probably seen the one from you, where you tell me how to find this place. If he's clever, there's probably enough to go on.'

'Is he clever?'

'Sometimes.'

'Is he on his way as we speak?'

'No, I don't think so. He can't leave the kids, can he?'

'Where was he when Noel phoned?'

'Arguing with Roly. I could hear them yelling at each other.'

Thea gave her sister a closer scrutiny. 'Is that part of the problem?'

Without warning, Jocelyn launched into explosive sobs, her breath restricted and her eyes flooding. Thea wondered at her own failure to observe the tension and misery behind the past days of apparent serenity. She hovered helplessly, waiting for the storm to die down, unable to think of a single consoling remark. Things were far too fragile for a confrontation with Alex, assuming he could find a babysitter.

To her relief, the storm soon passed. 'Sorry,' Jocelyn sniffed. 'It all got too much for a minute. I have no idea, you see, what I'm going to do next. It was so awful hearing Noel's voice. He was being so grown up and understanding, and I've hardly given him a thought since I left. I'm a lousy mother.'

'You do all right,' said Thea impatiently. 'Don't go all self-pitying on me.'

This robust sisterly remonstrance seemed to be restoring Jocelyn to a more equable condition, and Thea softened. 'Well, we'd better keep the hall table in front of the door, then, hadn't we – and tell Hepzie she's to guard us with her life.'

Jocelyn frowned at the floor for a moment. 'Thea...'

'Mmm?'

'Do you think anything'll happen? With this murder, I mean? Are we stupid to be staying here, with so much going on?'

'I think we'll have to trust Phil. We've told him the whole

story, and he's let us stay here. He must think it's safe. Imagine the scandal if we're murdered after all this.'

'Gosh, yes. That makes me feel much better.'

Thea grinned fleetingly. 'You're not seriously scared, are you?'

'Only on and off. It's difficult to feel scared all the time, isn't it. You sort of forget about it after a bit.'

'Same routine as before then: door open and shout if you think anything's happening. Even if I don't hear you, Hepzie will.'

'I need some distraction,' Jocelyn asserted. 'I'm going to go and cook us something.'

'If in doubt, cook?'

'It's force of habit, I suppose. You don't have to eat it.'

'I'll be delighted to eat it, and I might persuade Phil to stay as well. We can have it on our laps in front of the telly, can't we?'

Jocelyn grinned. 'That's another thing Alex hates,' she said. 'He thinks a family should have every single meal sitting up round the dining table.'

'He's right, in theory,' said Thea. 'But if you ask me, once a week is good going, these days.'

'That's what I said,' nodded Jocelyn.

While Jocelyn peeled potatoes, Hollis made himself at home at the kitchen table, playing with Hepzibah, who had her front paws on his thigh.

'My dogs don't jump up,' he said mildly.

Thea blinked slowly. 'You've got dogs? Why didn't you say?'

He grinned. 'A Welsh corgi and a Gordon setter. Possibly the daftest mixture you could wish for.'

'Could you go away for a bit,' Jocelyn requested. 'I can't cook with people watching.'

'Fine,' said Thea. 'We'll go into the lounge. Pity there's no gin.'

'There's sherry,' Jocelyn pointed to a rack of bottles in a corner of the kitchen. 'And plenty of wine. I vote we help ourselves.'

The living room was dominated by the words painted on the wall, turning it from a comfortable space in which a family gathered to relax and talk into a scene of invasion and contamination. The upward tilt of the writing, the ragged drips of the hurriedly-applied spray paint, the aggressive sentiment, all contributed to a chilly feeling of wrongness. 'Flora did that,' Thea said. 'At least, she didn't deny it when we accused her. I assume the poor girl wanted her house back.' She thought back to Flora's refusal to explain. 'She was angry with us for being here. I think that's really the whole reason. And if you saw her bedroom, you'd know she has a bit of a thing about painting on walls.' She looked again at the lettering. 'It isn't very nice, though, is it.'

'Help me shift the sofa,' Hollis ordered her. 'We'll sit with our backs to it.'

But Thea had no wish to sit with him on the sofa. Or rather, the wish was so powerful she couldn't afford to indulge it.

'I'll sit over here, where I can see you,' she said lightly, plumping into an armchair, having helped him move the sofa. The writing was still visible to her, but not full in her face.

He didn't like her choice of seat, raising one eyebrow, and muttering, 'It's entirely up to you.' She wanted to explain, and was annoyed that he didn't understand.

The dry sherry seemed to revive him slightly, but he continued to give an impression of weariness. Thea watched him sipping from the glass, marvelling at the solidity of him, the three-dimensionality. She wanted to assess and compare, to maintain a grasp of her reason, to behave sensibly, but everything seemed clogged by the fact of his body in the room with her, despite the physical distance between them. She knew she'd acted wisely in rejecting a place at his side. From where she sat, she could watch his face, noting the way his eyes were set into his skull, small and deep. His nose was long, with narrow straight-sided nostrils. A dry mouth, thin-lipped, and an odd chin, square-cut. The face of a man not given to indulgences. No broken veins or pouches beneath the eyes. No grooved signs of pain or rage. A quiet face, she concluded, that gave very little away.

What had become of the mother of his two children? Why had she made the unquestioning assumption that he was now single and available? Why was she still so certain that this was the case?

'You're not married, are you?' she blurted.

He gave himself a little shake, opening his eyes wider. 'That's a very direct question.'

'Well?'

'Divorced,' he said. 'Three years ago now.'

'Right. I thought so.'

'And otherwise unencumbered, for the record. Apart from the job, of course. That's rather an encumbrance.'

'And dogs.'

'Oh yes. Except that I actually share the dogs. They don't live with me full time.'

She waited for the explanation.

'I have a sister, you see. She's in Painswick and has some land. When things get busy, she takes them off my hands until I can be there for them again. It works very well.'

'Useful things, sisters.'

'So it would seem.'

Which would have been Jocelyn's cue to call that the dinner was ready, except that there was still a few minutes to go. Thea fiddled momentarily with some loose cording on a cushion tucked beside her, remembering the dead Siamese, which had very probably done the damage to the furnishings. Then she looked up at him, mouth opening to speak.

He was asleep. His head flopped loosely against the back of the sofa, and his eyes were firmly closed. He breathed slowly and deeply. Thea sighed, aware of irritation and embarrassment threaded into the surge of protective affection she felt towards him. People talked about total certainty in their relationships, unalloyed devotion, unwavering loyalty. She didn't believe it. Nothing could ever be that straightforward. She dreamed, for a minute, of setting up a permanent home with this man. Of waking in the morning and finding him there, of worrying when he was late back from his dangerous job, of the dickering about territory and control that every couple had to put up with. And the image of Carl, her real husband, the man she had actually lived with, floated before her eyes. It superimposed itself onto Hollis, and made her doubt whether she would ever feel wholly ready for somebody new.

She got up and went out to the kitchen. 'He's dropped off,' she said, quietly.

Jocelyn mimed laughter. 'How rude!' she said. 'How terribly unromantic of him.'

'That's what I thought,' Thea said.

They woke him up for the meal, which Jocelyn had managed to delay for ten minutes, and he briefly apologised, with minimal embarrassment. 'Call it a power nap,' he said, with a single uneasy glance at Thea.

'We were wondering if you think anything's going to disturb our sleep tonight,' Jocelyn said.

Hollis sighed. 'I hope not.'

'*Hope*,' Jocelyn repeated. 'Is that the best you can do?'

He flexed his shoulders, backwards and forwards. 'If things are going to plan, we've got the Innes boy under arrest by now, and he'll be locked up overnight. So that's one less worry.'

'Which Innes boy?' asked Thea.

'Dominic, of course.'

The news was startling. Thea felt a sharp pang of concern for the boy. 'Why have you arrested him?'

'A – because he broke in here and behaved threateningly, and B – because he's got a lot he can tell us and we'd like to get it out of him.'

'Are you going to keep him awake all night and then shine bright lights into his eyes?' Jocelyn asked, with some aggression.

'Leave him alone,' Thea chided. Jocelyn gave her a mulish look, but said no more. They concentrated on the spicy chilli con carne that Jocelyn had prepared so effortlessly.

Thea thought about the bereaved parents and her suspicions of the boy's father. There had certainly been irritation there, a bemused impatience with the person his son had been. She thought about Dominic Innes and his good-looking brother Jeremy.

'You know what,' she said, reverting to their earlier conversation, 'of all the people I've met this week, not one of them seems to want the canal restored. Which surely puts them all on the same side as Nick?'

'If it was only the canal, that might be true,' Hollis agreed. 'But we're hearing all sorts of tales about other schemes, which the locals think will wreck their way of life.'

'Such as?'

'Well, for one – Desmond Phillips wants to create a fishing lake, using the bed of the canal as the centre of it. Trout, apparently. Feeder streams, weirs, culverts, subsidiary ponds – all the trimmings.'

Thea choked on a piece of garlic bread, spraying crumbs across the table. 'He can't!' she yelped. 'He'd never get permission. That would *ruin* the whole canal project.'

'Precisely,' smirked Hollis. 'As well as causing even more disruption to the wildlife, and attracting visitors, and so forth.'

Jocelyn spoke. 'That must be why everybody's so irate with the Phillipses, then.'

'So it would seem,' said Hollis.

Thea groaned wearily. 'The plot is getting too thick for me. I'll be glad when I can leave. The prospect of another whole week is beginning to look rather daunting.'

'I'm not staying another week,' said Jocelyn.

They both looked at her. 'Aren't you?' said Thea.

'Of course not. I'm not that irresponsible.'

'Oh. When are you leaving, then?'

'I thought probably tomorrow afternoon. Before Alex comes to drag me home.' Thea wasn't taken in by the casual tone. There was a lot of painful choice-making behind the words.

'I understand, of course, that your family's needs take priority. It's just...' Thea pulled a face. 'You know.'

'Thea, I never expected to have to chaperone you or guard you against local delinquents. I thought I was the one in need of sanctuary. It's all got turned upside down, and I've had enough of it now. This morning, quite honestly, was the final straw. I don't want to have to go through anything like that again.'

'I thought you'd just taken it in your stride.'

'Have you ever had a strange man's arm tight around your throat? No. It's very unsettling, let me tell you. It shakes up some of your assumptions. Especially when...' she glanced at the silent Hollis and stopped.

Thea heard the unspoken words. *Especially when your husband's started to use physical violence on you as well.*

'Don't underestimate the effects,' said Hollis softly. 'Feeling vulnerable is a horrible thing. But Dominic Innes isn't going to do it again, and he's going to be very sorry before we've finished with him.'

'There!' Jocelyn triumphed weakly. 'I knew you were going to torture him.'

It was still light when Hollis left. Both the sisters went outside with him, Thea remembering her duties towards the pony. All forensic examinations of the stable complete, Thea wondered whether it would be a kindness to return him to his old home. His temporary quarters in the barn were cramped and insecure, and after the discovery of Flora, the barn felt vulnerable to intrusion and interference, even more than the stable did.

When they went to him, he seemed forlorn and abandoned. 'Poor old fellow,' crooned Thea. 'Not having a very nice time, are you? Come on then. Let's put you back where you belong, and see if that cheers you up a bit.'

Leading him with a halter, Jocelyn following behind, Thea watched for sore feet or other signs of sickness. He trod delicately, but appeared acceptably relaxed. Until, that is, he reached the door of his former home. *I am not going in there*, he said, in clear Ponyese. Jocelyn tapped him encouragingly on the rump, but still he baulked. Hepzie joined in, yapping behind him, to no avail.

'He's scared,' said Jocelyn. 'He remembers what happened.'

'I think he might prefer the barn after all,' said Thea. 'While the weather's hot, it's more airy in there. Not so many flies, either.'

They had both noticed the flies at the same moment. 'Um, Thea,' Jocelyn began, her nose twitching, 'isn't there rather a nasty *smell*?'

'Too right,' said Thea. 'We'd better have a look.'

The body was not difficult to find. A cloud of greenish flies buzzed above it, giving its presence away. The spaniel darted forward, but as rapidly retreated. Some things were too appallingly dead even for a dog's uncivilised tastes.

Thea edged closer, a hand to her nose. 'God, what a vile stink.'

'What is it?' Jocelyn had remained in the doorway, holding the pony's halter.

Thea tried not to see the heaving off-white movement in the decaying flesh, the skin shredding away from the skull and legs.

'I think it must be Milo,' she said.

Thea didn't sleep at all well that night. Despite an underlying anticipation of future delight, the fact of a murder close by persistently dragged her into darker thoughts, and another late night conversation with Jocelyn about men and violence and the fragility of trust had been unsettling, at the very least. The smell of the rotting cat lingered horribly in her nostrils, and the motive for leaving it there bothered her considerably. Nothing could be relied on, there were no guarantees of happiness, or even survival. Malice lurked behind every bush; people would kill to defend their own personal passions or perversions. In the deep of the night, she found herself reviewing a host of reasons to be afraid. The Phillipses were not as they seemed. People wished them ill. Thea had been lured into danger by substituting for Julia and Desmond. It was a betrayal, and she was angry about it.

She fell asleep on a whole new collection of thoughts, involving Jocelyn and Alex and the trouble ahead for them and their children. She admitted to herself that she disapproved in a free-floating way of people who produced five kids and then couldn't maintain a secure protective parental shield over them. It wasn't on, she thought, with a twitch of the lips, a brief rictus of condemnation.

'Well, we survived the night,' Jocelyn announced, at eight thirty the next morning. 'True,' Thea agreed. 'Although I can't pretend I slept very well.'

'Neither did I. Let's hope this business is settled quickly. I can't cope with much more.' Jocelyn was fingering her neck, pressing gently here and there

'Does it still hurt?' Thea asked her, thinking how long ago the previous morning seemed.

'Not really,' she said. 'Why is it always me, do you think?'

'No reason. At least, nothing personal. Your bedroom window's easier to climb through. He'd probably have opted for me, given a choice. I'm smaller.'

'Oh, hell. We can't go on like this, can we? We've got to face up to it all.'

'How do you mean?'

'We're in denial. If we don't do something, there'll be another murder. This house'll be set on fire, and the pony slaughtered. Your dog'll be shot, and my car tyres slashed. Bad people will do bad things to us. To be honest, I can't wait to get away. Although I'm not relishing home particularly, either.' She gazed miserably into her mug of coffee.

The peacocks had been quiet during the first hours of daylight, but were making up for it now. Their eerie cries gave an exotic backdrop to the yard and the wider area.

'I think I could get to like the sound they make,' Thea mused. 'It's rather lovely, in a way. Maybe they can sense thunder coming. The forecast said there'd be storms later today.'

'What? That ghastly screeching, *lovely*! You're mad.'

Thea smiled forbearingly and wondered why she was feeling so tense. The obvious explanation was Jocelyn's promised departure, and the unhappiness ahead if she went through with her decision to file for divorce. Plus the discovery of Milo's body in the stable had been sickening and frightening. Somebody had deliberately put it there as a message, and the obvious candidate was Jeremy Innes, since he'd been last to take possession of the corpse.

'I think I'll go to the Innes house,' she said. 'If that Jeremy dumped Milo on us like that, he needs a good talking to.'

'You'll report him to his mother, you mean? Isn't he a bit old for that?'

'I don't need his mother's support. I can deal with him myself. It was a disgusting thing to do.'

'And somebody should come and help us scoop it up,' said Jocelyn, rolling her lower lip in exaggerated horror. She paused. 'Don't you think we should tell the police about it? It's obviously connected to the murder in some way.'

'We should, and we will. But I don't think it's going to change anything. Phil seems to have all his plans laid already. And I have a very strong feeling we're about to see the whole thing settled during today.'

Jocelyn gave her a narrow look. 'Are you saying that to try to persuade me not to leave? You think I'll want to hang on here to catch all the excitement? Because if so, it won't work. I'll stay until after lunch, and then I'm off.'

'Alex hasn't been to collect you, then,' said Thea, with some obviousness.

'I did say he'd have trouble getting away. But he won't wait much longer. That's another reason I'll have to get my skates on. I don't want to be dragged home like a naughty child.'

Thea was walking over the grass, down to one corner, along to another, and back towards her sister. She'd done it four times so far. Jocelyn had been forced to close her eyes to avoid being driven mad. As the fifth circuit began, she cracked. 'Thea, please stop doing that. I know it helps you think, or something, but I can't bear it any more. It's neurotic.'

'Aren't I allowed to be neurotic in the circumstances? Every time I try to get going on something, I'm blocked. Thwarted.'

'I don't see that at all. What are you talking about?'

'Oh, never mind.' She flopped down on the grass, stretching her arms over her head, pointing her toes. 'This was meant to be *fun*. And I wanted to think, read, explore. When you showed up, that was meant to be fun as well.'

'Is that some sort of exercise you're doing?'

'Not really. It helps me feel free. Loosens the bonds.' She rolled over onto her front. 'And this weather! It's glorious. Why can't we just enjoy it?'

'I'm enjoying it, more or less. I'm definitely managing not to think about skin cancer.'

'Freedom's an illusion, you know.' Thea's voice was muffled, most of it directed into the grass. 'A meaningless concept.'

'Gosh. Are we doing philosophy this morning?'

'I'm thinking about you.' Thea sat up in a graceful feline movement. 'How can you hope to be free, with all those kids and everything? You're anchored, hogtied, imprisoned.'

Jocelyn grinned. 'You think so?'

'Don't you?'

'I think it's all down to how you look at it. I chose to have the kids. They define who I am, and make me proud of myself.

They're not stopping me from doing whatever I want to do. I'm not a *wanting* sort of person.'

'But you're not happy.'

'If freedom's a meaningless concept, then surely happiness must be as well? Listen, Thee – I'm not like you. I never did concepts and that sort of stuff. I know what things feel like. Sudden moments of joy, especially. I'm good at them. Take last week. One morning, when they'd all gone off to school and Alex was at work, and I didn't have to be anywhere. I'd cleaned the kitchen – everything shiny and smelling nice. I stood there, looking round at it all, and felt this great – well, *uplift* is the only word I can think of. As if I was standing on tiptoe, all buoyed up and pleased with myself. There was nothing more I needed at that moment, but a lovely clean tidy kitchen.'

Thea stifled a groan.

'I know. It sounds pathetic. And it wasn't exactly about the house, anyway. It was just knowing I had a place and was alive and at least some things were under control.'

'And then Alex whacked you with a cricket bat.'

'Right. It was that same day, I think.'

'It doesn't make any sense. You still haven't said why you think he does it.'

'He does it because he can. And because he thinks, like you, that there's no such thing as freedom, and he can't take it. He's trapped and it's my fault. He's scared of something – or everything. Just panicked and lost.'

'Has he said all that?' Thea was instantly absorbed, glimpsing a hint of an explanation for Alex's behaviour, at last.

Jocelyn shook her head. 'Not exactly. He doesn't like modern life, somehow. The supermarket shopping, the electronic games. He's like you and Carl in some ways. All for healthy outdoor living, and keeping life simple. I think he's terribly frustrated by the reality. He wanted a lot of kids, to show his own parents how it ought to be done, and then couldn't manage to live up to his own principles.'

'What? Was his childhood so miserable?'

'He always felt his mother was doing it wrong. She didn't listen to him, denied his feelings, told him lies. He wanted to be a much better parent than her.'

'That must be why most people have kids – if they think about it at all. They want to create some idyllic childhood – to have another go,' Thea mused. 'I never thought of that before.'

'And it's doomed. For one thing, the kids themselves never co-operate. And everybody's so tired, and society puts all that incredible pressure on you, and money runs out, or you lose the thread.'

'And that's why he hits out. Do you think?'

'Something like that. Maybe. It might be something completely different. I meant it when I said I don't care what his reasons are. Being here has shown me that I don't want him any more. He's faded in my mind, just in these few days. Quite honestly, I think he's been fading for ages.'

'Maybe that's why he hits you. To try to convince you he's not just a shadow or a phantom or something. He wants to make himself substantial. But none of that is any excuse. What keeps coming back to me is the feeling of *betrayal*. It shouldn't be too much to ask, to be able to trust your own husband not to hit you.'

Jocelyn closed her eyes again. 'I'm not going to stay with him, anyway,' she said calmly. 'I'm getting a divorce.'

'Oh,' was all Thea could think to say to that. This was another of those moments in life when everything changed from minute to minute, and the safest reaction was to wait quietly for the eventual outcome. Announcements were likely to be out of date within seconds, decisions altered and circumstances turned around in a chaotic whirl. Already she had lost count of Jocelyn's switches, staying and not staying, caring and not caring. It would be useful to know if and when her sister would depart from Juniper Court, but it wasn't crucial. Thea's place continued to be at the eye of the storm, despite the flurries of activity and alarming moments.

'What do you mean – *Oh*?' Jocelyn demanded. 'Can't you say anything more than that?'

'Like what? As I understand it, divorce is a protracted and

complicated exercise, particularly when there are children. It isn't enough just to say you're going to do it. It won't simply *happen* by itself. And right at this moment I've got quite a lot else to think about.'

Jocelyn went very still, turning away from her sister in a familiar huff. 'I'd have thought my marriage was more significant than the problems of a bunch of strangers,' she said.

'It's not a question of significance. It's more a matter of immediacy. Here we are, surrounded by all sorts of conflict and bad feeling and mysterious comings and goings, with people insisting that this is the final day, when it's all going to come to a head. To be honest, Joss, I'm getting really scared. Not just for myself but for Flora and Pallo and Hepzie. If you go off now, then that's up to you. I'm not pretending to be pleased about it. I'll cope. But don't ask me to get into deep emotional agonisings about you and Alex, because I'm not up to it today.'

'So why don't you get out of here as well? The Phillipses are giving you the runaround, let's face it. You don't owe them a thing.'

'I might just do that,' said Thea.

But half an hour later, the mood had lightened again. The sisters had gone out into the paddock with the dog, throwing sticks which Hepzie seldom bothered to retrieve and reviewing their options.

'I do feel a bit bad about leaving before the final act,' said Jocelyn. 'I can't help being intrigued by all these local goings-on. It's so very different from my own home life.'

Thea giggled, but soon reverted to seriousness. 'I find it hard to believe there'll be a conclusion as quickly as Phil says. How can he possibly know, anyway?'

'We've been kept dreadfully in the dark. Unfair, really. We don't know how worried we ought to be, or which people we can trust.'

'The sad fact is that we're irrelevant to whatever's going on. They would all obviously prefer us not to be here —'

'*Very* obviously. Every time I go into the living room it hits me all over again.'

Thea frowned worriedly. 'I probably ought to be doing something about that.'

'Not up to you, surely. Anyway, it's evidence. They'll want it left as it is.'

'Well, when's all this action due to start, do you suppose? I expected helicopters and men with megaphones by this time.'

'I hear an engine, as we speak,' said Jocelyn, nodding towards the road gate. 'But only a car. Helicopters would be too much to ask.'

Thea cocked an ear, assuming it would simply be a local resident driving off to work, or a delivery van with a parcel. But she was wrong. The familiar Mondeo swept into the yard. Thea started to trot towards it, behind the exuberant spaniel, who got there well ahead of her.

Two men got out of the car, and Thea realised she knew them both. Hollis had brought the Franklyn man to the scene of his son's death. She stared, collating the different remembered images of the face with the reality before her. The first time he had been wet and the light had been bad. Next he'd been in his car, staring ahead, his features wooden. Then in grief, with his weeping wife and tangled emotions. But always the same man, and one that Thea realised she had been suspicious of since the first glimpse.

'Hello,' she said warily.

'Thea.' Hollis was all briskness and control. 'You remember Mr Franklyn.'

'Yes, of course I do.' He looked ravaged, bemused, entirely dependent on Hollis for the next move.

'We won't be needing you,' the detective went on. 'We're just going into the pony shed for a minute, and then for a bit of a walk over the fields. You carry on with whatever you're doing.'

'Well, that's told us,' said Jocelyn, standing with folded arms. 'Best do as we're told, then. Check the pony, collect the eggs and do a bit of dusting.'

'He doesn't really mean it,' said Thea.

'What doesn't he really mean?'

'To dismiss us. He was just being professional.'

'Course he was,' said Jocelyn. 'And it might be nasty of me, but I can't help feeling pleased that we didn't clean up that smelly corpse.'

Thea clapped a hand to her mouth. 'God, I'd forgotten all about that. We should have warned them. He'll be *furious*.'

Jocelyn's expression was a classic.

The pony was standing passively in the barn, one front foot tilted so that only the tip of the hoof was in contact with the ground. His eyes were half-closed and his ears seemed droopy. Thea was reminded of a copy of *Black Beauty* she'd possessed as a child, which carried an illustration of a row of deeply depressed horses. They'd looked very much like this wretched Pallo currently looked.

'Hey, cheer up!' she urged him. 'Only another week to go. Don't go sick on me now, there's a good boy.' A wave of helplessness engulfed her as the animal refused to co-operate. He acted as if he had neither heard nor seen her, deep in his own gloomy thoughts. He paid no attention to the small quantity of corn and the two carrots she'd provided, either. Thea's scanty veterinary knowledge frustrated her – was he just having a mood, or had his condition taken a turn for the worse? Presumably the fact that he was still standing up was a good sign. Perhaps she'd overdone the starvation rations, one way or the other.

'Hepzie!' Thea called, glimpsing the spaniel sniffing around the yard outside. 'Come here, will you.' The faint hope that the fragile friendship between pony and dog might go some way towards enlivening Pallo was all she could come up with for the moment.

Hepzibah came obediently, looking up at her mistress for an explanation. 'Good girl!' praised Thea. 'Come and talk to poor old Pallo.'

But the pony ignored his new friend as comprehensively as he'd ignored Thea. 'Oh, for heaven's sake!' she burst out. 'What on earth is the matter with you?'

'Are you sure he's got clean water?' came a voice from the doorway. 'He looks rather dehydrated to me.'

It was Cecilia Clifton, dressed in a beige cotton jumper and dark brown trousers, standing with hands on hips, gazing critically at the pony.

Thea, feeling like an incompetent stable girl, went to examine the water bucket tucked in a corner between the feed trough and the barn wall. 'It's all a bit makeshift in here,' she defended. 'But I topped his water up last night.' The bucket seemed to be almost as full as she'd left it. 'It looks all right to me.'

'Ponies can be very fussy about their water. Where did you get it from?'

'The tap,' said Thea, resisting the following *of course*.

'Too much chlorine, probably. Isn't there a water butt somewhere?'

Thea couldn't remember a water butt. 'I'm not sure,' she admitted, before adding in a rush of self-pity, 'Gosh, he's a worry, this old chap. With everything else going on, I have to keep checking on him and keeping his spirits high. They're really worried about him, being so old, and having that disease, whatever it's called.'

'Laminitis?' asked Cecilia. 'Is that what they told you?'

Thea nodded. 'That's why he isn't allowed outside. Grass is bad for him.'

'He might have had a touch of it in the spring, but believe me, that pony hasn't a trace of laminitis now. He's as fit as a flea, apart from being old and crotchety and his feet needing a good trim.'

'That can't be right,' Thea argued, bewildered. 'Why would they lie about it?'

'To make you feel needed, I imagine.'

'But – what do you mean?'

Cecilia cast an exasperated glance at the sky, and said no more. Outside, Hollis and Franklyn were still in the doorway to the stable. Cecilia Clifton seemed not to be aware of them, which struck Thea as odd, as did her sudden coincidental arrival. 'Where's your car?' she asked.

'Oh, I left it at Frannie's and walked up. I thought I should come and see how you were. Is that a police car?' She indicated the Mondeo, but still didn't glance towards the two men.

'Superintendent Hollis,' Thea confirmed. 'He's keeping a good eye on us, but at the moment he's doing something mysterious that he hasn't explained.'

'Hmmm,' was all Cecilia said, accompanied by a brief shrug, as if the behaviour of the police was of total unconcern to her.

They found a metal trough, tucked against the far side of the barn, half full of greenish water. 'Surely he's not meant to drink this?' Thea protested. 'It's revolting.'

'It is a bit,' Cecilia agreed. 'But bring him out, and see what he thinks.'

Thea hesitated, feeling deeply uncertain. What if this was a callous ploy to get at Julia Phillips through her daughter's pony? If Frannie and Valerie were right, and just about everybody in the area disliked Julia, then it made sense to be cautious. 'Are you sure?' she said. 'I mean – it does look horrible.'

'He won't drink it if it's bad for him. Anyway, we'll get a better idea of how he is, if we take him for a little walk.'

Thea remembered his 'little walk' of the previous evening, but made no reference to it. Clumsily, she put the halter on the pony's unresisting head, and tried to chivvy him out of the barn. 'He doesn't want to move,' she reported to Cecilia, who was making no attempt to help.

'Smack him.'

With some trepidation, Thea did as instructed, slapping the pony's neck, hoping to push him towards the barn door. The effect was dramatic. Pulling the halter out of her hand, he tossed his head, dancing several steps sideways, before lashing out blindly with a vigorous kick from one back leg. The kick connected with a strut holding up the barn roof, but appeared not to do any damage. 'Oh, God!' Thea cried. 'Stop him, will you?'

With a jerky noisy clatter of hooves, Pallo easily evaded Cecilia in the doorway, and set off across the yard.

'Don't worry,' she said. 'He can't go far.'

Thea was in the first stages of an uncharacteristic panic. 'Of course he can!' she shouted. 'The road gate's open. The *field* gate's open. He can go *miles*, if he has a mind to.'

Where was Jocelyn? And Hollis? 'Help!' Thea shouted, uninhibitedly. This damned pony was her central responsibility. She was being paid to keep it safe, and she was going to do her absolute best to achieve just that.

'For heaven's sake,' tutted Cecilia tightly. 'Don't make such a fuss. At his age, he's not likely to make for the hills. Just nip round the back of the barn, and head him off. I'll close in quietly behind him. Grab the halter if you get a chance.'

But the pony wasn't interested in making a break out down the road. Nor did he seem to fancy the field. Instead, he headed purposefully across the yard to his old home. This struck Thea as seriously perverse, after his refusal to enter it only the previous evening. But it made the task of catching him easier – or so she assumed.

When Thea gave her yell for help, Hollis and his companion had been in the stable, and Jocelyn was in the house. Hepzibah was sniffing in corners at the other end of the barn. Suddenly, they all emerged in response to her shout. Hollis and Franklyn were met full on by the pony, who although not very big, seemed suddenly very determined. 'Grab his halter!' Cecilia called to Hollis. 'He's resisting arrest.'

Thea watched the resulting tug of war with some amusement. Managing to catch the halter only by its furthest extremity, the man was unable to prevent the animal from plunging and tossing his head. 'Hold it closer!' Cecilia ordered him, but without effect. Thea realised he was nervous of getting too near to the agitated pony. The Franklyn man had followed Hollis out of the stable, and was standing listlessly on the other side of the pony's head. As it stamped and lunged and then brought its haunches round in a sharp semi-circular swing, it caught him and knocked him against the doorpost.

It hadn't looked like a hard knock, and any sane person would have stepped quickly out of the way. But this man must have been consumed by the image of his son hanging from the rafters, or bemused by whatever Hollis had been saying to him, and in no condition for defensive self-protection. He let the pony's hindquarters press him more tightly against the unyielding wood, and then, when the animal detected the presence of yet another annoying human being, it kicked hard for good measure.

Cecilia Clifton had seen enough. 'Here!' she said, striding across the yard. 'What a useless lot you are.' She seized the halter, yanking it out of Hollis's hand, and crowded herself up to the pony's head. 'Behave yourself!' she snapped, with a vicious jerk on the leather.

Instantly peace was restored. The pony remained wild-eyed, but followed docilely when led to the water trough and tied to a convenient hook attached to the side of the barn. 'He can cool down there for a bit,' said Cecilia, wiping her hands together. 'Anybody would think he was a half-broken stallion, the way you people carry on.'

'But I thought he was a quiet little child's pony,' Thea complained. 'What on earth came over him?'

'That's anybody's guess. It looked to me as if he'd had enough of being messed about, and just wanted to get back to his old home. But I've never been much of a mind reader.'

Only then, walking back towards the shed, did the women understand that damage had been done beyond anything they'd expected. Thea had simply assumed that once the pony had been moved, Mr Franklyn would walk away unscathed, perhaps slightly abashed. Even in her scant experience of country life, she'd been kicked once or twice by cows and ponies. It happened, you whimpered for a moment and then forgot about it. This man was sitting white-faced on the ground, clutching his right knee with both hands. Hollis was squatting beside him, a mobile phone to one ear.

'Now what?' said Cecilia.

'He thinks his knee's broken,' said Hollis tightly. 'I'm calling for an ambulance.'

Thea resisted the general implication that Mr Franklyn's injured knee was almost entirely her fault. She had let the pony go, admittedly. Hollis was plainly angry about the thwarting of his plans for the morning, as well as embarrassed by the damage done to his witness. He phoned Mrs Franklyn immediately after summoning the ambulance, and arranged for her to meet her husband at the hospital. 'You can't imagine how difficult that was,' he told the sisters, when peace was at least partially restored.

Jocelyn had hovered uselessly in the yard throughout the fracas, and now seemed to feel that nothing of great moment had happened. Thea was much less tranquil. 'But why did you bring him here?' she counter-attacked. 'What were you hoping to achieve?'

Hollis shook his head. 'It was at his own request. He wanted to see the stable for himself. Then I was going to take him to the barn. It would have been useful,' he glowered at Thea. 'And now it's all turned into a bloody mess.'

Cecilia Clifton seemed to be withdrawing discreetly. It had begun to strike Thea as odd that she'd hung around for so long, despite her making herself useful with the pony and dog. The fifteen-minute wait for the ambulance had passed in a haze of first aid and reassurances to the injured man, with Hollis barely able to hide his annoyance and Thea striving not to argue with him. Now he was eager to leave, his head obviously overflowing with altered plans and difficult reports.

'Hang on,' Thea said. 'Can we get something straight before either of you leave.'

Cecilia and Hollis looked first at her and then at each other, surprised to find themselves referred to in the same phrase. 'Cecilia – you hinted at something a little while ago, that's niggling at me. That having me here to mind the pony was some sort of pretext? Is that what you meant?'

Cecilia stood her ground. 'More or less, yes. They could very easily have left everything under the eye of Frannie or even Valerie. There are plenty of horsey youngsters who'd have taken care of the pony.'

'So what am I, then? Why do you think they asked me here?' Thea felt herself growing agitated, her chest constricted, hands curled tightly at her sides.

Cecilia glanced again at the police detective. 'Look, Thea, I honestly don't know how the Phillipses were thinking. But all kinds of trouble have been brewing here for quite some time now, and it seemed like an odd moment to choose to disappear.'

'But they planned it months ago. Everything seemed completely normal here when I visited in May – and nothing's changed. Aren't you exaggerating?'

Hollis stamped an impatient foot. 'Thea,' he said, 'I can't hang about here. What's your point?'

Her stomach clenched again. 'I don't like feeling I've been set up somehow, that's all. I'm trying to get at the truth.'

'Well, don't ask me,' Cecilia spoke more sharply than before. 'I'm the last person Julia and Desmond would confide in. If you want to know what they're up to, you need to ask Robert Craven.'

'Enough,' Hollis ordered. 'Thea, you look pale. Go and have some coffee and calm yourself down. Miss Clifton, if you've got more information than you've already given us, please go along to the incident room in Cirencester and ask to speak to one of my officers there. Now, I really have to go.'

He took a few steps towards his car, before a thought gave him pause, and he turned back to Thea. 'And did you know there was something dead in there?' he accused. 'I thought Franklyn was going to be sick, even before his knee got kicked.'

'You didn't give us a chance to warn you,' Thea snapped back. 'We think it must be Milo – Julia's cat. Somebody's dumped his body here, just to make us feel really loved and wanted.'

Cecilia's startled inhalation could be heard across the yard. They all looked at her. 'B-But –' she stammered. 'He's been dead for nearly a week.'

'Too right he has,' said Jocelyn. 'And there's maggots to prove it.'

Cecilia's eyes went to tiny glittering stones in her head. 'Then they really do want you out of here, don't they,' she said.

There didn't seem to be any answer to that, and Hollis paid scant attention. 'I'll see you later,' he said to Thea, from his driving seat, and she wasn't entirely sure whether to take that as a threat or a promise.

Thea changed her mind about visiting the Innes establishment. 'I wouldn't know what to say to them,' she admitted to Jocelyn. 'And I don't think Phil would be very pleased if I interfered with his investigation.'

'Oh, bother Phil and his investigation,' Jocelyn snapped.

'Can't you think about anything else?'

'Yes, I can think about all kinds of things, if I try. And all kinds of people. I haven't forgotten I've got a life away from all this.'

'Well then,' said Jocelyn. 'When does Jess get back from wher-ever-it-is? And when does her police training start? And have you seen James and Rosie lately? How's her back? And what're you getting Dad for his birthday? He'll be seventy-five, you know.'

'Stop!' Thea ordered, laughing in spite of herself. 'Is this your way of saying I should get a proper job? That I live too much through other people?'

'Not a bit.' Jocelyn seemed genuinely surprised. 'I never looked at it like that.' She considered. 'But it's a thought, isn't it? I'm just as bad, with my feeble little efforts to earn some pocket-money. We don't *contribute* very much, do we?'

'We keep the wheels running smoothly. Or you do. I don't think I really want to analyse my own place in the world, just at the moment.'

'So what're we going to do then? I can't help feeling I need to leave here on some sort of high.'

Thea looked at her watch. 'It's nearly eleven. We could go for that walk in the woods I've been nagging you about. This is your final chance. We could have a quick drink at Daneway and back here for lunch – or the pub in Frampton Mansell, for a change.'

'You're not going to let me off that walk, are you?'

'I'm not going to *force* you, but it's nice, I promise you. It'll clear your head before you go home.'

'All right,' Jocelyn grudgingly agreed. 'But we are not to talk about the murder, my marriage, children or...or...well, that's about it. I might even let you tell me about the canal, if it keeps us off those other subjects.'

'Don't tempt me.' Thea stuffed some money into the pocket of her trousers, and they set out just as they were, Thea in train-ers and Jocelyn in flimsy sandals. 'We don't need a map,' Thea breezed. 'I can remember the way.'

They were quickly in Frampton Mansell, where Jocelyn paused outside the church with its oddly empty graveyard and decorative tower. 'Do you want to go in there first?' Thea asked. Before

Jocelyn could reply, Hepzibah had dived under the gate and was zigzagging over the bowling-green-quality grass, ignoring Thea's calls.

'Looks as if the decision's been made for us,' laughed Jocelyn. 'I don't mind a quick look.'

Leaving the spaniel to pursue her explorations, the sisters let themselves into the building. Thea found herself thinking about the way almost everybody still felt impelled to explore the church in any new place they were visiting, regardless of their religious proclivities.

'Errghh,' Jocelyn shuddered. 'It's horrible.'

'Plain,' Thea corrected. 'Not horrible.'

'I always forget how much I dislike churches until I'm inside one. I must be a real pagan at heart. Look at it!'

Thea drifted towards the table containing the ubiquitous information leaflets, finding a printed history. Skimming it, she extracted two or three basic facts. 'The church was threatened with closure in 1979 and the locals rallied round to save it,' she summarised.

'They needn't have bothered, if you ask me,' said Jocelyn.

Outside again, they called for Hepzie, who came into sight still sniffing interestedly at a cluster of headstones in an otherwise sparsely inhabited graveyard. Thea went towards her, pausing automatically to read a few inscriptions on the stones.

'Oh look at this one,' she called to Jocelyn, who was returning to the gate.

'Must I?'

'Not if you don't want to. It's a boy, Samuel Davy Willis. *Died in a tragic accident on the Thames and Severn Canal, 27th July 1933.* I wonder what happened?'

'How old was he?'

'Born 1919.'

'Fourteen. Doing something foolhardy, I expect.'

'As boys do. Sad, all the same. He must have been conceived right after the First World War. Somebody's pride and joy.'

'Oh, you. It's just one out of thousands. What's special about this one?'

'Nothing.' Thea left her contemplation of the gravestone. 'But it's something real, just the same. A little bit of human misery. I think it's the dates. Born just after the war, and died in the year they finally abandoned the canal altogether. It seems ironic somehow.'

Jocelyn seemed to shake herself. 'You're right,' she said. 'I'm being a cow. It must have been terrible for the poor people. Fourteen – he'd have been leaving school and getting a job, probably. One of the upcoming generation. Mind you,' she added, 'he would have been twenty when World War Two broke out. What would his chances of survival have been, anyway?'

'Not everybody went to fight. He could have been a grand old man in his eighties now with a host of grandchildren.'

'Stop it. I hate might-have-beens. They breed discontent.'

'Do they? You sound as if you've got some.'

'Not now. What did I tell you? That's one of the no go areas.'

'Sorry.' They left the church and continued along the small road, with Hepzie cheerfully running ahead of them. There seemed little risk of any traffic.

'Oh, there's a pony, look,' said Thea, pointing into a paddock. 'I wonder if it ever gets to meet Pallo.'

'Bound to, at the local gymkhana.'

'Tell you what,' said Thea. 'There's a better way, down past the pub. Come on.'

The railway line safely crossed, they traversed the southern edge of a field, which sloped downhill, to the valley of the River Frome, with dense woodland on the rising slope beyond. 'Gosh!' breathed Jocelyn. 'Isn't that glorious!'

'There are views like that everywhere you go, all over the Cotswolds,' Thea told her. 'Visually, it's an absolute paradise.'

Conversation proceeded at the same safe level, pointing out objects to each other, admiring the landscape until they were well into the woods. Dutifully they read the Wildlife Trust notices that appeared here and there, with pictures of otters and birds and flowers. 'Hey, see this!' Thea said, in outrage. '*After 200 years the canal closed, benefiting wildlife and enhancing the wetland habitat.* What a nerve! How dare they?'

'Why? What's wrong with that?'

'Canals are *wonderful* for wildlife. More banks and shallows for things like water rats and kingfishers and herons. More flower species. These idiots don't know what they're talking about.'

'I expect they do,' Jocelyn disagreed mildly. 'You're just biased.'

'I wonder what the canal restoration people make of it. This stretch is due for their attentions soon. There are some amazing locks just along that way.'

'Can we go along here instead?' Jocelyn asked, pointing to her left. 'If I'm remembering the map properly, it comes out at Daneway House.'

'No problem,' said Thea. 'Provided we can come back past the locks. Hepzie agrees with you, anyhow.'

They strolled through the woods, with the dog running ahead of them, checking regularly to see that Thea was still in sight. Fifteen minutes or so brought them to a small road, opposite the gates into Daneway House.

The house itself was not visible from the road, and they both felt too self-conscious to march up its driveway for a look. But they did take a footpath that curved around the back, from where they could see the medieval rooftops and chimneys, and the flamboyant gold-painted weathervane, in the shape of some odd mythical winged beast. Jocelyn professed herself satisfied at seeing it again.

'We'll have to have a quick drink at the Inn,' said Thea.

In the bar, the first person they saw was Jeremy Innes. At the sight of them, his eyes widened and he glanced round as if searching for somewhere to hide.

'Morning,' Thea said to him, her mind full of the decomposing cat. 'Listen, Jeremy – what did you do with Milo?'

'Nothing,' he said, avoiding her eye. 'What d'you mean?'

'Well, where is he now? Don't you think Julia will want him back?'

'My dad took him, if you must know. Said he'd dispose of him, and I was an idiot to talk about post-mortems. He said nobody deliberately killed him, and I should forget the whole thing.'

'Your dad,' Thea repeated. 'I still haven't met him.'

The *So what?* was almost uttered in the look he gave her.

'And what did he say he was going to do with him?' Jocelyn butted in.

'What's it to you?' Jeremy was trying to back away from them, aware of his mates listening to his humiliation at the hands of the two women.

'I'll tell you,' said Thea, impatiently. 'Last night we found the cat's body in the pony's stable, in a vile state. Somebody obviously brought it back to Juniper Court and dumped it, deliberately to upset us. There's a campaign to make us leave, in case you hadn't noticed. So don't give us that rubbish about your father, because it's obviously not true.'

One of the other youths sniggered. Jeremy flashed him a look, part pleading, part warning. 'Nobody cares whether or not you leave now,' he said. 'It's all too late now, anyway.'

'So what was all that macho stuff yesterday morning?' Jocelyn flared up. 'Your brother really overstepped the mark, didn't he?'

'And now he's been nicked, so you don't have to worry, do you?' Again there was as much pleading as anger in his tone.

'But *why*?' Thea insisted. 'What was the point?'

Jeremy heaved a deep sigh. 'Dom was angry about Nick, that's all.'

'Of course that wasn't all,' Thea snapped. 'He told us to get out of the house for our own good. Why was that? Is your gang going to burn the place down, or something?'

Jeremy forced an unconvincing laugh. 'Don't be stupid,' he said.

Thea gave up. 'Well, I don't understand any of it,' she admitted. 'But you ought to have known better than to drag a girl of fourteen into your activities.'

Jeremy's long-lashed eyes narrowed. 'We tried our best to watch out for her,' he said in a low voice. 'We didn't know —'

One of the other youths made a warning sound, part hiss, part cough, and Jeremy stopped.

Thea picked up the atmosphere immediately. 'So who is Flora's boyfriend?' she demanded. 'She said she wanted to phone someone she called a boyfriend.'

Jeremy shook his head. 'She hasn't got one. She talks big, that's all. Mostly she's just been a nuisance.'

'What, because her family are going to have to come back, and rescue her from the social services?'

He gave her a withering look. 'She's not with the social services. They took her to her mother, who won't be best pleased, according to my mum. Neither will Julia.'

'And what about her father? Can't he come back and take charge of her? It doesn't sound as if they're having much of a holiday anyway, all split up and him off fishing.'

Jeremy swallowed, and Thea thought he looked too young to be in a pub. She took pity on him. 'Never mind,' she said. 'We'll just have a drink and leave you alone. Sorry to have been so pushy.' The boy looked at her with a relief that was almost gratitude.

They drank their beer quickly, both feeling they were simply passing the time until Jocelyn took her leave of Thea and Juniper Court, and Hollis pulled the rabbit out of his pocket, and made everything right with the world again. The air was humid and still. Male laughter wafted down the garden from the open pub door.

'That gravel car park used to be a big canal basin,' said Thea. 'Did I tell you that?'

'I expect so. Please don't say you want to go back for another look at that tunnel.'

Thea shook her head. 'No, I'm more interested in the flight of locks. I think they're absolutely magical.'

'You would. Come on, then. I think those black clouds are coming this way after all.'

They took a footpath that began right beside the Daneway Bridge. Within two minutes, heavy raindrops began to fall, splashing noisily on the treetops overhead.

'We'll probably be reasonably sheltered here in the woods,' said Thea, with blithe optimism. 'We might as well keep walking.'

'Or we could go back to the pub and wait until it stops.'

'I don't think I can face that boy again. No, come on. It won't be much.'

Another two minutes, however, saw the storm dramatically increased, with the trees a less than perfect protection. 'Hey! This is quite exciting!' laughed Jocelyn. 'I haven't been out in a good storm for ages.'

They dodged along, trying to stay under the broadest thickest trees, and succeeding to some extent in avoiding a total soaking.

'I'm not sure we're going to think it's fun if it lasts much longer,' Thea said. 'Look!' She pointed to the sloping woodland to their right, where rivulets of water were already forming, and running down towards their path. 'We'll have very wet feet at this rate.'

A thunderous roll from the sky overhead seemed to endorse her trepidation. Jocelyn squealed, partly from fear, but mostly from a surge of exhilaration. The noise of torrential rain on the tree canopy was growing louder by the minute, until they had to shout to be heard. Hepzie was having second thoughts as to the pleasure quotient in quite so much of a deluge. Her ears hung limply and her feathering disappeared, making her seem half her former size.

'Watch where you're going,' Thea warned. 'It's slippery.'

The world had changed completely since their walk in the other direction less than an hour before. A greenish light filled the woods like a toxic cloud. Even if they had been able to see far ahead, the relentless rain forced them to duck their heads and hunch their shoulders. Neither had jackets. Thea wore a T-shirt and light cotton trousers. Jocelyn had an open-necked short-sleeved shirt and knee-length jeans. Thea had trainers, which gripped the slippery path reasonably well, but Jocelyn's sandals were smooth-soled and useless. Twice her foot skidded from under her, in the sudden mud.

'How much further is it?' Jocelyn asked, after a few minutes of blundering along.

'I don't really know where we are. It all looks different. If it doesn't stop soon, we'd better find a good place to shelter.'

And then everything happened in a bewildering rush. The path seemed to narrow. A minor torrent of water was gushing downhill and across the path. Too late, Thea observed the abrupt drop into one of the canal locks, on their left. As Jocelyn tried to stride over the rivulet ahead of her, her foot slid sideways, her arms flailed, and she disappeared over the edge of the lock that neither of them had noticed was there.

'Aarghh!' screamed Jocelyn as she flew through the air, followed by a nasty silence.

Thea's first thought was that at least the landing would be fairly soft, in the thick mud that lined the bottom of the lock. Her next was that it was a sheer drop of fifteen feet or more, and the original handholds or ladders attached to the walls must long since have disappeared. The dense growth of brambles, nettles and small shrubs blocked both ends where the gates had once been.

'Joss?' she shouted, carefully inching towards the top of the lock. 'Where are you?'

Water flowed everywhere, down inside her clothes, over her face, over the lip into the lock. What would have been rather a joke on a fine dry day had been transformed into a disaster by the force and noise of the thunderstorm.

But she quickly located her sister, despite the rain, and was relieved to see her sitting comically in an expanse of dark brown mud. There were water weeds growing all around her, some of which had become draped across her head.

Jocelyn looked up, her hair plastered to her skull and her front entirely coated with the sludge of the lock bottom. Only then did Thea realise that she was cradling her right arm in her left, a rictus of agony pulling back her lips.

'Did you hurt your arm?' Thea called. The noise of the rain was maddening, and the bad light obscured all the finer detail of what she could see.

Jocelyn nodded. 'I expect it's just sprained or something. And my ankle hurts just as much. I landed all sideways.' The need to get as close as possible to her sister made Thea first squat and then actually lie down on the brink of the lock, hanging her head over the edge. It did make the distance seem a lot less than before, but Jocelyn was still quite a way below her.

'You won't be able to get me out,' Jocelyn said. 'You'll have to go and fetch somebody.'

Thea experienced the classic dilemma of all calamities taking place out of earshot of the passing crowd. A dilemma that mobile phones had in a stroke reduced to virtually zero. 'I don't suppose you've got your mobile with you?' she called down to Jocelyn.

The answering shake of the head came as no surprise. 'Neither have I.'

Another crash of thunder only added to her sense of crisis and helplessness. More water surged down the bank towards them, and she realised there was a culvert cut across the towpath, channelling much of the rainfall directly into the canal just beyond the lock. It was flowing invisibly under the vegetation, but efficiently raising the water level just where Jocelyn was sitting. Before long Jocelyn would be finding herself in something rather more fluid than the present sludge.

'Okay,' she decided. 'I'll have to run and find somebody.' But the dog? Suddenly Hepzibah was dreadfully in the way; an insupportable nuisance. 'Come here,' she said to the bedraggled creature. 'You'll have to stay with Jocelyn.' Thankful for the habit of always slipping a lead into her pocket, she tied the spaniel to a tree two feet from the brink of the lock. Hepzie hated being tied up at any time. Now, in pouring rain with some obvious calamity going on, she was desolate.

'I'm leaving Hepzie here,' she called down to Jocelyn. 'She'll be somebody to talk to.'

'More like a hostage, to make sure you'll come back,' Joss said, again barely audible. 'Hurry up, will you. This arm bloody hurts.'

'I'm going.'

But which way should she go? Onwards towards Frampton Mansell, and its silent ghostly aura, but enough houses for somebody surely to be in – or back to Daneway, where there was at least a pub that she knew to be open? The distances, if she'd remembered accurately, must be almost equal. The deciding factor was the railway line at Frampton. Somehow she felt reluctant to cross it in pouring rain, where she could neither see nor hear properly.

It was horrible having to maintain at least a trot, and now and then a faster run, despite several near falls in the slippery mud. She was thoroughly soaked and cold. The distance seemed endless, and although she couldn't see how any real harm could come to Joss, it felt completely wrong to leave her alone in her prison. Her lungs were searing and her legs aching when she finally emerged onto the road over the Daneway Bridge. Water cascaded along the roadsides, and dripped from the trees, but by some miracle the deluge had in fact stopped. Only now did Thea become aware of this, with a mixture of thankfulness and self-rebuke at the awful timing of the woodland walk.

She was too breathless to speak coherently when she finally reached the road at Daneway. Her initial instinct had been to go to the pub and rally a group of people to come and haul Jocelyn out of the lock. But the pub looked unaccountably deserted from where she stood, and there was a house rather closer.

Nobody answered the door when she rang the bell attached to the doorpost. In desperation she tried the handle, planning to step inside and shout, but the door did not yield. How dare they be out, she inwardly raged. It felt as if hours had passed since she'd left Jocelyn, and now there was a nightmare delay where the world was empty and nobody would help. Water gurgled and slurped down the sides of the road, dripped off the trees and turned the ground to mud. Her clothes clung to her, making her feel naked.

There was no option but to try the pub. When the front door opened easily, and she stepped into a bar still half full of drinkers, Thea felt completely stupid. Of course they would all have retreated indoors when the rain started. And it was still not quite two o'clock, according to the large clock on the wall.

'Somebody help me!' she shouted, feeling all vestiges of self-control running away with the rainwater that dribbled down her legs and into her inadequate shoes. 'Please come and help.'

Everybody looked at her. 'What's up, love?' asked an older man, the kindness scarcely bearable.

'My sister – she fell in one of the locks. I can't get her out. She's hurt her arm and her ankle.'

The effect was unforgettable. Men leapt to their feet and hurled instructions at each other. The older ones seemed particularly galvanised. In seconds there was all the succour she could wish for, the party led by a man on a chunky vehicle that resembled a ride-on lawnmower. He waved at her, indicating that she should take a seat behind him, like the pillion on a motorbike.

All she could do was cling to him and hope her sodden condition wasn't causing him too much discomfort. All she could think of was Jocelyn crouched in the mud of the pit, staring at the sheer brick wall above her, wondering how she'd ever get out. And her shivering uncomprehending dog, almost certainly whining and yapping for Thea's return.

It seemed to take no time at all to get back to the place. Behind the lawnmower, which she faintly remembered was actually a thing called a quad bike, surged men with blankets, mobile phones and encouraging smiles. No ladders, she noted, with a twinge of anxiety. Jocelyn would enjoy all this, she thought. So would Hepzibah, in all probability.

By a process that looked to have been effected by pure magic, the rescuers simply walked into the lock from the farther end, pushing their way through plants that grew to armpit height. Of course, Thea realised, the bottom of the canal must be level with that of the lock, at the lower end, so the barges could get into it. Then the water level was raised, the boat floated upwards, until it was able to leave the other end, having climbed the twelve or fifteen feet necessary. From Chalford to Daneway the sea level rose by something like fifty feet, which the canal had to accommodate somehow. Whoever invented locks was in Thea's pantheon of absolute geniuses. What had appeared to be a completely impenetrable barrier was nothing of the sort.

Feeling faintly foolish for not having worked this out sooner, she watched as Jocelyn was gently carried onto the muddy towpath. The rain had entirely stopped, and the light was greatly improved. She knelt beside her sister, who was white and shivering, but still talking.

'This is all very exciting,' she was prattling. 'I feel ever so important. And you're all so *organised*. Does this happen a lot?'

Something in the atmosphere changed. One or two of the men seemed to draw back as if a nerve had been hit.

'Not often since the canal was dry,' said one with an attempt at humour. 'This is a bit unusual.'

'But it hasn't had water in it for decades,' said Thea.

'Thank goodness, some might say.' They were rubbing Jocelyn

dry, carefully avoiding the damaged areas. It had been decided, it seemed, that she could ride on the quad bike, back to the road where she could be taken to hospital. 'There should be an ambulance turning up any time now,' said somebody. The men were hard to distinguish, with hair plastered sleekly over their heads, and shapeless rainwear covering most of their bodies. Thea kept glimpsing one who seemed familiar, but he wouldn't stay still long enough for her to have a good long stare.

'Didn't you see the signs?' the last speaker demanded. 'We spent quite a bit putting these up, I can tell you. All in the interests of health and safety, of course.'

Thea gazed around. 'No,' she said. 'What signs?'

The man pointed to a board, which presumably had lettering facing away from where they were gathered. 'There's one,' he said. 'It tells you to be careful of the locks.'

'It was so wet,' Thea defended. 'We were walking with our heads down. And it was terribly slippery underfoot.'

'It's a sensitive issue around here,' he continued. 'One that you two haven't helped.'

'Well, gosh, I'm sorry,' Thea defended heatedly. 'We'll be more careful next time.' Crossly, she went to untie Hepzie from the tree, devoting herself to the dog for long enough to make the point that she had no more to say to these overbearing locals.

The whole party was on the move by this time, Jocelyn balanced on the wide back seat of the quad bike. Within two or three minutes, they were met by two paramedics, carrying a stretcher and other paraphernalia. Despite Jocelyn being vertical and fully conscious, they insisted on running checks on her before letting her continue any further. She was then escorted solicitously to the ambulance where she was driven to a hospital in Cirencester. Thea had been all set to go with them, when the presence of Hepzibah raised serious objections. 'I can't go without her,' Thea stated, implacably.

'Well, it can't come in the ambulance,' said the paramedics.

For a moment, Thea felt like screaming. The prospect of a long muddy trek yet again through the woods to Juniper Court was unbearable. 'Here,' said the man she thought she'd recognised,

'I'll drive you home.'

The men were rapidly dispersing, their task accomplished 'Thank you!' Thea shouted after them. 'You were wonderful. One or two flipped dismissive waves at her, the others just kept walking. Thea watched their retreating backs with a wild array of emotions. It was humiliating being the subject of a silly accident, the one in need of rescue, and even more uncomfortable to be indebted to a bunch of strangers. Threaded through this was a sense of transgression. She and Jocelyn had done something that angered and even sickened the locals.

The offer of a lift was too good to refuse. 'We'll make the car horribly muddy,' she worried.

The man just shook his head as if nothing could matter less. 'You've forgotten who I am, haven't you?' he said.

She looked more closely at him, trying to place him. 'Robert!' she said. 'Frannie's husband. I am sorry – it seems such a long time ago that I met you.'

'Less than a week,' he grinned. 'But I gather quite a lot's been going on.'

'You could say that,' she agreed.

The drive back to the house took little over five minutes, the small road running along the southern edge of the woods, parallel to the canal, and into Frampton Mansell. There was no time for much conversation, and besides, Thea's head was much too full of worries and questions and plans and more worries.

'I don't think her arm's broken,' Robert offered. 'Nor her ankle. From the things the ambulance people were saying, I got the impression she isn't badly hurt at all.'

'I hope not. She was planning to go home this afternoon.'

'Really? Where does she live?'

'Just outside Bristol. She's got five children.'

'Heavens! And you?'

'Just one.'

She was hardly hearing her own words, speaking automatically, her thoughts elsewhere. Perhaps, she thought later, it was in an effort to capture her attention that Robert said what he did.

'You'd better go home yourself.'

'Why?'

'It's all such a mess.' He was suddenly vehement, smacking the steering wheel. Thea could see the village just ahead, and opted not to take him up on his outburst. But she did have an urgent question.

'Why were they so angry?' she asked. 'As if we'd broken some taboo.'

He didn't take his eyes off the road ahead. 'People have died in that canal,' he said, gruffly. 'My uncle, for one.'

'Oh dear. Do you mean where – or when – there was water in it?'

'Obviously. But that's all I'm saying. This is where I drop you.'

'Thanks ever so much for driving us,' she gushed. Hepzie had been kept firmly on her lap, to avoid muddy pawprints on the upholstery. 'I can't wait to go and have a hot shower. I can't remember when I've ever been so wet. And then I suppose I'll have to go to Cirencester and find the hospital.'

They drew into the yard of Juniper Court, through the open gate, and pulled up behind a silver-grey people carrier which Thea did not recognise. 'Good God, who's this?' she groaned.

Then a man got out of the driver's seat, looking as if he had been waiting a very long time.

'Christ almighty,' said Thea. 'It's Alex.'

'Where's Jocelyn?' he said angrily, before noticing Thea's condition. 'What the hell's been happening?'

Thea turned to Robert, leaning down through the open passenger door. 'Thanks again,' she said. 'You've been really kind. I'm sorry we caused so much trouble.'

Instead of a polite acknowledgement, he gave her a hard look. 'You don't know the half of it,' he said. Then he nodded at the irate visitor. 'You'll be okay, will you?'

Thea almost laughed. Between the two of them, she wasn't at all sure which would be the safer bet. At least Alex was family. 'Oh yes,' she said. 'He's my brother-in-law.'

Robert said nothing more, but reversed back into the lane and sped away. Thea stared after him, thinking of all the other questions she wanted and needed to ask. Then she took a deep breath, and walked towards Alex. 'Come in,' she said. 'I've got to change out of these clothes.'

'Where's Jocelyn?' he demanded again. 'Her car's here.'

'She's been taken to hospital,' Thea flared, wanting to shock and alarm him, remembering that he had been guilty of behaviour that could have sent his wife for medical treatment. Hoping, almost, that he would think this had indeed happened; that an injury caused by him had turned septic or proved unexpectedly serious.

'What? Thea – what did you say?'

It could have been the absence of any expletive, the fear in his voice and eyes, that thawed her icy manner. 'She's all right. We can go together to see her, when I've changed. Why don't you make a pot of tea or something? The kitchen's through there.'

Tiredly she climbed the stairs, feeling the clammy comfortless weight of the clothes against her skin. It took a long time to peel them away, shivering in the bathroom, burdened by questions and obstructions. She wanted to be free to get to know Phil Hollis without the tangle of the murder investigation dragging him down. She wanted Jocelyn and Alex to go home together reconciled and safe. She wanted Pallo and Hepzie and all the poultry and furry pets to flourish under her care. She wanted Milo to be alive again, and the Cotswold Canal to regain its former glory. All these wants jabbed at her, with the hot water from the shower head.

Downstairs again, in layers of dry clothes, too warm for the outside temperature, she confronted Alex as he stood in the kitchen doorway. 'God, what a day!' she sighed. 'How did you find us, anyway?'

'You put it in an email to Joss. I meant to come sooner, but I couldn't just abandon the kids.'

Foolishly, Thea looked around as if expecting to see them strewn about the house. 'So who's looking after them?'

'Oddly enough, your mother.'

This was deeply unwelcome news. 'What on earth did you tell her?'

'That we were having a bit of a crisis, and I needed some time alone with Joss.'

'Does she know she's with me?'

He nodded. 'Why not? It isn't a secret, is it?'

Thea couldn't begin to explain the complexities of any answer she might give to this. Jocelyn had always been their mother's favoured child, giving rise to resentments and compensations that could never be fully untangled or explained. And Thea knew her mother would somehow blame her, would find cause for reproach and criticism. Just as she knew that if she voiced this to any of the siblings, or to Alex, they would laugh and accuse her of fantasising. They would say her mother only had her welfare at heart, and never for a moment thought her to blame for anything. And Thea would feel worse, and shy away from encountering her mother for another chunk of time, until the natural family force sealed the rift again and normality resumed.

'Listen, Alex,' she said, leading the way into the living room, only to discover the still wet and muddy spaniel curled forlornly and damagingly on the sofa. 'Oh, hell,' she moaned. 'Look at the mess she's made.'

'Never mind the dog,' he spat, from outside the room. 'Just tell me what's happening.' He took a step down the hall towards the front door, but needed to say more to Thea before he could leave.

'Quite a lot,' she returned, pulling Hepzie off the cushions and brushing uselessly at the large damp stain. 'You awful dog! Look what you've done!'

'Thea,' called Alex warningly.

'Oh, for heaven's sake.' She went to the hallway to face him. 'We went for a walk in the woods. It started raining – torrentially. A thunderstorm. Water everywhere. Joss slipped on the towpath and fell into a lock. She hurt her arm and her ankle and I couldn't see how to get her out. I ran for help, and a whole lot of men came to the rescue, and called an ambulance. We all got very wet.'

'Has she broken anything?'

'I don't know, but that chap who just brought me home said he didn't think it was very serious. She's been taken to Cirencester.'

'How far's that from here?'

'Not far. Six or seven miles, I suppose.'

'Well, I'm going to see her. Now.'

Thea paused, sensing a chink of release. 'If you go, then maybe I don't need to,' she said, recognising a familiar pattern: two parents discussing which of them should rally to a needy child. 'We needn't both go,' she said, echoing a line she and Carl had often used.

Alex gave this a moment of thought. 'Right,' he said uncertainly. 'Or maybe we could phone them and ask how long she's likely to be there?'

'You can try. I doubt if they'll tell you, if she's still in casualty.'

He dithered, and Thea suspected he was suddenly nervous of meeting his wife face-to-face without Thea to moderate them. 'I'll have to bring her back here to collect her car,' he worried.

'She probably won't be able to drive.'

'So – how are we to manage?'

Thea's teeth clenched involuntarily at the helplessness of men. 'I have no idea,' she said. Alex and Jocelyn were no longer her problem. She could wipe them off the crowded whiteboard that was her jumble of obligations and concerns. 'I've being paid to watch over this place. And believe me, that's quite enough to be going on with. You probably didn't know that there was a murder here on Monday.'

He barely reacted. *Murder*, after all, was not a word that tripped lightly into normal daily discourse. There were no pre-ordained rules as to how to deal with it. If anything, he seemed to think she was joking, or using the word in some new and metaphorical sense.

'Did you hear me?' she repeated.

'You mean – somebody was killed?' As she had just done, he looked vaguely around the room as if expecting to see a dead body.

'Yes, I mean somebody was killed. Look at that!' She pushed him into the living room where he couldn't fail to see the daubed writing on the wall.

'Get out of here,' he read, with a bewildered frown. 'That's not written in blood, is it? Where are the police? Why are you still here? What about *Jocelyn*?'

'I assure you the police are very much involved. Joss was keeping me company, otherwise I don't suppose I'd have stayed.'

'Thea,' Alex said slowly. 'Wasn't there a murder in the last place you did this house-sitting nonsense? Isn't that a terribly big coincidence?'

She inhaled deeply. 'A bit,' she admitted. 'But we think there could be some sort of explanation for that.'

'We?'

'The Detective Superintendent and me.'

He snorted. 'Sounds like a music hall song,' he said. 'Now, I'm sorry to leave you with all this trouble, but my place is by Jocelyn's side. I've left it much too long as it is.'

'Don't be so pompous.'

Something in her tone alerted him. He paused, one hand on the doorknob. 'She told you then?'

'That's right, Alex. She told me.'

Rather to Thea's surprise, news of Jocelyn's accident reached Hollis by the middle of the afternoon, leading to a phonecall to enquire about her progress.

'She's not too bad. They've done X-rays and the arm isn't broken. Her husband showed up in the middle of it all and he's going to take her home.'

'You mean this evening?'

'So it seems. Joss phoned me only ten minutes ago. He'll bring her back here for her clothes and things, and then take her back to Bristol.'

'So you'll be on your own.'

'At some point, I will, yes. I don't know precisely when, though.'

'Would you phone me, as soon as they've gone?'

'If you like.'

Several middle-sized worries persisted: the dirty mark on the seat of the sofa, the requirements of the pony, the increasingly unsettling silence from Julia Phillips and her family and what to wear for Hollis. Plus whether or not to cook for him, and if so, what. A bigger worry was the sense of a murderer close to discovery,

just beyond the front door. There had been unusual traffic movement past the gate, she'd noticed when outside seeing to the live-
stock, which might well be plain-clothes police officers gathering
for the kill.

Except that if that was the case, Hollis would hardly be taking
time off for some canoodling – as she hoped and believed was his
intention.

The thunderclouds a dim and scarcely credible memory, it was
turning into a fine warm evening. Catching Hepzibah skulking in
the kitchen after her chastisement, Thea saw no option but to
give the dog a thorough wash. At home, this would be done in the
bath, but the resultant splashes could turn the whole room into
something resembling a mud-wrestling aftermath, so it seemed
more sensible to do it outdoors, if she could find some sort of
tub for the purpose.

She found one eventually – a galvanised steel hipbath hanging
on the wall in the barn containing the freezer and the
Lamborghini.

It was a makeshift bath compared to their usual ritual. No dog
shampoo, no carefully warmed water. 'Serves you right,' she told
the spaniel. 'You should have known better than to sit on that
sofa in your condition.'

Five minutes later, a pathetic shivering little animal gazed
reproachfully at her, pretending to be at severe risk of hypother-
mia. Thea gathered her into the towel she'd found upstairs, hoping it would not show any telltale signs of use after she'd washed
and dried it again.

'How sweet,' came a voice from the gateway. 'I seem to have
missed all the fun.'

It was Valerie Innes, smiling in a genuinely friendly way. Thea
was almost pleased to see her. 'You would have got very wet,' she
said, noticing that the cuffs of her sweatshirt were unpleasantly
damp from bathing the dog. 'It's a day for getting wet.'

'I know – that rain! You weren't out in it, were you?'

'I'm afraid so. That's why I've had to wash the dog. She got
dreadfully muddy. And Jocelyn fell into one of the canal locks.'

Valerie's face was a riot of feelings. Horror, disbelief, amusement and something like calculation in the narrowing of her eyes. 'I don't believe it,' she said. 'Nobody would be such a fool.'

'She couldn't help it. The path was awash with the sudden downpour and she just skidded in sideways. The foolish bit was when I didn't realise I could have got her out from one end.'

'Was she hurt then?'

'A bit. Nothing too serious. What's so incredible about falling into a lock?' She remembered the reactions of the rescuers and Robert Craven's partial explanation.

Valerie crossed her arms over her stomach, as if nursing a special story. 'Around here, it's a very sensitive matter,' she said. 'Plenty of people have good reason to detest the canal and its locks.'

'But why? There hasn't been water in the thing for fifty years or more.'

'Fifty years isn't very long for someone who's lost a precious son. The ripples last much longer than that.'

'Do they?' Thea wondered whether Carl's death would still be resonating in 2050. For Jessica, his daughter, she supposed it would. 'Who lost a precious son, then?'

'Quite a few people, as it happens. For instance, there was a very affluent mill-owner from Chalford, somewhere around the turn of the century, who had a son and three daughters. The son was the baby of the family. He was going to inherit the business. And then he fell into one of the locks at Cowcombe and drowned. The heart went out of the old man, the business failed, the daughters had smaller marriage settlements than they expected, so their lives were affected. The mother's sister had a fine upstanding son of her own, which bred jealousy between the two women. And so it went on. There've been others, too, rather more recently that that. The main one was right here, in Siccaridge Wood.'

'Samuel Davy Willis,' muttered Thea.

'What?'

'There's a grave in the churchyard of a boy. It says he died in the canal.'

'Samuel Davy Willis was the older brother of Robert Craven's mother. See what I mean? Living with a canal isn't all rosy and romantic. It can claim lives, and there are plenty of people around here who do not want to see it restored.' Valerie smacked her own upper arm in emphasis. 'Now do you understand?' she repeated, as if it was important.

'I'm not sure,' Thea said slowly. 'What exactly are you trying to tell me?'

'That feelings against the canal are very strong, even now.'

'And your sons are prominent in the campaign against its restoration. You must hear a lot of talk about it in your house.'

Again, Valerie's expression was of real emotion, the prime one akin to fear. 'They won't listen to me,' she complained.

'You mean you told Dominic not to break in here and try to intimidate us? Last I heard he was in police custody. That must be very upsetting for you.'

'His father's absolutely furious. But he's out again now. They couldn't keep him, of course.'

Thea remembered that this was not Dominic's biological mother. 'What about Jeremy? I saw him today and he seemed very bothered about something.'

'Of course he is. He was fond of Nick Franklyn, for one thing.'

'So who killed Nick?' Thea burst out, with the single burning question that had to be answered. 'If everybody liked him so much and agreed with his opinions, why did he get himself strangled?'

Valerie pushed her face closer to Thea's. '*You* don't have to worry your pretty head about it, do you? You can just carry on your cosy little affair with the handsome detective and let us worry about the important things.'

Thea rode the wave of fury, and hugged the damp spaniel closer to herself. The infuriating part was that the woman had a point. The murder really wasn't any of her business. But the intrusiveness, the sense of being watched and judged sickened her. She cast politeness to the winds.

'Mind your own business,' she shouted. 'All I want is for the truth to come out. It's going to be dreadful for poor Julia, coming home to all this mess. What do you want from me, anyway? Why don't you just leave me alone?'

Valerie behaved as if Thea had not even spoken. 'I came, actually, to warn you,' she said, with an air of adult forbearance in the presence of a hysterical child. 'If you're thinking of staying here alone tonight, my advice is, don't.'

'Why? What's going to happen? Why do people keep talking about a crisis that's going to happen here?'

'You'd better ask your nice friendly policeman about that,' said Valerie, before she strode away.

Centuries ago, Thea remembered, before she and Joss had embarked on their ill-fated walk, Hollis had said something to the effect that he expected the whole murder investigation to be resolved before the end of the day. That didn't leave him much time. Or had the two accidents – to Franklyn's knee and Jocelyn's elbow – set the whole thing back? Or had he shelved it in favour of a rendezvous with Thea, alone at last, when they might drink wine, and tell stories about their lives…her insides turned warm and liquid at the thought.

Instead, the sound of an approaching engine caught her attention and she paused on the doorstep. Other traffic did pass the gate, of course, and she was no expert on the sounds of differing types of vehicle, but something made her think it was Alex bringing Jocelyn back to collect her things.

And she was right. 'Here they are,' she said to Hepzie, before they'd even turned in through the gate.

Jocelyn's arm was in a sling, bound tightly to her body, remarkably disabling. 'And it really isn't broken?' Thea asked for a second time. 'Why do you need all these bandages, then?'

'It's *chipped,* I told you,' said Jocelyn. 'It needs to be kept in exactly the right position, so it can heal over properly. Elbows are very complicated,' she added importantly. 'If I started trying to use it, it could grow a spur, or something. It'd lead to trouble later on.' Thea refrained from querying this typical vagueness.

'How long is all this for? And what about the ankle?'

'Ten or twelve days, they think. It's not like being in plaster for six weeks. I have to go and have another X-ray before they take the bandages off. And the ankle's only sprained. They've bound it up tight, and it hardly hurts any more.'

'Well, you won't be able to drive,' said Thea.

'Or cook or wash up or change sheets or about a million things,' said Jocelyn with some smugness. 'It's worse than having no arm at all, in a way. They told Alex I had to be treated like a porcelain doll.'

Thea glanced nervously at her brother-in-law, who was sensibly keeping his distance, much to Thea's relief. Having to cope with the response of a violent husband to his wife being likened to a china doll was an irony too far, under the circumstances.

'Shall I make us something to eat?' she offered, hoping they would decline. Surely they were eager to get home, see the kids, relieve the babysitting grandmother of her duties? But it seemed not. Jocelyn and Alex both responded enthusiastically to the suggestion.

Suppressing a sigh, Thea listed the options. 'There's sausages and bacon, and some frozen fish – though I'm not sure we ought to eat that. It looks a bit special.'

'Sausages will be fine,' said Jocelyn. 'Somebody will have to cut them up for me.' She giggled.

'And eggs,' Alex added. 'Could you find us some eggs?'

Jocelyn snorted. 'The place is overflowing with them, thanks to all those birds outside. More than we know what to do with.'

Jocelyn had become a different person in the presence of her husband. She was tense and self-effacing. When he spoke, she flinched. Thea scanned her memories of recent visits to them, wondering if she'd failed to notice this changed behaviour. After half an hour she was almost ready to punch her sister herself.

The question was, had she become like this because of the violence, or had the way she acted provoked the assaults? Surely it could only be the former. Which left the same bewilderment as to what exactly had motivated Alex in the first place.

She told them about Valerie Innes's visitation, just for something to say. But Jocelyn had evidently withdrawn all interest from the murder investigation, and when Thea attempted to run a few theories past her, she waved them away as if they were annoying insects. Alex showed a polite attention, but it was clear that his own thoughts left little space for evildoing in a remote corner of the Cotswolds. Hepzie, mindful of her bath and the trauma in the woods, kept her distance, turning her back on human beings until they saw the error of their ways and apologised.

But Thea could not ignore the rising crescendo of excitement inside her. Hollis was going to spend the evening with her. She would have him to herself at last. Even if they spent the time discussing the killing of Nick Franklyn, they would be learning about each other, joking, smiling, and possibly even touching. Her emotions leapt from anticipation to anxiety, through impatience, self-mockery and a nameless sense of falling away from promised light back into the grey flat place she had inhabited a year ago, because anything else was too much to expect or hope for.

'We'd better go,' said Jocelyn, the meal concluded. 'You'll be all right, won't you?'

'I expect so.'

'Come on. Don't be like that. Lover Boy's probably hiding down the lane, just waiting to see us leave.'

'Who?' Alex frowned at them both. 'Has Thea got a

boyfriend?'

Jocelyn closed her eyes for two long seconds. 'Sort of,' she said. 'It's the chap in charge of the murder inquiry.'

Thea desperately wanted to ask Jocelyn if *she* would be all right. Parting from her was suddenly much more difficult than expected. Something vital was missing between her and Alex: the spark that linked married couples, despite the usual frictions and frustrations of ordinary life. They weren't looking at each other, and kept a space between them. When Alex hovered beside her, conscious of the injured ankle, trying to help her, she cringed away from him. It seemed blatant to Thea now, and horribly important. How they could sleep in the same bed, or even ride in the same car, was beyond her.

'I'll phone you tomorrow,' Thea said. 'To see how you are. And I'll keep you posted on how it all turns out here.'

'Yes,' said Jocelyn. 'You do that.'

They finally left at eight o'clock. Jocelyn's car remained at Juniper Court until arrangements could be made to retrieve it. The sisters hugged gingerly, paying due regard to the damaged arm

'I'll phone you in the morning,' was all Thea could manage to say.

'At last!' moaned Hollis when she phoned him. 'Are you all right?'

'Tired,' Thea admitted. 'It's been an extremely long day.'

'Poor you. Well, give me ten minutes. I'm afraid the day isn't done with yet. And keep the doors locked, will you? Don't let anybody in except me.'

She laughed and promised to comply.

He was there in nine minutes, enfolding Thea in his arms the moment she'd opened the door. It felt like two pieces of jigsaw finally interlocking, settling down in their allotted places after a long frustrating series of setbacks. They clung and sighed and rocked for a whole long minute.

'Hello,' she said, eventually. 'What happens now?'

'What happens now is that I pull myself together, remember

who I am and what I'm meant to be doing this evening. I've got a whole team of officers out there, waiting to make a move, all relying on me for their instructions. And everything's been held up because of your highly annoying sister.'

'Surely not? Why is she so important?'

'Because I need to get you out of here, without attracting any notice.'

'I see,' she lied.

He smiled down at her and her heart went soft and light, and she had to swallow down the yearning simply to take him to bed and never let him go.

'Oh dear,' she said. 'Why's this so difficult?'

'It'll be fine. We're almost there now. Just a few more twists and turns through the maze and we'll be out in the sunlight.'

'Lord, don't tell me you're a poet!'

'No danger of that. I just have an unfortunate liking for metaphors. Look, we'll have to go.'

'We? Go?'

'Yes, I told you. I can't leave you here, it isn't safe. I shouldn't be telling you anything, by rights, but I can just say we've set up a sort of ambush at the barn. There's almost enough evidence for a conviction, but my orders are to go for belt and braces.'

She watched her expectations shrivel, leaving her drained and passive. 'Why can't I just stay here and wait until it's all over?'

'Because there are a few unpredictable elements. We still can't work out why Franklyn's body was brought here hours after the killing. There's some sort of message there, and one reading of it is that it's a warning to anybody at Juniper Court.'

She was reminded of the Phillipses. 'Have you contacted Julia again? Is Desmond answering his phone? Is it right that Flora's been sent to Liverpool?'

He pulled a face. 'Mrs Phillips is in serious trouble. She's checked out of the hotel where she was staying with the three younger children, and didn't leave word as to where she'd be. The Garda have been looking for her all day.'

'She can't be that hard to find, surely? You've got the number of her car, haven't you?'

'Ireland's an easy place to lose yourself. They will be found, but it's annoying, and time-consuming.'

'And it looks bad,' Thea agreed. 'Maybe they've just gone to join Desmond. He's off fishing in the mountains somewhere, isn't he?'

'So it seems. He's certainly a dedicated fisherman.'

'So they don't know about Flora? She said she told each parent she was with the other one. Maybe Julia's set off to try to find her, with Desmond not picking up his phone messages. That would make sense. It's bound to be perfectly innocent.'

Hollis smiled forbearingly. 'I'm not sure anything in this case is perfectly innocent,' he said.

He explained briefly that the burden of suspicion for the murder of Nick Franklyn lay squarely on the Innes brothers, who were known to be part of the Rural Warriors, with Nick as leader. That there had been friction in recent weeks over the prioritising of campaigns. When questioned by the police, Frannie Craven had freely acknowledged her own involvement, and had described meetings where tempers had flared – in particular between the Inneses and Nick. She had listed nearly twenty local people who were either active members or regular sympathisers, including Cecilia Clifton, Flora Phillips, the landlords of both the nearby pubs and the Master of Foxhounds. But not Desmond or Julia Phillips.

The barn, owned by the Innes family, was one of the meeting places, where some of the more sensitive equipment was stored, including balaclava helmets, climbing equipment, placards and leaflets. When Valerie Innes, owner of the barn, had been questioned, she professed to have left her sons to their own devices, having been assured by them that they would not break any laws.

'Did she know Nick was actually *living* there?'

'She called him an illegal squatter, so I guess she did.'

'But that husband of hers would have evicted him, surely? It must have been a direct ploy to stop him converting the barn.'

'Too risky. If the media got the story there'd be a lot of sympathy for Franklyn and not much for Innes. It suited him better to bide his time and do things in his own sneaky way.'

'But it gave you the idea that his sons could have had mixed feelings about Nick,' Thea realised. 'Family loyalty in conflict with their protest activities. And Jeremy's basically a law-abiding lad, with a lot to lose. Plus a mother you wouldn't want to get on the wrong side of. Does she know they're your chief suspects, by the way? And what about the influential husband? What's he saying?'

'He's tying himself in knots, pulling every string in Gloucestershire to protect them. He forced us to release Dominic before we wanted to. He's got a top lawyer standing by to thwart every move we make.'

'Hence the belt and braces,' Thea realised.

'Precisely.' Hollis spoke with relish. 'And we'll get them, you see.'

'But I still think they didn't do it,' she said, surprising herself with this abrupt certainty.

'Oh, don't you?'

'I can see the logic, from your point of view, and all the evidence and so forth. But we know they were all in the barn together on Sunday night, plotting their strategy. So there's sure to be traces from Dominic and Jeremy anyway. Why them, incidentally, and not one of the others?'

'There are only two others who ever met at the barn, and they can prove they were at home all Sunday night.'

'What about Nigel Franklyn? You believe his story now, do you?'

'I do, as it happens. It's vague enough to be credible. And there's no trace of him at the barn. He swears he didn't know anything about it and I believe him. The client at Bisley backs up his story and says he was quite calm and focused. If he'd just killed his son and then hanged his dead body from a stable roof, I think he'd be in rather a state, don't you?'

'You're saying the same person killed him then hanged him here?'

'Actually, we've still got an open mind about that.'

'And how many hours between the two events?'

'Impossible to say for sure, but it must have been after midnight when he was killed. Possibly as late as three or four in the morning.' He looked hard at her. 'But you don't believe I'm right?'

She shook her head. 'It feels wrong to me. With all those people on Frannie's list, it's too simple to just dump everything on Jeremy and Dominic. It leaves too much out – like why take the body to Juniper Court?'

'To divert attention from the barn. They must have hoped we'd never discover that Nick was dossing there.'

Thea wondered about this. 'That would work if the suicide idea had stuck,' she nodded. 'They must have underestimated the intelligence of the police, in that case.'

Hollis grimaced. 'Most people do,' he said. 'Sometimes with good reason, to be honest. If things had been busy, and the killer just slightly more clever, it could have worked.'

She nodded. The same set of thoughts went around yet again: that somebody had brought Nick's body from the barn to Juniper Court, hiding somewhere until Thea left for her walk, and then lugging the corpse up into the loft. 'But it's so *horrible*,' she shuddered. 'I keep imagining the dead weight of him, being winched up like that.'

She heard her own words. *Winched up*. She had not in fact visualised it happening like that until now. She'd imagined the killer on the upper level, holding the rope and pushing the body over the edge with the noose around its neck, the roof beam taking the weight. Now she realised the body could have been at ground level, the rope slung over the beam, and hauled steadily up to where she had found it. 'Could one person have done it alone?' she wondered.

'We re-enacted it,' he said unemotionally. 'It would be awkward, but possible.'

'It sounds as if you've opted for the simplest explanation,' she said. 'A falling-out amongst the protesters. Dominic and Jeremy strangle Nick, and then leave him here as a warning to Desmond not to go ahead with his fish farm idea. Simple. Nick's father maybe heard there was trouble brewing, which is why he was suddenly so keen to find him. Valerie's such a control freak, she thinks she can just bully everybody into doing what she wants – is her husband as bad as her?' She frowned. 'That would be unusual. Women like that generally have wimpy little husbands.'

'He's not a wimp,' Hollis smiled. 'He's a big noise in the Planning Office, as it happens.'

'Heavens! That must make for some good old family rows.'

'That's where your theory might hold water. It seems he doesn't discuss his work with anybody. He's a Freemason, as well. Friends in high places. And a very nice slice of old money, inherited last year from his father.'

'Those boys didn't do it,' said Thea again.

'You mean, you've looked into their eyes and judged them to be pure?'

'Pretty much that, yes,' she said, meeting his gaze full on. 'You're taking Dominic's attack on Jocelyn as indicating he's capable of violence. But actually, it's just the opposite. He was very uncomfortable with it, none of that craziness you'd have to have to kill somebody.'

'But the method. Coming up behind his victim and grabbing them by the neck.'

'Is that how it was with Nick?'

'Must have been. A length of strong cord was pulled tight from behind him. No signs of any chance to defend himself. Not a bruise on him anywhere. Just quick and probably completely unexpected.'

'Premeditated, then.'

'Looks like it.'

They were still in the hall, talking fast, watching each other's faces, aware of snatching time before Hollis got on with his job. Now he went to the front door, waving her to accompany him. 'We should have left ages ago,' he tutted.

'But – how do you know they'll be there? What are you going to do? Won't I be in the way?'

'We have information,' he said inscrutably. 'They're meeting at the barn, and then there's talk of making some sort of attack on Juniper Court, for reasons we still don't understand at all.'

'Something to do with Flora,' Thea said. 'Jeremy hinted at

something when I saw him today. He was going to say more when one of his mates stopped him.'

'Well, we won't let it get that far. You're going to sit tight in the car until it's all over.'

'And what about Hepzie?'

'What?'

'If it isn't safe for me to stay here, then it isn't safe for her. I'm really sorry, but I can't just leave her. Not after what happened at Duntisbourne. Do you understand?'

He groaned with some melodrama, and ran a hand through his hair. 'This is getting worse by the minute. Bring the damn dog, why don't you. Just promise me she won't bark or want to pee at the critical moment.'

'Absolutely,' Thea promised, with an inward tremor.

She sat in the front passenger seat of the Mondeo, with the spaniel on her lap. Within moments they were driving down a narrow track with dense trees on one side. 'Where are we?' she whispered.

'Only a few hundred yards from the barn. Nobody's going to see you here.'

'That's a relief.'

'Listen,' he told her. 'I won't have time to say this twice. You're to stay in the car unless I expressly tell you to get out. If that happens, you're to take the dog and run for the nearest trees or long grass or woodpile – anything you can find that'll hide you. Stay down until I come calling for you. However long that takes.'

Thea giggled in spite of herself.

'It's not funny, love. As far as we know, nobody's armed. This is all meant to be very calm and low key. But there are still uncertainties, and I don't want anyone to take any risks. Understand?'

Thea hadn't really heard anything beyond that sweet-sounding *love*, but she murmured assent, anyway.

'I'll leave the key in the ignition, so you can open the windows if you want.'

Then he was fishing in his pocket for a mobile phone. Thea had a disconcerting image of another one ringing loudly just outside the barn and betraying its owner to the killer inside. Then she remembered that they could be set to vibrate silently instead of ringing.

'Jack?' Hollis muttered into his phone. 'I'm in place now. Can you talk?'

Apparently Jack could, as Hollis listened intently for a few seconds. 'Right. Good. Give me two minutes.'

He opened his door delicately, whispering to Thea, 'We've got them under surveillance now, in the barn.'

'Good luck then,' she said. An irritation was settling on her, compounded of disappointment and weariness. The man was playing silly games when all she wanted was his arms around her.

Hollis leaned back into the car. 'Be very quiet!' he ordered. 'This is important.'

'Good luck,' she repeated, meaning it this time.

She waited in the car, annoyed with herself, but still sensing something ridiculous in the situation. Why hadn't she just gathered up the dog and gone home the day she found the body? The ensuing week had been an ordeal of painful frustrations, with Jocelyn to cope with and Hollis simultaneously seductive and unavailable.

Slowly she began to doze, with Hepzie curled warm on her lap. Images flickered in her head, making little sense. She wished for a cushion, or permission to play music. Even a Radio Four play would have been welcome company. Outside the light was fading, the trees losing detail, all the more so for the steaming up on the inside of the windows as she and Hepzie breathed.

A man's voice brought her awake, and without thinking, she wound down the window beside her, the whirr of the electric motor sounding loud in the twilight.

'They're at the barn now, look,' said the man in a low voice.

'I said they would be. I don't know why we had to come and make sure, when it was never in any doubt.'

'Stupid buggers.'

A second voice replied. A voice that was more familiar to Thea. 'They're after the Innes boys, just like Frannie said. She's a clever girl, is my Frannie. This is all thanks to her, you know. She's really led them up the garden path with her stories of feuds between the lads. Lucky for you, mate.'

The first man laughed. Thea wondered how they could possibly not have noticed her, only a few feet away in a whacking great car. She tried to locate them, using the wing mirror, but could see nothing. Cautiously, she turned, sticking her head a little way out of the window.

There were footsteps and more conversation. 'We can't stay here,' said the second man, who had to be Robert Craven from the voice. 'We ought to get back. We've seen enough to know what they're up to.'

And then Thea saw them, and they saw her. She pulled her head back, too late. 'Flora!' cried the man who wasn't Robert. 'Darling, what are you doing here? They said you were with Maggie.'

He ran to the car and pulled the door open. Hepzie raised her head and grinned. Thea met the man's eyes and knew who he was at last.

'Good God – Desmond Phillips,' she said.

'You're not Flora,' he realised, his jaw slackening. 'Who are you?'

'This is your house-sitter,' said Robert, with a hint of amusement. 'She does look a bit like Flora in this light, I suppose.'

'But —' Desmond was evidently thinking fast. 'She's seen me,' he stuttered. 'She knows I'm here.'

'Bad news,' Robert sympathised.

'What did you hear just now?' Desmond demanded of Thea. Even as he spoke she could see him working out that it was an ill-advised question. She tried to remember precisely what she had heard, and what it had implied.

'You killed Nick Franklyn,' she said, before grasping just how very stupid her own words were. 'Everybody thinks you've been in Ireland all week. You've scarcely been mentioned or thought of.' She lowered her head, hugging the spaniel to her. 'Oh dear.'

'Now what?' muttered Robert. As a henchman, Thea was beginning to judge him sorely inadequate.

'Get in,' Desmond ordered. 'Back seat.' He ran round to the driver's side and threw himself into the car. Before Thea could make a move, he had started the engine and was reversing down the track. Surely, she thought, Hollis would hear them and give chase? But she could see no other headlights, or even torch-beams, in the gathering darkness. Hollis was busy with his cat and mouse game, with no attention to spare for the woman and dog waiting obediently in his motor.

She had never taken the time to wonder what it would be like to be held captive, under any circumstances. In a car with two men, it was turning out to be entirely terrifying. A car supplied complete freedom to go anywhere. They could drive to the north of Scotland or the centre of London. Even if word went out to the police across the country, the procedure for identifying and intercepting them was bound to be cumbersome. But that was the rational part, which was crowded into a small corner by the more primitive dread of being separated from her familiar life. Even though her precious dog was with her, she still felt like a small child snatched from the pram in the garden by wicked fairies.

'We'll have to dump the car,' Robert urged from the back. 'They'll find it in no time.'

Desmond made an inarticulate sound of rage and indecision. He smacked the steering wheel, before swinging it violently, manoevring the car into the country lane that led back towards Frampton Mansell.

'Des,' Robert repeated. 'Leave it, and we'll walk.'

'She's got a dog,' Desmond snarled, as if only just realising this fact. 'A bloody *dog*.'

Thea hugged Hepzibah tighter and said nothing. She was searching her memory for useful information from films or books that might help her to cope. All she could come up with was how unreal such depictions were. The victim would whine and plead for a few minutes, before gathering her wits and asking for details as to how and why the murder had been performed. This sort of behaviour was well beyond Thea's capabilities. Her insides were cramping, hot and tight, making her fear for the security of her bowels. People on films never soiled themselves – or if they did it was soldiers under ferocious bombardment, and never a female person. They were far too dignified for such appalling loss of control.

She glanced at Desmond's face, trying to reconcile it with the tall smiling husband and father she had seen a week before. Now it was taut and damp with sweat. His hands were claws, his voice thick with panic. This, unlike the half-hearted Dominic of Thursday morning, was the real thing. This man could kill. The difference was that between a tiger and a hamster, a Cape buffalo and a newborn fawn. Her bowels surged more powerfully, and she struggled to contain them.

The women on the movies would start by accusing. 'How could you kill that innocent young boy?' Then they'd bargain. 'I promise I won't say a word, if you'll just let me go.' Then they might threaten. 'You can't possibly hope to get away with it, you know.' None of these tempted Thea. They all seemed designed to further enrage her captor. But one strategy did seem viable, and she twisted slightly in her seat.

'Robert?' she croaked. 'Please – Robert.' Full sentences were beyond her.

'He thought you were Flora,' Robert explained superfluously. 'That's why he showed himself.' He seemed to be wondering at the way events had turned. 'The sort of thing you couldn't possibly predict,' he went on. Thea began to doubt Robert Craven's sanity, despairing of him as a potential saviour.

'She's like Flo, though, isn't she,' Desmond said, joining in the wonderment. 'You couldn't blame me.'

'Nobody's blaming you, Des. Just dump this bloody car, will you.'

The headlights had finally been turned on, as they put a half-mile or so behind them. Thea made no attempt to work out where they were going.

'Leave it at Sapperton,' Robert said. 'We can walk back from there.'

Desmond made another wordless gargle, which could have been agreement. Thea's body began to misbehave in another direction. 'I'm going to be sick,' she said. And before anybody could react, she was. Even as it was happening, she managed to acknowledge that it was marginally preferable to losing control of the other end.

Vomit seemed to fill the car. It went on Hepzie, the seat, the floor, and Desmond's trousers, as she leaned helplessly towards him. Somewhere behind her Robert was half laughing, half registering disgust. When it was over, Desmond was still driving, but much more slowly.

'Urgghh,' said Thea.

'Now we'll *have* to dump the car,' said Robert.

The next hour was full of the stuff of nightmare. A strange dark route led downhill through fields and then into woodland. The men took an arm each and marched her along, ignoring stumbles. They complained about the smell of vomit at first, but soon all three of them grew used to it. But the worst thing, by far, was Hepzie. She had been left behind in the car, and when Robert had pointed out that she would bark and bring notice to the vehicle, Desmond had wrapped a white handkerchief tightly around her muzzle. The dog's shocked response to this piece of violence had broken Thea's heart. 'She'll suffocate,' she had wailed. 'She'll die of thirst.'

'I'll kill her now then, shall I?' Desmond had flexed his strong tense hands. 'That might be a better idea anyway.'

Thea had gone silent then, and ice cold. 'No, no,' Robert had protested lightly. 'No need for that. Don't get carried away, like you did with the damned cat.'

For which mercy, Thea was already eternally grateful to Robert Craven, whatever he might do to her in the coming night. Learning that it had been Desmond who had run over the Siamese was shocking in itself, but not on her immediate list of things she had to think about.

The nightmare became even more unreal when they reached their destination. A waxing moon combined with the last moments of daylight was giving enough illumination for Thea to recognise where they were, just before she was pushed down into squelchy sludge that reminded her all too vividly of the accident in the lock earlier that day. 'It's the tunnel!' she said, surprise jolting her into lucid language. 'The canal tunnel.'

'Right,' confirmed Robert. 'And I can promise you nobody's going to find you in here.'

A new thought hit Thea. Hepzie would find her. When she was eventually released from her prison, she would detect her mistress's scent and lead the police directly to her. But the hope this generated was tainted by dread that the spaniel would be intercepted and strangled by Desmond, before anybody could stop him. And in any case, it would be hours and hours before that could happen. The car had been tucked into a gateway, where it could remain unseen for days. The dog could die before anybody found her. Virtually all the fleeting hope drained away, and Thea slumped between her captors, not caring if she fell in the stagnant mud.

The clinging remnants of vomit on her clothes made Thea abhorrent to herself. Her body cringed inside the besmirched garments, struggling to get away, to shrivel into a smaller protective shell. She was stiff with the effort, hardly knowing herself in these extremes of fear and dread.

Inside the tunnel, to a distance of some twenty or thirty yards, a platform had been erected, stretching across the whole width. It was raised only a foot above the floor, giving enough headroom to stand up, although Desmond had to crouch slightly. It smelled of rotting vegetation and mouldering stone and was almost completely dark. 'They'll never find us here,' said Robert again. There was a boyish glee in his voice, a pride at having discovered the perfect hideaway.

'Quiet,' said Desmond.

Thea watched the pewter flickers of light on the watery mud at the mouth of the tunnel, miserably aware that their footprints had already disappeared. It was, as Robert had said, a very good hiding place.

Slowly she grasped that the next phase had not been planned. The men had no idea what to do with her. She was a spanner in the works, and nothing more than a panicky instinct to hide had brought them here. Although, she suspected, this must be where Desmond had spent the greater part of the past week. Had he been here when she and Jocelyn had come to look at the tunnel? The thought exhausted her with its implications and ironies.

She tried to conjure Hollis, the concerned professional, who would institute an efficient search unclouded by emotion. He would find his car – of course he would. He would have patrols out searching at this very moment. It wasn't late – not much after ten. Things could not possibly be as desperate as they seemed.

Robert spoke, his voice echoing in the closed space. 'I'll have to get back. Frannie's going to worry. I told her I was only going for a drink. If she thought I'd been with you —'

'You're not going anywhere,' Desmond grated.

'Come on, Des.' The forced lightness did not quite conceal the nervousness beneath. 'Frannie isn't going to take much more of this. She hasn't liked it from the start. If she knew what had really —'

'Shut up,' Desmond snarled. 'Frannie's not my problem.'

Thea edged up against the dank brickwork, curling herself into a small huddle of misery. When this was over, she thought, her account of how she'd behaved would be deeply unimpressive. She imagined Jocelyn's disappointment in her. 'Didn't you give them a good telling off, like you did with that Dominic?' she'd say. The idea made her shudder, and once begun, she found she couldn't stop. Her whole body began trembling violently.

Desmond detected the vibrations. 'You're not going to spew again, are you?' he asked her.

'I don't think so,' she stammered. 'I'm just cold.'

'Can't you phone her?' Desmond returned to Robert and his troublesome wife.

'And say what? How do I explain a quick pint turning into being out all night?'

Desmond gave up arguing. 'Well I want you here. No more to be said.'

'Why, though? What good's it going to do? We can't stay here forever.'

'Let me think.'

Thea kept her eyes on the mouth of the tunnel, willing someone to come, ready to scream at the slightest sign of anyone. Desmond's uncertainty had given her a fleeting sense of possibility, if only she could get her brain to work. But not being able to see the men's faces was a severe handicap. They sat on the platform, shifting their weight from time to time, but moving little. She had no idea what provisions there might be, although she'd felt a piece of fabric as they'd lifted her into place, which suggested some sort of mattress or bedding. A dark shape at the further end was just visible, which could possibly be a box containing food or drink. Or guns, knives, ropes...

'Listen,' Desmond ordered. 'They'll have arrested the Innes lads by this time, and have them charged with killing Nick. Once that happens, they're not going to worry about any more investigations. They still think I'm in Ireland anyway. I can get away tonight, and disappear.' He spoke tightly, forcing the words out through rage and the panicked frustration of the fugitive.

'Disappear,' Robert echoed. 'Big change of plan is that, Des.'

'Thanks to this bitch,' Desmond snarled, thumping Thea in the ribs. 'I ought to throttle her and leave her here. They'd never find a body behind the landslide further up the tunnel.'

'They might,' Robert warned. 'For God's sake, don't make things any worse.'

'I thought it was Flora,' Desmond grieved at his own fatal mistake. 'She looked like Flora.'

'Right. She did. I thought it was her as well. Especially —'

'Especially what?'

'Well, being near the barn. I mean, that's where Flora would go, isn't it.'

'That bastard!' Desmond's voice went high with hatred. Thea heard the passion of the killer and her shivering increased. 'I'd do it again, Rob. Knowing what he was up to with Flo – he deserved what he got.'

'Yeah,' Robert endorsed. ''Course he did. Her being so young, what else is a dad meant to do?'

Thea barely registered that she'd just heard the explanation for Nick's killing. That hadn't mattered to her for quite some time now.

'Okay, here's the plan,' Desmond inhaled shakily. 'We stay here till midnight or a bit after. Tie this cow up and leave her here. You can go home and explain to Frannie – say you got playing cards in the upstairs room or something. I'll have to —' Thea could hear the sudden understanding in his silence. She knew what he had done. With her alive he would never be safe. Given that he trusted Robert never to reveal the secret, he could have reappeared as if returning from the Ireland holiday, and simply carried on his normal life. Working on the assumption that the police would persist in prosecuting Dominic and Jeremy, even if they were eventually acquitted, the lapse of time would remove both evidence and urgency from the case. It was shaky, but probably worth the risk.

'Jesus!' Desmond exploded. 'I'll have to kill her. You see that, don't you?' Thea wasn't sure whether he was addressing her or Robert, and couldn't see that it mattered. She'd worked it out ahead of him, anyway.

'Wait,' Robert urged. 'She might not talk. Explain it to her. She'll see it your way. Nick Franklyn was a slimy little pervert, no good to anybody. You did the world a favour. She doesn't have to go running to the police.'

Thea remembered the glimpse she'd had of Nick Franklyn, a solitary limping figure she'd taken for a vagrant. She hadn't felt drawn to him, hadn't really cared even when she'd found his body. If it meant she might be spared, she didn't think it was beyond the limits of her conscience to agree to Robert's suggestion.

'Yes,' she said.

'Yes what?' Desmond snapped.

'Yes, I can see it your way.' Talking hurt her throat, roughened by the vomiting and constricted by fear. She realised she was very thirsty.

'You'd say anything now, though, wouldn't you?' he sneered. 'What about for the rest of our lives? I don't think so.'

'I would – for Julia and the others. Such a nice family. And Flora. Lovely girl.' She was gasping for breath, not knowing if she was making any sense.

Suddenly he was shining a torch in her face, hurting her eyes with it. 'You called the cops soon enough when you found her, didn't you? What d'you do that for?'

'No choice,' breathed Thea. 'Ask her.'

She was still thinking about Nick and the fulsome promises she was eager to make. Was it too great a betrayal to conceal a murderer? Could the dead possibly care about justice? She visualised his pale face above the damaged neck. Surely he was beyond it all now. Surely it couldn't matter what she vowed – provided innocent people weren't imprisoned because of it. Already she knew she couldn't go as far as that. She frowned at the light, still bright through her closed eyelids. 'Switch it off,' she said.

'Anyway,' Robert said. 'You've got the alibi. It'd be her word against yours.'

'You won't let me down, then, Rob?'

'No way. It's all sorted. Cast iron. Nobody can be in two places at once.' He laughed grimly.

To Thea's relief, the torch was switched off. When she opened her eyes again, she couldn't see the tunnel mouth any longer. Everything was deeply black. Death must be like this, she thought.

Silence fell, while the situation impressed itself on the three of them. Some of the tension seemed to lift in the absence of sights or sounds. Thea waited, barely thinking. There was certainly nothing further she dared say, until Desmond revealed his decision.

'We'll stay here quietly for a bit,' he ordained.

'That's fine,' said Robert. 'Doesn't do to be too hasty.' But Thea could hear worry, and remembered his wife expecting him at home.

For the first time, Thea understood the meaning of the term 'to marshal one's thoughts'. They had to be tightly controlled in order for them to be bearable. The first one to be bound and gagged was any idea of Hepzie. To entertain an image of the frightened dog locked in the car, thirsty and hungry and miserable, could only lead to hysteria or despair. And Hollis was a no-go area, too. Intent on his mistaken quest for the wrong people, he had abandoned her to her fate, and might never redeem himself. Which left the murder itself. A murder case now solved and explained, but perhaps never to be closed. Except – she jerked spastically at the fresh thought.

'Why did you hang him in the stable?' she croaked, before she could consider.

Desmond reached out and gripped her upper arm. 'What?'

'The body. Why did you hang him up there hours after he was dead?'

'I didn't,' said Desmond, his voice oddly blurred. 'Somebody else did that.'

'Who?'

Desmond didn't reply. After a long pause Robert spoke. 'We don't know,' he said. 'We don't bloody know.'

Time passed in a stupor, with Desmond now and then shining the torch on his watch and prevaricating as to his best course of action. Nothing had been resolved, but Thea permitted herself the conclusion that she was not shortly to be strangled. The dangerous energy of panic had dissipated, mainly thanks to Robert Craven and his very ordinariness. Although it hadn't been stated, she somehow assumed he had not been present at the killing of Nick Franklyn. Robert was an accessory after the fact, but not an active accomplice. But Desmond was still to be feared. Whatever that elusive element that maintained civilised behaviour in daily transactions might be labelled, it was missing in this man at this point in time. He had laid violent hands on another human being, and in doing so had crossed a line that set him apart. And he knew it. Something inside him was broken, and Thea suspected he was only just understanding the implications.

Surely, she craved, it must be midnight. She was stiff and cold and smelly. The moon had moved across the sky and no light filtered through the entrance to the tunnel. Robert was shifting restlessly, now and then humming mindlessly to himself until Desmond told him to stop.

And then the voices came. And a bright light, flickering across the entrance but not directly into it. There were people on the canal towpath, just outside the tunnel. It was so unexpected that Thea took it for a dream and made no move. A woman spoke, clear in the silence of the night.

'I'm going to jump down there and have a proper look.' A dull splash followed, and the torchbeam was suddenly pointing directly at them. 'Robert!' came the voice. 'Are you in there?'

Robert did not answer, and Thea wondered whether the beam was reaching far enough to make them visible. 'There's something in there,' the woman called to her companions.

'Is it him?' It was the younger voice of Frannie Craven. Thea almost laughed. Beside her Desmond gave a hiss, like a cornered rat.

'I can't see. Wait a minute. Robert!'

'It's my mother,' Robert muttered, barely audible.

Thea never quite knew where the strength came from, but thought it had to do with the realisation that there were now more women on the scene than men. That altered the balance and changed everything. 'He's here,' she called. At the same time, she roused herself and jumped off the platform, expecting to be rabbed back by one of the men.

But she wasn't. Wading through the mud, slipping and staggering, she approached the woman. 'Hello!' she called. 'Can you see me?' The torchlight seemed to be dimming, the tunnel mouth further away than she'd thought.

'Who's this?' came the older woman's voice. 'Where's Robert?'

'Go on,' muttered Desmond. 'Leave me, and don't say I'm here. I can still do some damage if I want to.'

Thea and Robert obeyed like frightened children. 'Ma – we're coming,' Robert called. 'Get out of the mud, will you.'

They pushed aside the flimsy barrier across the tunnel entrance and a confusion of hands reached down for them, and helped them onto the towpath. Voices and lights came and went. Thea took some time to register that there was a second familiar accent. 'Cecilia?' she queried. 'What are you doing here?'

'Never mind that now,' came a tone of brisk authority. 'Let's just get you warm.'

They had to half carry her back to the Daneway pub. Questions went unanswered, the voices lowering as they approached the pub and neighbouring houses. Except for Robert's mother, who repeated, 'I knew where you'd be, my lad. Always did come to this daft tunnel when things got a bit rough. Thought I'd forgotten, I suppose. But a mother never forgets. When Frannie phoned me to ask if I knew where you'd got to, it only took me a minute to think.'

It made little sense to Thea and she didn't care. All she wanted was her dog, and Hollis and a nice safe bed.

She tried to make her priorities clear, appealing to Robert for an assistance that he seemed deeply reluctant to provide.

'We have to rescue Hepzie,' she repeated. 'She's in Superintendent Hollis's car, in Sapperton.'

Mysteriously nobody seemed to hear her. Cecilia drove her own silver vehicle in a direction that Thea was sure did not lead to Sapperton. Frannie and Robert were with her in the back, one on either side.

'Please!' she tried again. 'Robert, tell them. Where are we going? I must get my dog.'

Again, nobody responded. Thea drew breath for a scream, wondering as she did so whether she had been right, and this was actually just a dream all along.

Then Cecilia spoke. 'Thea, please calm down. Robert will go and get the dog for you. Everything's under control.' Thea heard exasperation and impatience in the voice, along with a reassuring strength of purpose.

But the absence of explanations began to strike Thea with a deep foreboding. Had she escaped from Desmond only to fall into a new kind of captivity? Did Frannie know what was going on, or had she been told to keep her questions for later?

'Where are we going?' she asked again. 'What's going on?'

'You're quite safe,' Cecilia threw the words over her shoulder. 'I told you, it's all under control.'

Control. The word fixed itself in Thea's head. Cecilia Clifton was in control. Frannie was under her command, and Robert's mother, whatever her name was, was a friend. They were Night Riders, vigilantes, righters of wrongs, in the silence of a Cotswold night. Everything was indeed under their control.

'What about Valerie?' she asked, aware of a missing figure. Nobody gave an answer, and Thea went back to worrying about Hepzibah. Only then did she remember that Desmond Phillips had the key to Hollis's car. He had click-locked it and pocketed the key. Robert would have to break into it to retrieve the dog. And Robert was unlikely to want to do this. Alarm filled her as she realised that Desmond was liable to return to the car and use it to make his escape. Before driving off, he would eject the animal, or – if in a certain mood – strangle her to rid himself of the nuisance.

'I want my dog,' she wailed. 'Let me go and fetch my dog.'

Cecilia heaved a loud sigh. 'Thea, dear, do be quiet. We're on delicate ground here, and we certainly don't want to draw attention to ourselves. Now poor Frannie has been dying to know just what you and her husband were doing in that tunnel, but she's got the good sense to wait until Robert can explain it all to her at home.'

Thea made a sound of outrage at being given such a low priority.

'I'm joking,' laughed Cecilia. 'We know what a loose cannon you've been, right from your first few hours here. The fly in the ointment and that's a huge understatement. You know,' and she turned round quickly to emphasise the point, 'you almost scuppered everything. If we'd had any idea that you'd seen Nick at the barn, it would all have been different.'

'Hold on,' begged Thea, convinced that she would never catch up with these complexities. 'You make it sound as if you were all in the murder together. Some awful great conspiracy, the minute Juniper Court was empty. Except — ' She had been on the brink of adding something about Desmond, before remembering that he was the real wild card in the matter. Even if she didn't betray him directly – and she was already wondering why in the world she shouldn't – there might be a more effective moment to do it.

'Nothing of the sort,' snapped Cecilia. 'The Innes brothers killed him. Some drastic falling-out in the cell led to it. I can see now that it was coming on for some time, but I never dreamed – well, too late for that now. Justice is being done, thanks to the magnificent Superintendent Hollis. Given how influential and noisy their father is, I had my doubts.' She sighed again. 'And of course I had hoped they might escape detection. They're *my* boys in a lot of ways, and I grieve for them.'

Thea leaned back in the car, overwhelmed with frustration. 'They didn't kill him,' she breathed, half expecting to be ignored as before. 'And I want my dog.'

'Of course they killed him,' Cecilia shot back. 'And you have yourself to thank for their arrest.'

Thea almost didn't take this up, tempted just to lay her head back and close her eyes. But nobody liked to be blamed for something they felt innocent of.

'How on earth can it be my fault?'

Cecilia sighed gustily. 'If you hadn't directed the police to the Inneses' barn, there'd have been no evidence against the boys. The fact of the body hanging in the pony shed would have caused hopeless confusion, with no leads or clues.'

Thea tried to match the two accounts she had heard that evening, and make sense of them. She tried to see Robert's face, but it was too dark. He knew the truth, and must be quaking with the dread that she would disclose it.

'So why do you think Robert was hiding in the tunnel?' she asked, feeling that she had at last found something intelligent to say.

'Loss of nerve, I assume,' said Cecilia. 'Keeping himself out of harm's way.'

Robert's wife and mother each made sounds, but spoke no actual words. Robert himself muttered 'Hey, steady on,' in a feeble protest.

'Sorry, Rob,' Cecilia threw over her shoulder. 'I'm sure you had your reasons.' She turned the car abruptly to the right, announcing, 'We're here now, look. We'll go inside and have a milky drink, and find Thea a bed for the night. It's all going to be fine, dear. Believe me.'

Thea barely glanced at the house as she was bundled in through the front door. It was old, with subtle lighting and small rooms. She was settled into a soft old sofa facing a fireplace that looked as if it was well used in winter.

Seeking an ally, she focused on Robert's mother, a wiry little woman in her mid sixties, whose eyes followed her son constantly. When Frannie came into view, the eyes would harden briefly and the lips tighten. In calmer circumstances, Thea would have found the trio fascinating. As it was, they were merely obstacles to her urgent quest, unacknowledged captors side-stepping her concerns. It seemed the only one willing to speak to her at all was Cecilia.

It was barely thirty minutes since they'd left the tunnel. Desmond could well still be lying low there, waiting until he was sure everybody had gone. But he wouldn't wait forever. He was liable to work out for himself that Thea's silence would be fragile. Then he would run along the path to Sapperton, retrieve Hollis's car, and do unspeakable things to Thea's dog. She sat on the sofa, rerunning this scenario in a fever of foreboding, until she had gathered the energy to act.

The others were in the kitchen, muttering amongst themselves. Their confidence that she wouldn't jump up and run out-

ide screaming for help was annoyingly patronising. She almost
ɔpted for that very course, before pausing to think.

The crucial nugget in the story was undoubtedly the universal
nsistence that Dominic and Jeremy had murdered Nick. Cecilia
ɿad sounded as if she genuinely believed it to be true. Examining
his from all sides, Thea reached a decision.

She went to the kitchen doorway, and stood waiting for them
ɯo notice her. She felt Robert's eyes on her, and knew she had to
ɑct swiftly, before he understood what she was about to do.

'Cecilia,' she said. 'You're quite wrong about who killed Nick.
It was Desmond Phillips. He was with me and Robert just now in
the tunnel, and he locked my dog in DS Hollis's car. It's at
Sapperton. It's unjust for the boys to be charged with the murder. And I do not want Desmond to get away with it. He was
threatening to kill me.' She paused, fighting down the hysteria
that made her want to say it all again, only louder.

Cecilia stared at her, mouth working as she repeated the words
silently to herself. 'Desmond?' she echoed. 'Don't be so stupid.'

'It's true. Ask Robert.'

'It can't be. For heaven's sake, why would I go to all that trouble to save bloody Desmond Phillips' skin? I did it for Jemmy
and Dom.'

Thea finally grasped who it had been who removed Nick's
body from the barn and restrangled it in the pony shed at Juniper
Court. Robert Craven, evidently, had just reached the same conclusion.

'Damn it to hell!' he shouted. '*You* hanged him in the stable.'
His eyes bulged as he confronted Cecilia.

The woman was not intimidated. Her head twitched to one
side as if tossing away an irritating strand of hair. 'Of course it
was me,' she agreed. 'Who else?'

'We thought... I mean...' he floundered.

'You can't have done it alone,' Thea said. 'You'd never had got
him into the stable by yourself.'

Cecilia pressed her lips together, apparently dumbfounded by
the sudden turn of events. Five people snatched alarmed glimpses
of each other before finding a neutral point in the room on which

to rest their gaze. Even Thea felt afraid of what she might observ
on the other faces. Confessions were working their way to the
surface like erupting boils, full of malignant contagion. To Thea
it felt like a miasma of potential betrayal, one person's words
casting another into disgrace and shame, wrecking lives forever.

It was abruptly much easier to think. The events of the previous weekend were laid out before her with crystal clarity. And
another rapid glance around the room revealed to her that this
put her in a unique position. With the possible exception of
Frannie Craven, who looked weirdly relaxed and unconcerned,
the others were still grappling with new ideas. They were slowly
setting aside assumptions, and replacing them with Thea's accu-
sations, testing for validity and assessing implications. Thea
watched the process, with a dawning apprehension. It might well
occur to Cecilia that Thea's version was unacceptable; that the
bearer of such stories was best kept out of sight and sound.
Having escaped the clutches of the actual murderer, she was now
in those of someone almost as ruthless.

But Cecilia's rage had already found a different object.
'Desmond?' she repeated breathily. She looked to Robert, who
had his own gaze firmly on the carpet. '*Desmond.* My God. Have
you known this all along?' Shock turned to fury, and Robert
cringed. 'You've been hiding him, have you? Helping him.' She
stood up, looming over the seated man flanked by his wife and
mother. 'I'll *kill* you, Robert Craven. You weak stupid treacher-
ous little *bastard.*'

'Hold on Ciss,' Mrs Craven senior came up fighting. 'That's
enough of that. Give the boy a chance.' She got to her feet and
faced Cecilia at a distance of a few inches. 'It doesn't have to be
so bad.'

'If I'd *known,*' screeched Cecilia. 'If only I'd *known* — ' She
quivered with passion, eyes flashing. 'Why didn't you *tell* us?
What did you want to shield him for?'

Robert shrugged at the impossibility of explaining. Cecilia's
eyes narrowed. 'Were you there when it happened? Did you help
him? Are you a murderer as well? I wouldn't put it past you.'

He shook his head. 'No I wasn't. I never even saw Nick after-

vards. Desmond called me and made me meet him and find him
fresh clothes. He ran over the cat,' he added as if this fitted vitally
into the story.

Frannie squawked at this. 'Milo? Desmond killed Milo?' Thea
flinched, remembering Cecilia's dismissal of Frannie as not worthy of consideration. It was far from true: Frannie Craven was a
force to be reckoned with. 'Tell us everything, Robert,' she said.

Thea was calculating days and times. 'How *could* he have done
it?' she demanded. 'The ferry didn't dock in Cork till Sunday
morning, which is when the cat was killed.'

'He flew back in a private plane. He left Julia and the kids the
minute the ferry landed, and was back here by nine.'

'And Julia didn't object?'

'It was part of the plan. He'd invented a story about a fishing
trip, with an early start on Sunday. If Flora hadn't mucked everything up, he'd have gone back days ago and finished the holiday
with them.'

'So what was he driving?' said Frannie.

'What?'

'When he ran over Milo. His car's in Ireland, and don't tell me
he used the Lamborghini.'

'He hired one. I was waiting for him at our gate, while you had
your Sunday lie-in. I saw the whole thing. It ran in front of the
car and he steered right at it. He was in that sort of mood.'
Robert shrugged, as if knowing he was describing something that
no woman would understand. 'He never liked Milo,' he added.

'Never mind the cat,' Cecilia snapped. 'It's Desmond I'm
interested in. He planned the whole thing – is that what you're
telling us?' She focused intently on Robert. 'Where was he all day
Sunday?'

'In the tunnel,' said Robert, as if this was obvious.

'And it was all planned – killing Nick at the barn, and giving
himself a cast-iron alibi.'

'Right,' Robert nodded almost eagerly. 'He spent weeks setting
it all up. Paid a bloke to impersonate him, sitting for hours fishing on a riverbank. Made sure three or four witnesses would
swear it was him. Desmond's clever. And he always gets what he

wants.'

'But *why*, Robbie?' his mother demanded, taking his hand. 'You're going to be in terrible trouble for hiding him as you did.'

'Why what, Ma?'

'Why did he kill the Franklyn boy?'

'Because of his fishing lake,' asserted Cecilia. 'He thought the Warriors would put a stop to his plans and wanted to break them up. He knew we'd all blame the Innes boys.'

Robert shook his head. 'No, that's not it. It was Flora. He thought Flora and Nick were – you know. And she's only fourteen.'

The silence lasted an unbearable time. Thea tried to speak, but could not find words.

'But that wasn't true, was it?' Cecilia whispered. 'None of them touched Flora. I told them not to, and they laughed and said I didn't need to worry.'

'It might have been true,' Frannie offered. 'Flora was an awful little flirt.'

Thea was watching Robert, and the flush suffusing his face. A grim suspicion overtook her. 'Yes, she's only fourteen,' she said. 'And she was worried enough to come back here to try to stop her father. She *knew* what he meant to do. And when she got here, all she could think to do was hide away in the car and hope she wasn't too late. With me and my sister in the way, she couldn't really protect anybody. It wasn't until we found her that she knew she'd got there too late. Poor little thing.'

'Poor little thing!' Frannie protested. 'She's a devious little menace. One of those girls who make men mad.' She too looked penetratingly at Robert and a chill descended. '*You* told Desmond she was sleeping with Nick, didn't you?' she accused. 'It can't have been anybody else. And why would you do that?' All trace of the ditzy young wife so subservient to her husband, which had been Thea's initial impression of her, was long since discarded. The truth only made her stronger. 'To throw him off the track. Robert. Oh, Robert.' The last words were uttered in a voice full of knowledge and despair and a kind of resignation. Everyone knew – even Thea had somehow understood it from the first –

hat Robert Craven liked young girls.

'Robbie?' his aghast mother spoke. 'It isn't true – it can't be rue. What's Frannie saying?'

Robert recoiled. 'I never – she isn't – we didn't — ' He rallied slightly. 'Look, you can examine her. She's not – I mean, it was only — ' He subsided again miserably, unable to name the acts he'd committed with the girl. All four women understood well enough without any graphic language.

'Oh Robert,' they seemed to sigh in unison.

After that, Robert became a broken man. Nobody protested when Thea lifted the phone and keyed the number for Hollis. She was patched through to his bedside, where he woke from the first deep hour of sleep, muzzy with exhaustion and total failure to understand.

'Phil, we need you here,' she said. 'Wake up, will you.' She had expected an alert cry of relief at hearing her voice. After all, as far as he knew she was still a hostage somewhere, in his car. Why wasn't he on the road searching for her?

'You took my car,' he remembered. 'Why did you do that? Did you get sick of waiting for me? Where did you go? I was frantic, wondering what might have happened to you. We checked the hospitals. We searched for hours, in the dark. I've got the alarm set for four, so I can go and start again.' As he shook off the effects of exhausted sleep, his true feelings began to surface.

She almost laughed, but anger took precedence. 'I was *kid-napped*, you idiot. He almost killed me. I thought you'd be out there looking for me.' A cold sense of abandonment gripped her, along with several dreadful might-have-beens.

'What? Who?'

'Desmond Phillips. He murdered Nick Franklyn, Phil. And he's got my dog, and your car. He's very dangerous, and very clever. I'm at Cecilia Clifton's house. The car was at Sapperton, but he might have moved it by now.'

'Thea, Thea,' he pleaded. 'The Innes boys killed Nick Franklyn. We've got them in custody. They'll be charged tomor-row. I've had his mother trying to scratch my eyes out.'

'Serves you right,' she said, meaning it.

That woke him up even more thoroughly. 'Explain it to me again,' he invited.

But she had had enough of explaining. 'I need you to go to Sapperton and find the car. It's locked – if it's still there. I hope you've got a spare key? But Phil, I think Desmond will have taken it away by now, and I can't bear to think what he might do to Hepzie. He tied her jaws shut. She might suffocate.'

'Can you get there?'

She looked around the room, which seemed full of dazed and terrified people, who were even so still potentially hostile to Thea herself. 'No,' she said. 'Come here first and collect me. Cecilia Clifton's house.'

'And where's that?'

'Oh, for God's sake,' Thea cracked, and threw the phone at Cecilia. 'Tell him this address,' she ordered. 'And tell him to be here fast.'

In the car, Thea had a flash of foreknowledge at how the effects of the night would rebound on her for many months to come. Her revival after the escape from Desmond had been rapid, bringing her to the point of issuing orders to a police superintendent and calling him an idiot. Rapid, but also transitory. For the present, her whole being was focused on the rescue of the dog. She leaned forward, as if this could make the car go faster. She held a vision of Hepzie curled patiently on the car seat, trusting her mistress to come back for her. *It'll be all right* she repeated silently to herself. Because any further turn of the screw would not be bearable.

Hollis tried to question her, especially on the matter of Desmond. 'I'll give you the whole story tomorrow,' she promised. 'You should have arrested Robert this evening, I suppose – but I don't think he'll be going anywhere. His womenfolk aren't going to let him get into any more trouble.'

'Robert?' Hollis echoed. 'Robert Craven, do you mean?'

'Shut up,' she pleaded. 'And drive.'

Her vision was almost realised. The car was where they'd left it, the dog stretched limply across the back seat, breathing shallowly. Thea ripped off the binding from her jaw, and cradled her, oblivious of everything else except for the powerful stench of her own vomit. When the tail wagged and the tongue came out for some much-needed panting, she dissolved into tears that threatened never to stop.

Against all protocol, Hollis took Thea and her dog back to his own home in Cirencester. He removed her vomit-covered clothes, and wrapped her in a pair of pyjamas that smelled of airing-cupboards. He gave her a large glass of whisky, telling her she had to drink it in bed, and then go straight to sleep. Hepzibah was placed on the duvet beside her. 'I'll see you both in the morning,' he said.

He woke her at nine with a mug of tea. 'Sorry I can't leave you to sleep any longer,' he said. 'But I ought to be somewhere else already.'

'You don't believe me about Desmond,' she stated flatly. 'If you did, you'd have been up all night hunting for him.'

'How do you know I wasn't?'

'Because you've obviously had nearly as much sleep as I have.' He was shaved, and smelt of soap. His hair was tidy and his shirt new-laundered. 'And you're much *much* cleaner. I still smell of sick.'

'So the story isn't over,' he summarised regretfully. 'I've been thinking it all through again, and need you to make an official statement. You called me an idiot,' he reminded her.

'Yes. Sorry.'

'I'm beginning to think you might have been right.'

She hoisted herself up and sipped the tea. 'Hepzie's going to want to go out,' she said. 'I don't remember if she had a pee last night. She must be bursting.' The spaniel showed no signs of discomfort, nestled in the duvet, one eye half open. 'Lucky she didn't do it in your car.'

'I don't think it would matter, given that it's awash with vomit already.'

'Is it your own, or just one of a whole fleet belonging to the police?'

'It's mine, but the police paid for it. I'm foolishly fond of it, actually.'

'I expect it'll clean up all right.'

She finished the tea, knowing he wasn't going to allow her to prolong the cosy interlude. 'You're being very patient with me,' she smiled. 'It must all be very confusing.'

'You said we'd have to arrest Robert Craven. At least, I *think* you said that. But he didn't kill Franklyn?'

'He protected Desmond, knowing he'd killed Nick. And he had sexual relations with Flora Phillips, who is only fourteen. That, more or less, is what started the whole thing. He put the blame on Nick, and Desmond was enraged and killed him. Flora came home when she suspected that her father might not be where he said he was. She probably thought he meant to kill Robert, who she must have been fond of, if not utterly in love with.'

'Thea,' Hollis said warningly. 'Stop talking, have a shower, get dressed and come with me. Now. The dog stays behind. You can come back for her later.'

'Dressed?' she repeated, looking down at herself in his roomy pyjamas.

'Ah,' he paused. 'It'll have to be a bit makeshift. I haven't washed your things yet.' He produced a passable brushed cotton shirt and a pair of jeans that were ludicrously big on her.

The first surprise was that they did not get into his replacement car, but set out on foot. 'It's only five minutes,' he said. 'Very convenient.'

The next was seeing him in action with his colleagues. As he walked into the building, people materialised, all anxious to speak to him, but maintaining perfect order. Thea had assumed that she was his priority, but instead he directed her to a row of chairs and asked if she would wait fifteen minutes or so. It had not until then occurred to her that there would be other crimes needing his attention, that the world had not simply stopped while the murder of Nick Franklyn was resolved.

Finally, and most startling, was the appearance of Julia Phillips, walking in through the front entrance as calm as could be. Wihout thinking, Thea jumped up and went towards her. 'Julia!' she called. 'Hello!'

Julia gave her a cold look, turning her face away.

Too late, Thea understood that there could be no happy reason

for Julia's being there. The mislaying of her daughter, the allega-
tions of sexual misdemeanours, the interruption of her holiday
and above all the actions of her husband – no wonder, Thea
thought charitably, she isn't feeling very friendly.

'Sorry,' she faltered. 'I shouldn't have said anything.'

'No, ' Julia agreed.

Hollis returned as promised and led her into a small office, where
she made her statement, describing everything she could recall of
the previous evening. Although he remained with her, prompting
her with questions, scratching his nose from time to time, his
thoughts seemed to be partly elsewhere.

'You don't seem terribly interested,' she complained eventually.

'Oh, I am,' he assured her. 'But I'm not happy.'

She looked at him. 'Why not?'

'I'm not sure we'll ever manage to make it stick. Your evidence
is hearsay. Robert Craven might refuse to confirm what you've
told us, and not one of those three women has any reason to back
you up, either. If they construct a viable account and stick to it,
you'll be a voice in the wilderness. You'll sound like a hysterical
fantasist.'

'What about Flora?'

'Flora is fourteen years old, and already on record as disturbed
and rebellious. Her testimony isn't going to persuade anybody of
anything.'

'So we just abandon it, do we? Let Desmond escape, as well as
Robert and Cecilia? Don't tell me you'll stick to the charges
against the Innes brothers.'

He put up his hands. 'Whoa! It's not as bad as that. We know
you were taken away in my car, against your will. Your dog alone
is proof of that. We can lay charges against Phillips for abduction,
if nothing else. But — ' he sighed. 'The rest of it isn't nearly so
simple.'

'Julia's here,' Thea remembered. 'She seemed furious with me.
How much of all this does she know?'

'That remains to be seen. She's being interviewed as we speak.'

Uneasy at her dual role of witness and – what? girlfriend? –

Thea got up to go. Then she remembered that she had no transport, and no obvious destination. 'Um,' she said. 'You're busy, aren't you. I should let you get on with it. But what happens next?' She sagged at the weight of the decisions and complex logistics. 'My clothes and car are at Juniper Court. Hepzie's at your place. Where am I meant to be?'

'Wait here a while. I've sent someone to fetch Craven and Miss Clifton. I ought to be here for their questioning. And I can't leave the Innes boys dangling for much longer with their father raising hell the way he is. Plus there's a new case just breaking, and nobody else but me is available to oversee it. But I want to take you back.' Their eyes connected; rueful, forgiving, thwarted looks were exchanged.

'You haven't got time,' she said briskly. 'I can walk to your place, collect the dog, and find a taxi back to Juniper Court. I can't just abandon it – although I suppose Julia — '

She faltered under his gaze. Nothing at the Phillips house seemed to matter any more. The pony and rabbits might be hungry and thirsty, the poultry vulnerable to foxes, but Thea had no lingering sense of obligation to them. Julia was home now, anyhow. She could feed her own damned animals.

'Well,' he hesitated. 'That would save me some time. I'd send a PC with you, except — '

'You'd rather nobody knew I'd left my dog and clothes at your place,' she finished.

He grinned self-mockingly and took a step closer to her. 'Just for now,' he agreed. 'If it wouldn't be too unchivalrous of me.'

Thea swallowed a wave of self-pity, as she remembered what had happened to her barely twelve hours earlier. She had not sought solicitude, had valiantly concentrated on the police investigation, and even now had as much concern for Hollis's reputation as her own wellbeing. Somewhere in all that, there was something missing.

'Okay then,' she said lightly. 'I think I can find the way.'

He fished in his pocket for a key to his front door. 'Leave it under the dustbin when you go,' he said. She forced a laugh at that. Already he was almost at the door, needing to be elsewhere, intent on his duties. He had given her shelter and hot water and clean clothes, kept her safe and provided sustenance. Perhaps he thought that was the limit of his responsibilities towards her.

The streets of Cirencester felt strange in a number of ways. She was reminded of the first time she had gone out alone after giving birth to Jessica, when crossing a street seemed impossibly dangerous and her body felt tender and unfamiliar. The people all around her were remote, uncomprehending, knowing nothing of what she had so recently endured. She could be a ghost or a time traveller, operating in a wholly alien reality.

A taxi was summoned by a phonecall from Hollis's hallway, her filthy clothes bundled into a black bin liner, and her dog attached to her by a length of string located in a kitchen drawer. It all seemed to take a long time. Her head was thick with the muddle of the past week's events. Nothing was going to get settled as it should. Hollis, she admitted to herself, was not a proper policeman at all. He didn't behave a bit like films and books ordained that he should.

For the first time in many days, she thought of her brother-in-law James, another Detective Superintendent who, now she thought about it, was often just as laconic and disorganised as Hollis seemed to be. James would be concerned, alarmed, even reproachful when he heard the story – and with any luck he might throw some light on some of its more shadowy areas.

When the taxi finally delivered her to Juniper Court, it was with a bizarre sense of d j vu that she observed another brother-in-law standing in the gateway, looking as if he might have been there for some considerable time.

'Alex!' she shouted, stumbling out of the car, Hepzie entangled with her legs. His familiarity and strong male presence were entirely welcome in those few seconds before she remembered his abuse of her sister and the new relationship she must henceforth construct with him.

To his credit, Alex asked almost no questions, but instead briefly explained that he'd come back for Jocelyn's car. He had knocked at the door of Juniper Court and received no response, then explored all the buildings, and found nothing but a hungry pony and some birds roosting on the straw of the stable loft. The fact that Thea's car remained in the yard, alongside that of his damaged wife, gave him confidence that Thea would eventually return.

'But how did you get here?'

'Train, bus, and then Shank's Pony. It's a lovely day for it.'

Thea hadn't heard the phrase 'Shank's Pony' since school. Typical Alex, old-fashioned, slightly maladroit, and disconcertingly likeable. Perhaps, she thought wistfully, Jocelyn would be able to forgive him, and everything would revert to normal after all. It would be a pity to lose him from their lives.

'I've got to pack all my stuff,' she told him. 'Will you wait with me?'

He gave her a narrow look, but still suppressed all curiosity. 'If you want,' he agreed. 'But I shouldn't be too much longer. Joss can't do much for herself, and she's got all the kids there.'

The kids can do everything, then, Thea thought impatiently, surprised at the implication that Alex was still under the same roof as Jocelyn. Then she realised that there had barely been time for any other arrangement. 'You haven't wasted any time coming back for the car,' she said. 'You only left here last night.' It seemed like weeks ago.

'We didn't know how much longer you'd be here,' he said. 'Or what your people might think about minding a strange vehicle. It seemed best to get a move on.'

He hovered in doorways and passageways as she scoured the house for any of her possessions that might have escaped from the bedroom. 'I should wash my sheets,' she worried. 'And look at the mess Hepzie's made of the sofa. I was going to clean that.'

'You really have to go now, do you?'

She turned to face him, aware of his admirable restraint. 'I'm sorry,' she said. 'I owe you some explanation. Things have been very – dramatic, I suppose – since you left yesterday. We know who killed the boy, and who hanged him in the stable here. But they haven't actually been caught yet. I've given a statement this morning, and I don't think I'm needed any longer. The woman of the house has come back from her holiday early, and I don't want to be here when she gets home. She's at the police station as well – or she was.'

'It sounds a total mess. You're well of out of it, if you ask me.'

Only then did Thea think ahead to the rest of the day. She felt herself grow pale and cold at the idea of simply returning to her own home in Witney, reliving the drama all on her own.

Alex watched her face. 'You'll come back to us, of course,' he said, as if it only needed this light confirmation. 'I don't think Joss can cope otherwise.'

She spent the next days recuperating at her sister's house, each of them wondering how they'd possibly have managed without the other. On the Tuesday, Thea agreed that she should remain there until the weekend, after which she really would have to go home.

On the Sunday evening, Thea had taken the children and Hepzie into the garden for a wild game of french cricket while Jocelyn and Alex talked. He had then gone upstairs and packed a bag before leaving at nine o'clock. He and Jocelyn both showed obvious signs of weeping, which only two of the children observed. 'What's the matter?' Noel had demanded, his eyes wide.

'We'll explain it all to you tomorrow,' Thea had told him, jumping in before Jocelyn could speak. 'Don't worry, darling. Just let's get everyone to bed for now, okay?'

Little Roly, Jocelyn's pet, had approached his mother warily and put a finger to her cheek. 'Does your elbow hurt?' he asked, with huge concern.

'It does rather,' Jocelyn agreed, with a damp smile. 'Off you go to bed now, angel. Auntie Thea might read to you if you ask her nicely.'

It was after ten before Thea returned heavily down the stairs, remembering her own mistreatment and wondering if she'd ever feel normal again. Then she reminded herself that she was an old hand at surviving disaster, and things would one day be sweet again.

'What did you decide?' she asked.

Jocelyn was on the sofa, her feet up, her eyes red. 'As you see. He's gone,' she said. 'With you here there isn't a spare bed, and I can't endure him in with me.'

'Where did he spend last night then?'

'Here,' Jocelyn nodded at the sofa.

'But he hasn't gone because of me? The kids could bunk up if they had to. You could have one of them in your bed.'

'Obviously.'

'So?'

'So I don't know. There isn't going to be anything neat and tidy about this, however much we might want it to be. I can't tell you anything, except I'm already glad he's gone and I want to go to bed.'

'Right. Me too. But tomorrow we're going to have to explain things to the kids.'

Jocelyn moaned. 'God knows how, when I can't even explain it to myself.'

'I'll help,' said Thea.

She kept her promise, sitting with Jocelyn and the whole family overflowing the living room, with solemn faces and flurries of tears. They gave no false assurances, Jocelyn admitting her own uncertainty. 'We'll just have to struggle through a day at a time,' she said. 'But I'll tell you one thing – I'm bloody glad it's the holidays.'

Toni, a slender child with dark eyes and careful manner, considered this. 'Why?' she said.

'Because if it wasn't we'd have to keep Auntie Thea here for weeks, washing your school clothes, walking you to the bus, getting you to bed on time.'

Toni turned her gaze to Thea. 'But now you'll have to cook all our food, and find us things to do,' she said. 'That's probably going to be worse.'

Thea couldn't help feeling there was meant to be a laugh somewhere in this exchange, but she couldn't readily identify it. 'Just you wait,' she said. 'I've got about fifty ideas for holiday activities.' Nobody laughed at that, either.

But she did organise a selection of projects, remembering how her father had done the same for his large brood. 'Don't you remember?' she chided her sister. 'All that nature study he made us do. No wonder I married Carl, with his environmental enthusiasms.'

'I remember,' nodded Jocelyn. 'But there isn't much scope for that sort of thing round here. I haven't seen a rosebay willow herb for years.'

'You can't have looked, then. I saw a clump of it at the edge of the Sainsbury's car park only this morning.'

'Well, I'm not sending Roly out there, even for you. Besides, they're not allowed to pick wild flowers these days.'

'Nor collect birds' eggs. I know. But we can't just let them watch daytime television or play ghastly alien-zapping games the whole time. It'll rot their souls. Don't they make things any more? Don't they *ever* go outside?'

'Noel does. He goes to cricket club and he says he's going sailing later on. I forget who with. And no, I don't think making things features much these days.'

'I hadn't realised. Remember all that *Blue Peter* stuff with cereal boxes and pipecleaners.' Thea sighed her nostalgia.

'I was never as interested as you were.'

Thea gave the matter some serious thought, and came up with a list of ideas for constructive play which the children greeted with suspicious interest. First was a theatre, to be constructed from scratch, with a set, curtains, actors, and a play to perform.

'My God!' groaned Jocelyn, privately. 'You were born a hundred years too late, d'you know that? You'll be making us all play charades next.'

'Good idea,' said Thea, pretending to write it on her list. 'You have to admit, though, they're intrigued.'

'I admit it. My worry is having to sit through the finished product at the end of the week.'

'I'll pretend you never said that.'

The subject of the killing of Nick Franklyn took a while to emerge. Thea had a startlingly horrible dream on the Tuesday night, and couldn't refrain from relating it to her sister next morning. 'Desmond Phillips was holding me down in the sludge at the bottom of the canal, and when he forced my head below the surface I saw Nick's disembodied head snarling at me. It was so *real*.' She shuddered.

'Post-traumatic stress,' Jocelyn diagnosed. 'You'll get flashbacks as well, I expect.'

'Thanks very much. I wonder why Phil doesn't call. The story isn't really finished yet. What if they never catch Desmond? I'll spend the rest of my life frightened that he'll turn up one day.'

'You could call him,' Jocelyn suggested. 'He might be waiting for exactly that.'

'He'll be busy. I don't want to disturb him.' She sighed, and missed Jocelyn's next remark. 'Sorry?' she said, belatedly aware of an expectant silence.

'You're lovesick,' Jocelyn accused with a teasing grin.

'Shut up.' Then she softened. 'But it would be nice to hear his voice.'

The anticipated voice was finally heard the next morning, along with its owner's face and body and full physical presence. Noel was the first to announce him. 'Auntie Thea! A man has just parked outside. Come and see!'

She met him a few feet short of the front door, and faced him without touching. They spoke simultaneously, with very similar sentiments, to the effect that both looked a lot better than they had on Sunday.

'Amazing what a good sleep can do,' he said, adding, 'How's Hepzie? And Jocelyn?'

'They're fine. The kids won't leave Hepzie alone. Jocelyn's going to have to get a dog when I leave.' Her voice lowered. 'Alex has moved out. It's all a bit grim, to be honest. And I'm having nightmares.'

His gaze locked onto hers. 'Well, I might be able to do something about that,' he murmured. 'I thought you might want to hear it in person.'

'That sounds encouraging. Come in. Have some coffee. Meet the family.'

Thea's theatre project was in its final stages of completion on the dining room table, when she went to find Jocelyn. Her sister was using her good hand to hold the end of a tape measure for Abby, who wanted to ensure the proscenium curtains were precisely the right length. 'Having fun?' said Thea.

'The little beast has cut up one of my shirts for a costume,' Jocelyn pouted.

'Mum! You said we could!' Abby protested.

'Only under torture. Actually, it did have a hole in it, and I think I bought it in 1979, so it hasn't done too badly.'

'Phil's here.'

'So I gather. Hi, Phil.' The detective had followed Thea into the room and was scanning the contented activity with disbelief.

'What's going on here?' he said.

'Oh, this is Thea's influence. She's really missed her vocation.'

'School teacher?'

Jocelyn shook her head. '*Blue Peter* presenter.'

The laughter was just loud enough to betray the tension still below the surface. Even the children joined in, while passing quick looks between themselves.

Thea made coffee and took a cup to Jocelyn before settling in the kitchen with Hollis. Jocelyn had indicated with a sisterly look that they could have all the privacy they could wish for, for as long as they liked. 'You released the Innes boys, I suppose?'

'On bail. They've been charged with a few minor infringements, but they're not killers. You were right about that.'

'Their mother must be relieved. What infringements?' She found her brain was slow to get into gear, to summon the faces of Jeremy and Dominic and all the other people she'd come into such close and unwelcome proximity to. 'Oh, yes. Silly me,' she rushed on. 'You mean Dominic's intrusion. Everything else is sorted, then, is it?'

'All but a few details. It's been keeping us up late, but we're more or less there.'

'And I was right, wasn't I? Desmond Phillips killed Nick because Robert Craven told him Nick was having sex with Flora. And all along, it was Robert who was abusing her – he lied about Nick.'

Hollis nodded. 'Flora confirms all that, more or less, but she won't agree to testify against her father or Craven. You were right there, too. She's hopelessly in love with the bastard.'

'What about Cecilia? Is she as powerful as she seems?'

'She won't say anything, either. But everything appears to lead back to her. She's quite a woman. Two years ago she appeared in a Planning Appeal hearing, doing all the legal work for a group of local protesters, rather than spend thousands on a barrister as most of these groups do. Her side won, needless to say. Since then, she's been in demand as a sort of unpaid consultant for a whole range of conservation groups. She runs an internet service as well. And her biggest enemy is Angus Innes.'

'Father of Jeremy and Dominic?'

'And Planning Officer for the county. Inclined to give permission for a large number of developments that Cecilia finds unacceptable. She has clashed with him countless times.'

'And delighted in turning his sons against him? Nasty.'

'More or less. If the boys could be implicated in the Rural Warriors, seen as breaking the law and opposing perfectly legitimate projects, it could reflect badly on the father. My DI is convinced that she wanted to get Innes removed from office, due to divided loyalties.'

'But she *loved* them, in her way, despite what she told us about students.'

'Huh?'

'She used to teach Jocelyn – didn't we tell you? She said she never liked the students much.'

'Jeremy and Dominic aren't students, though, are they?'

'True. And I still don't properly understand why she moved the body.'

'I think it was mainly panic, trying to shield the boys. In a way, it worked against her own interests. It would have sullied the whole Innes family, given the barn such a terrible image that nobody would ever want to live there if it was converted. All things that she probably wanted.'

'And how on earth did she know Nick had been killed, anyway?'

Hollis reached across the table and took hold of her hand. 'We've examined the record for Phillips's mobile phone,' he said. 'He made a call at 4 a.m. on that Monday morning to Cecilia Clifton. Ten minutes later he phoned Robert Craven's mother, Lottie.'

Thea went blank. 'So?' she muttered, trying to see the significance.

'Try this. He could have disguised his voice to Cecilia. If he simply said something like *Go to the Innes barn right away. The*

Warriors need you urgently, that might have had the desired effect. She rushes over there, finds the body, realises how bad it would look for the boys and decides to move the body and try to make it look like suicide.'

'But why would Desmond phone her like that? He wouldn't know what she'd do.'

'Just to get a witness to the time of the murder, to make best use of his alibi. Otherwise, Nick might have lain there for days, for all he knew.'

'But could she do it all by herself?'

'You forget. Phillips also phoned Lottie Craven.'

'What? And said the same to her? Why her, though?'

'I'll come to that. She buzzes over to the barn as well, finds Cecilia and the body, agrees with the suicide idea, and helps drag poor Nick into the car and over to Juniper Court.'

'You've got evidence for this?'

'Hairs, blood and flakes of skin in Cecilia's car,' he nodded. 'She had it cleaned, but not well enough.'

'But why Juniper Court?'

'Probably a matter of convenience. Plus the Phillipses were one of the few local families not involved with the Rural Warriors. It seemed like a good idea at the time. They hung about on the side road for hours waiting for you to go out, apparently. Amazing that nobody saw them.'

'If they did, they wouldn't have thought it odd. Cecilia's a familiar figure. People would just give her a wave and forget they'd seen her.'

'Probably. Anyway, that's more or less it.'

'Except Lottie. Why did Desmond phone her?'

'To give himself a lever over Robert, we think. Robert was the only person who knew the whole story about the Irish alibi. He was a danger to Desmond – so by implicating his mother, he made it less likely that Robert would ever betray him.'

Thea stared at the floor, absently rubbing her thumb over the back of his hand. 'It doesn't feel as if it's finished though – not while Desmond's still on the loose.'

'As it happens — ' he began, before his phone trilled in his pocket. With a little smile, he answered it.

'Thanks,' he said after a lengthy silence spent listening to his caller. 'That's made my day. Well done. Oh, and Jack – try not to call me again today, okay?'

He turned to Thea. 'Where were we? Something about Desmond being on the loose?'

He wasn't fooling her. 'You caught him,' she crowed. 'How?'

'That was Jack. We had to play a little trick on friend Phillips, I'm afraid. You'd probably call it entrapment.'

She ducked her head, in an exaggerated apology. 'I don't care how you did it,' she said. 'You could shoot him in cold blood and I'd be perfectly happy.'

'Luckily for us, his wife feels rather the same. We had to involve her, to make it work.' He shivered. 'The capacity women have for treachery never ceases to appal me.'

Thea laughed. 'What did she do?' She realised she'd almost forgotten about Julia, the bumptious, high-flying, careless stepmother.

'She set him up in the simplest way. Told him she'd have killed Nick Franklyn herself if she'd realised what had been going on with Flora, and Desmond got so sucked in, he openly admitted it to her. What he didn't know was that there were two plain-clothes officers listening to every word.'

Thea hugged herself, wondering why she didn't feel happier. 'And that counts, does it? It's proper evidence?'

Hollis held up a finger. 'Belt and braces,' he said. 'Remember? Our people approached him there and then, replaying the tape recording they'd made, and scaring him so badly he went along to the station and made a full confession. That was what Jack just called to tell me.'

'And Julia —'

'When she heard the whole story, and caught up with Flora, she couldn't do enough to help us.' His face grew serious. 'To be honest, she scared the life out of me. I'm still not sure what made her so enraged. I've never seen anything like it.'

'He ruined everything for her, humiliated her, embarrassed her,' Thea supplied. 'And committed a murder because of what he hought was happening to his daughter. Her reaction sounds airly normal to me.'

Hollis made a thoughtful face, sucking in his lips as if tasting the argument. 'Am I missing something?' he said eventually.

'Jealousy,' Thea explained. 'Julia's jealous of Flora. If Desmond had killed to defend *her* honour, she'd feel completely different.'

'I see,' he said doubtfully.

Hollis stayed for lunch, and then suggested to Thea they go out for a drive. 'I've got an idea I'd like to run past you,' he said. 'And I think we've already exhausted your sister's patience, hogging the kitchen for so long.'

She agreed with enthusiasm, the heady sense of relief at Desmond's capture colouring everything. The air felt sweet and balmy, the future a sunny landscape. Only Jocelyn's predicament tainted her sense of optimism, and even that could yet turn out to be salvageable. Already her sister was making references to Alex which seemed to imply some mellowing.

With Hepzie on a lead, she followed him out to his car. Only then did she realise it was already occupied. On the back seat sat a large black and tan dog, with a domed head and floppy ears. Peering closer, Thea saw a smaller yellow dog flopped beside the first one.

'You left them out here in the sun,' she accused. 'Poor things.'

'I parked in the shade, and the windows are open,' he defended. 'They're fine. Let me introduce you.'

He opened the car door, saying 'Stay!' in a firm manly voice. The dogs looked at him, then at Thea, then at Hepzie who had jumped onto the seat and was cavorting seductively around them. 'Claude and Baxter,' said Hollis. 'Baxter's the big one.'

Thea watched the well-trained setter and corgi turn with total dignity away from the undisciplined spaniel. 'Hello boys,' she said. 'Come here, Hepzibah, before you make a bigger fool of yourself.'

Settled in the front seat, the spaniel in her usual place on Thea's lap, they drove off. 'Where are we going?' Thea asked.

'To the nearest beach that allows dogs. I think I know the very place,' he said. 'It'll take forty minutes or so.'

'Plenty of time for you to explain this big idea, then,' she said comfortably. 'And don't try to put me off until we get there. I want to know this minute what it is.'

'Well...' He kept his attention firmly on the road, not venturing the briefest of glances at her face. 'I've got a week's leave in October. And it so happens that an aged aunt of mine died at the beginning of this year, leaving me as her last surviving relative in this country. She had a cottage in a village called Cold Aston, not far from Stow-on-the-Wold and I'll have to go and sort out the contents and then sell it. I should have done it ages ago, but it kept getting put to the bottom of the list. It's quite a task – she was a real old hoarder, poor thing. Now, what I was wondering – and tell me if this is out of order – is whether you'd like to come with me? I think the place will still be habitable – a local woman goes in and airs it now and then. I had the electricity and phone disconnected, that's the only thing. And I would insist on taking my dogs. It's their holiday as well.'

Thea laughed. 'So we'll need the camping gaz. But October – that's ages away.'

'I imagine we can snatch a few mutually agreeable encounters between now and then.'

'I hope so.'

'So do I.' He reached out a hand, and she took it and squeezed it before he needed it back for a gear change.